www.MinotaurBooks.com

The premier website for the best in crime fiction.

Log on and learn more about:

The Labyrinth: Sign up for this monthly newsletter and get your crime fiction fix. Commentary author Q&A, hot new titles, and giveaways.

MomentsInCrime: It's no mystery what our authors are thinking. Each week, a new author blogs about their upcoming projects, special events, and more. Log on today to talk to your favorite authors. www.MomentsInCrime.com

GetCozy: The ultimate cozy connection. Find your favorite cozy mystery, grab a reading group guide, sign up for monthly giveaways, and more. www.GetCozyOnline.com

MINOTAUR BOOKS

Praise For Cathy Pickens And Her Mysteries

HUSH MY MOUTH

"No slim Pickens with this author...*Hush My Mouth*
is fabulous."
—*The Best Reviews*

"Add to the growing shelf of Southern sleuths the
proud name of Avery Andrews."
—*Wilmington Star-News*

HOG WILD

"Death with eccentric Southern charm."
—*Charlotte Observer*

"Murder and mayhem, served up with Carolina barbecue and hush puppies."
—*Kirkus Reviews*

"A mysterious, a little bit crazy, and a completely
enjoyable read."
—Dixie Cash, author of
I Gave You My Heart, but You Sold It Online

"The batter thickens on this highly seasoned chicken-
fried clue fest."
—*Publishers Weekly*

DONE GONE WRONG

"Richly atmospheric...[a] finely crafted cozy."
—*Publishers Weekly*

"Fans of Southern down-home regional mysteries
will want to read *Done Gone Wrong*...The courtroom scenes are exciting."
—*Midwest Book Review*

"[A] fast-paced Southern mystery with plenty of
grit and humor."
—*Mystery Lovers Bookshop News*

"An enjoyable, edgy cozy, and the descriptions of sites and sounds in Charleston made me want to be there."   —Iloveamysterynewsletter.com

SOUTHERN FRIED

"[An] assured debut, a cozy with some sharp edges...This strong start augurs well for future books in the series."   —*Publishers Weekly*

"The world of Dacus, soaked in tart atmosphere, is well worth a visit."   —*Kirkus Reviews*

"Has a welcome and surprising sharpness of observation mixed in with its cozier qualities...definitely has the look of a keeper."   —*Chicago Tribune*

"A spicy mystery...this is a must-read."
                    —*Romantic Times BOOKreviews* (top pick)

"Smooth writing and a very engaging and wonderfully imperfect heroine."   —*Mystery News*

"Tidy plotting...gossipy humor, colorful characters, and Southern ethos. Highly recommended for most collections."   —*Library Journal*

"A good old-fashioned murder mystery!"
                    —*New Mystery Reader* magazine

ALSO BY CATHY PICKENS

Hush My Mouth

Hog Wild

Done Gone Wrong

Southern Fried

CAN'T NEVER TELL

A Southern Fried Mystery

Cathy Pickens

St. Martin's Paperbacks

This is a work of fiction. All of the characters, organizations, and events portrayed in this novel are either products of the author's imagination or are used fictitiously.

CAN'T NEVER TELL

Copyright © 2009 by Cathy Pickens.

All rights reserved.

For information address St. Martin's Press, 175 Fifth Avenue, New York, NY 10010.

EAN: 978-0-312-35445-9

Printed in the United States of America

Minotaur hardcover edition / February 2009
St. Martin's Paperbacks edition / December 2009

St. Martin's Paperbacks are published by St. Martin's Press, 175 Fifth Avenue, New York, NY 10010.

10 9 8 7 6 5 4 3 2 1

ACKNOWLEDGMENTS

Dana Berlin Strange is a real person—and a restaurateur of the first order, owner of Jestine's Kitchen on Market Street in Charleston, South Carolina. Readers who've followed Avery's adventures know her penchant for Jestine's Co-Cola Cake. In this book, a character has borrowed Dana's name. The real Dana is as warm and welcoming as her namesake in this book, though much younger, and, as far as I know, the real Dana never ran away with the carnival.

Thanks to her bidding generosity for a worthy cause, Nancie Phillips has had her name co-opted by a sassy television reporter. Except for their shared name, the two share no other similarities, as far as I know. Thanks, Nancie, for your generous bid!

Many thanks to all who continue to help Avery on her way: Catherine Anderson and the mean bunch of women: Ann Wicker, Terry Hoover, and Paula Connolly. She wouldn't go far without you.

The amazing teams at Minotaur Books and the Jane Rotrosen Agency continue to work their magic:

Ruth Cavin and Toni Plummer, Hector DeJean and Jessica Rotondi, Matthew Shear and Matt Baldacci, Meg Ruley and Christina Hogrebe. Thanks so much!

For there is still a vision for the appointed time; it speaks of the end and does not lie.

—Habakkuk 2:3

ONE

Thursday Evening

"I thought this was supposed to be scary."

My niece Emma made her pronouncement with the derision only a seven-year-old can muster.

I looked down at the top of her dark red hair, plaited in a thick ponytail down her back, unruly curls escaping around her face. Nothing much scares her, so the tableaux of faked horror in the carnival fright house didn't stand a chance.

Four teenagers caught up with us in the dark, one couple in a clutch so tight they could have entered the three-legged race. The other couple trailed behind, self-consciously holding hands. The girl in the impossible clutch used every dilapidated fake prop as an excuse to shriek and grab tight to her scrawny boyfriend.

In a few years, would a prepubescent Emma visit a fake fright house looking for thrills of that sort? I shuddered, but knew I had little reason to fear. The look on Emma's face and the disgusted flip of her ponytail as she made a faint gagging sound told me the real worry was that she'd leap from seven to eighty-seven and join her great-great-aunt Aletha without any stops in between. My own little Attila the Hen.

The carnival had rolled into Dacus, bolted together its rides, slid up the doors on the concessions, and opened for business today at noon.

Emma and I had waited until early evening before we ventured out to the Fourth Festival and its carnival midway. By that time, the sun had sunk low enough to cool the late June heat down some, and the darkness and the dancing lights turned the tawdry traveling show to magic. Still, the inside of the trailer was humid and smelled like a dirt-floored basement tinged with mildew.

The first fright house tableau displayed electric arcs popping, strobing lights, and automated mannequins in an operating room scene. One mannequin wore a blood-spattered smock and held a roaring toothless chain saw aloft. The other mannequin, lying on the operating table, jerked and screamed, accompanied by an awkward mechanical clank. It all looked a bit halfhearted.

The teenagers, wanting a thrill a second, scooted past us in the dim room, almost as though we were a not-very-scary part of the display. Not that anything in the place was scary.

As the teenagers reached the narrow room's exit, a loud pop from one of the arcs gave the teenaged girl leading the foursome yet another reason to jump. She was half a head taller and fifty pounds heavier than her slim-hipped date. She grabbed him with such energy that he stumbled against a third mannequin levitating beside the exit door. This mannequin held a chain saw over the doorway, the small engine producing a constant putter and whine.

The boy's bravado slipped, and he jumped out

of the mannequin's reach. From a safer distance, he glanced up at the figure clad in a butcher's apron and overalls.

The other guy in the foursome, who was also smaller than his amazon of a girlfriend, kept one arm around her waist and nestled up under her ample endowments. Judging from his expression, he wasn't thinking whatever fifteen-year-old boys usually think when they have their arm around a garden of earthly delights in a too-tight Wrestlemania T-shirt.

I followed his frozen gaze to the floor.

"Man!" His shocked whisper was followed by a glance at me and a shifting dance on his feet. The two girls were the last to notice and, by then, their dates had pushed them underneath the puttering chain saw and through the doorway.

The mannequin's leg lay on the floor. It had slid from the now-limp pants leg.

"They broke it," Emma said, condemnation in her tone. "And now they're running away." The foursome couldn't help but hear her, even in the next room.

"I'm sure it's fallen off before," I said.

Emma stepped closer. I reached for Miss Fix-It's shoulder, intending to steer her out of the stifling trailer and toward a fried elephant ear coated with powdered sugar.

She stooped and, before I could issue a motherly "Don't touch that," she said, "It's real." Very matter-of-fact.

I'm obviously not as quick as my brilliant but quirky niece. It took me a minute to see what had attracted her notice.

The lace-up work boot had walked many a mile before it retired to the sideshow. What stuck out the top wasn't a pale pink, smooth plastic mannequin leg.

It was weathered brown, like old cracked leather, and covered with thick, curly hairs. At the top, protruding from the leathery stump, was a gleaming white knob, roughly the size of the silver-tipped cane Mr. Brown carried to church on Sunday.

The top of a leg bone. For the first time, the fright house gave me a genuine jolt of adrenaline. The mannequin was real—and very dead.

TWO

Thursday Evening

I grabbed Emma's arm and jerked her to her feet. A silly reflex, I know, since it couldn't hurt us. But I wanted to get her away from what had become the most realistic fright house I'd ever encountered.

As we ducked under the chain saw and through the curtained doorway into the next room, I couldn't help but glance up at the face. I hadn't paid any attention to it before, but now the shrunken cheeks and shriveled lips made me shiver. The eyes were half-closed, the lips slightly parted, the wiry ginger hair sparse.

As a chain-saw-wielding maniac, he was completely unconvincing. As a real blood-chilling fright, he worked.

I bent protectively over Emma and tried to hustle her past the next exhibit, a fake graveyard. She didn't budge.

"Shouldn't we hide the leg?" she asked. "Somebody might steal it or mess with it."

I took a deep breath to slow my galloping heart rate. "Um—sure."

That was a good idea, but I needed a second to

get my well-calibrated fight-or-flight response under control.

"You stay right here," I said. She didn't argue.

I left Emma standing in the fake graveyard and let the curtain fall closed behind me before I slid the leg—surprisingly lightweight even with its heavy work boot—under the dusty curtain that draped the wall. Thanks to the baggy leg of the man's overalls, visitors likely wouldn't notice the missing boot. If they did notice, it would blend well with the general shabbiness of the rest of the fright house.

I put my arm around Emma and headed out the exit into the dusky blue twilight. The evening air felt cool, catching the perspiration on my arms and face.

I speed-dialed Rudy Mellin, chief deputy of the Camden County Sheriff's Department. No way I wanted to explain to a 911 dispatcher what we'd found, and I certainly didn't want it broadcast to every scanner addict in the county.

"Rudy, can you come over to the carnival? There's a little problem here."

"A–vry Andrews, why the hell don't you find somebody else and ruin his night off?"

Emma glanced up at me, so I knew she could hear both sides of the conversation.

I turned my back on her, hoping that would block Rudy's irate replies. "Emma and I just discovered a dead body in the fright house. He's not fresh. He's been there awhile. Didn't see any reason to cause a stampede by calling 911."

He gave a dramatic and exasperated sigh, but this time he didn't cuss.

"You still at the carnival? Meet me at the front gate. I'm about five minutes from the fairgrounds."

I mentally debated whether to tell the kid taking tickets at the fright house entrance about our discovery, but decided to let Rudy take charge of that. The place had no patrons lined up, clamoring to get in.

Emma and I retraced our steps along the midway, her hand in mine. The strands of lights outlining the rides and booths brightened as night fell. Rock music pulsed from the Tilt-a-Whirl. My chest pounded in time with the music as we passed.

"Who is he?" Emma's tone was matter-of-fact, as if she routinely spent Thursday evenings discovering desiccated human remains. "How'd he get there?"

Something about her straightforward curiosity made me shudder. She raised the puzzle with the same tone she would use to ask my dad how a toilet flushed or what a shotgun football offense was. Her face, upturned and waiting for an answer, showed no sign of false bravado or unacknowledged angst. She seemed to accept the puzzle as it came.

That left me the only one tamping down the willies. I knew too much about what followed a mysterious death. I could tell myself that was the reason, or I could just admit that it creeped me out.

Rudy pulled up outside the gate as we walked up to the chain-link fence. He didn't bother searching for a parking space. He was driving his personal car, not a county issue, though this one too was a sizable sedan in a nondescript color.

He walked around the front of the car and bent over to talk to the woman in the passenger seat. He straightened and tucked his shirt tight as she slid over into the driver's seat. His wife, I supposed, though I couldn't see her clearly.

Wearing a short-sleeved striped shirt and dark slacks, Rudy didn't look quite like himself without his khaki sheriff's uniform. He looked like a guy on a date. Maybe I just missed the authority the uniform implied.

"Thanks for making me miss dinner."

The badge clipped to his belt and his gun in a tidy holster on his hip helped reestablish his authority.

"Yeah, well, I haven't had my elephant ear yet. This wasn't on our schedule either."

For the first time, Rudy registered Emma's presence. He gave her a curt nod. She simply stared, her hand still in mine.

Another deputy pulled up outside the fence as Mrs. Mellin pulled away.

"Where is it?" Rudy asked. "Did you get them to shut it down?"

"No." Nobody'd given me a junior detective badge. "I didn't tell anyone what we found."

Rudy gave an exasperated huff. "This isn't some kind of prank, is it?"

I shrugged. "Who knows? All I know is they've got what's left of a human body dressed up and holding a chain saw in the fright house. Didn't seem like it ought to be there."

Rudy frowned. "How the hel—" He glanced at Emma. "How do you know it's real?"

"The leg fell off. Even Emma knows what the condyle on a lower leg looks like."

Emma nodded gravely. "Some kid bumped into it and the leg fell off. They all ran away so they wouldn't get in trouble." Miss Law-and-Order wanted to make sure all the miscreants were implicated.

Rudy looked concerned. "Did the kids realize what it was?" He asked me rather than Emma, though she might have been paying more attention to their reaction than I had.

"I don't think they noticed," I said. "They just thought he'd broken one of the displays."

"Would you recognize these kids?"

"Don't know. There were four of them—two guys, two girls. One of the girls was wearing a Wrestlemania T-shirt." Kids that age can all look alike, despite the time they spend on dressing to distinguish themselves.

"The one who bumped it had on square-toed orange sneakers," Emma said.

Both Rudy and I stared at her. Rudy couldn't know, but Emma has this thing about shoes.

"So where is it?"

We turned down the midway—which wasn't much. The Fourth Festival, held July Fourth week every year, was a modest affair at the county ballpark. A carnival midway, some local craft booths, and a hot-air balloon ride crowded the grassy lot, along with civic clubs and churches selling barbecue, pound cake, assorted home-baked goodies, and raffle tickets for a quilt or some fishing tackle. It couldn't really compete with Hillbilly Day up in Mountain Rest, with its greased pig, greased pole, and clogging contests, but it provided a garish bright spot in the heat of summer.

I studied the fright house with more interest as we approached it. It appeared to be constructed from a couple of trailers joined in the middle, probably easy to dismantle for the trip to the next town.

Lining the side of the trailers were a series of signs urging patrons to come inside and see the CHAMBER OF HORRORS! ZOMBIE GRAVEYARD! CHAIN SAW MASSACRE! NOT FOR THE FAINT OF HEART! Tinny screams and maniacal laughter played on a recorded loop.

"Step this way! These two lovely ladies will be glad of a big strong man to protect them." The barker at the ticket booth gave us his singsong spiel. The young kid who'd taken our tickets had been replaced by this gray-haired man who acted like he really wanted our business.

It took a second for him to spot the badge and gun.

Rudy leaned over and spoke quietly. "We're going to have to ask you to shut down for a few minutes, sir."

The ticket-taker wasn't inclined to be so quiet. "I can't do that! Whatever for? You can't roust me!" He stood almost as tall as he was wide, his polyester pants belted squarely around the widest part of his bowling ball middle. His head, a smaller bowling ball, perched atop his sloping shoulders.

He glared at me. Maybe he'd seen Emma and me enter earlier and thought we'd complained about something in his show. Come to think of it, we had.

"Sir, I need to check inside. Please don't sell any more tickets for a few minutes, until I get back."

Rudy looked around the booth, emphasizing without saying a word that there wasn't exactly a stampede demanding admission to his fright house.

I quietly told Rudy where I'd hidden the leg. I didn't want to take Emma back inside. A second visit might reinforce the reality and take it from mere puzzle to the stuff of nightmares. My brother-in-law Frank was already concerned that I could be a bad influence on his daughter. I didn't need to add to his list of my questionable actions an experience that might require long-term counseling.

Emma and I stood off to the side, away from the baleful eye of the fright house barker.

Not that he turned away any paying customers during the interminable ten minutes we waited. This was the first night of the week-long carnival and the crowds were sparse yet. Respecting Rudy's request, he stopped yelling his pitch, studiously avoiding us as he propped on his wooden stool and took sips from a cup underneath his podium.

Rudy came back out the entrance in what was, for him, a rush. Rudy normally moves with a big man's deliberation. While inside the trailer, he'd acquired a sense of urgency.

"Sir, we will have to close this attraction until further notice. Certainly for the rest of this evening."

"You can't—!"

"Yessir, I can. I'll also need to see the manager or owner or whoever is in charge of the entire midway."

"This is my attraction, my meat and potatoes. You can't sashay in here and take away a man's next meal." His protests were drawing more attention than his sideshow spiel had.

"Sir." Rudy kept his tone even and leaned close to the irate bowling ball. "What can you tell me about the dead man in your trailer?"

That shut him up. His eyes bugged out and he froze with his mouth open. Under the blinking bright lights of the midway, he turned a sallow shade of pale.

Rudy replaced his cell phone on his belt. He'd apparently alerted the troops.

"If you cooperate, we can do this the nice way, wait until after closing to bring in crime scene and not alarm the guests. Or we can do it the hard way and shut down the whole midway. Your choice."

He stared up at Rudy, wanting to argue but quickly calculating the cost. He then grabbed either side of the top of his rough podium and scooted it in front of the steps leading into the trailer. He flipped down a CLOSED sign and said, "This way."

"We'll be off," I said to Rudy, cocking my head in Emma's direction.

Emma hadn't let go of my hand, which worried me a bit. She wasn't the clingy type.

"Can you hang around for a little while? Just in case?"

"I'm kind of hungry," Emma said quietly. "And you promised we'd ride the Runaway Bobsled."

She must have sensed my hesitation about staying. I'd wondered about the best way to make the evening's events seem less out of the norm and therefore less scary. Sugar, fat grams, and the threat of throwing up. Couldn't get more normal than that.

"Sure," I said to Rudy. "I've got my cell phone."

Emma dropped my hand and headed toward the lemonade booth first, without waiting for me.

THREE

Friday Morning

I discovered that tough little seven-year-olds and experienced medical malpractice attorneys share something in common. Maybe it was a hereditary toughness. I'd refused to let on that I was queasy after the first medical autopsy I'd witnessed. Emma, in turn, didn't let a leg bone that could have appeared in a museum display case diminish her appetite.

We skipped the corn dogs with salt-and-vinegar fries and went for the fried elephant ear doused in powdered sugar I'd been craving. We then jumbled it around inside our stomachs on a couple of rides before we wandered over to watch the giant balloon rise and descend on its tether a couple of times, its insides periodically glowing in the dark sky, whooshing with hot air.

It hadn't taken much to talk ourselves out of buying tickets for a balloon ride, so I wasn't forced to learn if I was afraid of those kinds of heights.

After an hour, I called Rudy to tell him we were heading home, to call me if he needed anything. He sounded as though he'd forgotten he'd asked us to stay.

Emma spent the night with me, sleeping on the trundle bed in my room rather than the daybed in the next-door sitting room. I didn't want her to have a bad dream from her fright house visit—or from her culinary adventures. Or maybe it was in case I had a bad dream. In the dark before we fell asleep, we chatted for a while about the new clubhouse I'd promised to build for her.

The next morning, Emma seemed to take finding mummified remains completely in stride. For breakfast, we grabbed granola bars from my meager stores in the kitchen Melvin Bertram and I share. He and I have mirror-image downstairs offices and upstairs apartments in the Main Street Victorian that had begun life as Melvin's grandfather's house, served for a time as the Baldwin & Bates Funeral Home, and had reincarnated as the offices of Bertram & Associates and Avery Andrews, Attorney-at-Law.

Melvin was in Fort Lauderdale, meeting with a client in a mansion somewhere on a yacht canal, so we didn't have to worry about disturbing him on our way out. As we walked down the front walk, Emma detoured a few steps off the sidewalk to my giant stone angel statue. She patted the statue's foot, where it peeked out from under its draped stone robe.

"I like her," Emma said. "Even if Aunt Letha says she doesn't know where you got your sense of propriety."

I nodded, certain Emma knew what "propriety" meant. The eight-foot angel did defy convention. It had been destined as a grave marker, but a client decided she'd be happier if the angel moved to my front yard. It now serves as an unusual signpost, with AVERY ANDREWS, ATTORNEY-AT-LAW discreetly carved on her pedestal.

"Do people see the angel sign and come in?" Emma looked up, her hand still resting on the intricately carved bare foot.

"Yep." Surprisingly, the number of people who felt an urge to update their wills had really picked up since the angel had taken up residence.

I'd had to do a crash refresher on trusts and estates because I had never written a will before I'd returned to Dacus in November. Eight months ago, I'd been a successful trial attorney in Columbia, until my world had unexpectedly changed. What I'd planned as a temporary return to Dacus had become unexpectedly permanent. Spending time with Emma and my family—something I hadn't been able to do with the work schedule required by complex trial work—was a decided plus. As long as the angel kept bringing in clients needing wills and no one painted over my number inked on the walls in the Law Enforcement Center's intake cell, I might make it. Not the kind of money—or pressure—I'd been used to, but I might just make it.

This week, even though vacations are difficult to arrange when you're self-employed, I'd pledged to take some time off. With granola bars in hand, Emma and I climbed into my 1964 Mustang convertible—my grandfather's late-life fling—and headed north up Main Street to where the road began to climb into the Blue Ridge Mountains. We were joining her parents and some of their friends for a pre-Fourth of July picnic at Bow Falls.

"Who all's coming? Do you know?" I asked after I straightened out of the first curve in the road. We drove with the car top down. By late morning, the day would be too muggy.

"Some people Dad teaches with, I think. And Jack."

She clipped off Jack's name. I wasn't sure what that tone meant. "Who's Jack?"

"This kid in my class."

"Is he the only one your age who's coming?"

She shrugged. "Probably." That didn't bother Emma. She lived in a world of grown-ups.

"What's Jack like?"

"He's a freak."

I didn't ask if that was good or bad. Not knowing might make me a freak—the bad kind, the uncool-aunt kind.

I opted for a safer question. "What makes him a freak?"

I glanced at her in time to get the full effect of a dramatic eye roll. By the time she got to be a teenager, she would have that polished to perfection.

"You'll see. He's easy to spot. He wears a cape."

I could see her point. "He'll be in the second grade next year?"

"Uh-huh. That's okay. No one beats him up or anything. They just know that's him. He hangs upside down on the monkey bars for most of play period. But he's okay. For a boy."

High praise indeed.

From what I understood, this picnic was a mid-summer ritual for some of the professors and spouses that Frank knew from the university. Most of them didn't teach in the summer, spending their time on research projects—or goofing off. Who knew what they did? Years ago, when this group had arrived as young professors, they had formed a bond and usually had a mountain picnic the weekend before the Fourth of July, as well as a gathering at Lydia's and Frank's around Christmas.

Partying with a bunch of professors didn't sound particularly exciting, but I hadn't had any better offers. The closest I'd come was at the last Fourth Festival planning meeting when Adrienne Campbell, the festival president, had yet again tried to fix me up with Todd David, the city attorney. Professors who might lapse into quoting *Beowulf* in the original Old English after a few beers was infinitely preferable.

We hung a wide right onto the cutoff over the hill to the Bow Falls road. I hadn't been here in, gosh, years. As we topped the hill, I strained to catch a glimpse of the lake in the distance, but the hazy air and the now-tall trees blocked the view off the overlook.

When we pulled onto the rough asphalt leading into the parking area, I noticed how deafening the tree frogs were. Had they always been this noisy? They seemed louder in town recently, especially in the late evening when I often take walks. The rhythmic pulsing would drown out New York street traffic, given the chance. Unlike traffic, though, this pulsed, almost like breathing, as though the world and all that was green inhaled and exhaled in a loud chorus.

I handed Emma the money to stuff into the fee collection box. Not a voluntary act on crowded weekends because parking lot monitors wandered about. I understand the economics of rationing access to wilderness areas, but paying to walk out to see a waterfall seemed a bit . . . unnatural. Judging from the crowds, the parking fee didn't keep anyone away.

"I hope somebody brought potato salad without green crunchy things," Emma said as she gave a mighty heave to the long car door.

She walked a few steps ahead of me, and I noticed that I hadn't done a very neat job braiding her ponytail.

Lydia's fingers would itch to fix it as soon as she spotted it.

But Emma had brushed her teeth and said her prayers last night, without any prompting from me. So she hadn't completely fallen apart while she was in my unpracticed care, despite what my brother-in-law Frank feared.

"There's Mom and Dad!" Emma took off running, her sneakers kicking up behind her with each step.

I caught up with them on the narrow paved path just in time to hear her announce, "—found a dead body." She paused for dramatic effect. "It was sca-ree." Complete with dramatic hand gestures to emphasize the last two syllables.

First I'd heard that she'd found it scary.

Frank's and Lydia's gazes went from their theatrical daughter to me, their mouths slightly agape, their eyebrows raised.

I offered what Granddad would have called a mule-eating-briars grin.

"He looked like a mummy, all dry and crusty," Emma continued. "His leg fell off."

From the looks on their faces, I could see that the grapevine hadn't carried news of the discovery as far as their house.

I filled them in on the evening's activities, downplaying the drama. "He'd apparently been there for a while. It wasn't like there was any danger."

That last sounded defensive, but I couldn't help it. Frank's runner-lean face was pulled into that stern frown I saw too often from him.

We'd almost reached the top of the gentle slope that ends in the first look-off to the falls.

"There's Jack," Emma announced. She made a skip, the prelude to a full-tilt run to join a skinny redheaded kid, who stood with his parents and a picnic basket at the overlook.

"Emma!" Lydia called her back. Emma froze midstride and spun around, struggling not to look frustrated.

"It would be best," Lydia said, "if you didn't say anything about this, especially to Jack."

Emma's shoulders slumped forward and her mouth fell open. "Mo-om."

"You don't know the whole story. It's best to wait until you do."

Lame reason to keep a good story to yourself, I thought, *especially when Jack looked like such a promising audience.*

"The police are investigating," I said to help out. "Once that's finished . . ."

One side of Emma's mouth knotted in a thoughtful frown, but she nodded and spun into a run.

Frank hefted their picnic basket and walked on ahead.

Lydia waited until he was out of earshot. "Avery, how could you get her involved in something like that? She's only seven!"

"I didn't get her involved. We went into a really cheesy, stupid, very unscary fright house at the fair and a mannequin's leg fell off while we were standing there. End of story."

Lydia gave me a dismayed frown.

I tried to chide her into remembering she'd been a kid once. "Think what a great what-I-did-on-my-summer-vacation essay she'll have when school starts."

Lydia bit her lip and covered her mouth to hide her smile, maintaining a facade of decorum. "We'd have killed to have something like that to write about, wouldn't we?"

"Lots better than making up stuff."

Emma eyed us as we joined them at the overlook, probably both relieved and suspicious at our laughter.

Lydia introduced me to Jack and his parents, then Frank and Jack's dad trudged on up the path toward the top of the falls.

I overheard Emma whisper to Jack, "She's a lawyer, and she's going to build me a clubhouse."

He stood stock-still, assessing me with a steady blue-eyed gaze. He didn't look impressed in the least.

"She's the one with the angel statue in front of her office," Emma continued in a stage whisper.

From the cock of his head and his continued stare, I assumed that raised me a tiny notch in his consideration. I liked the looks of Jack, with his pale red hair and freckles and his magnificent purple cape.

"Why do you have that angel?" he asked me.

"I like her. She watches over me."

He studied me a moment and nodded. For a kid in a cape, I guessed just liking something was reason enough.

"Let's go." Lydia waved Emma and Jack along. "We've got to finish setting up."

I hung back a minute, leaning against the rail fence worn smooth by uncounted hands. The hillside fell steeply off the overlook and rose again on the opposite side of a deep draw. Framed in the middle distance by thick summer green was Bow Falls, the tallest waterfall in the eastern United States. The sound of the water tumbling on the granite rocks carried faintly to where I stood. The rains on Wednesday had fed it full.

I remembered when the path from the parking lot to the overlook had first been paved, a blasphemy in my mind. Too civilized. Too easy for people to get here now—not that it had ever been hard, as long as you drove slowly and didn't knock a dent in your oil pan as you dropped off onto the unpaved entrance road. Now, though, it was all very civilized—and crowded. I was joined by a chattering bunch of college kids, not serious hikers, just a carload passing on the way to somewhere else. Hard to get a moment to commune alone.

Dad said he remembered being able to drive along the path that clung to the hillside and even across the top of the falls. As I walked along that same path, now strewn with boulders, I couldn't imagine how that was possible. Maybe the boulders had been blasted loose when the state built the road that now ran above my head, invisible in the thick trees on the steep hillside. I listened to a car pass on the highway above and was glad they'd stopped letting people drive along this track. I was sure many had objected to that change. Always a balancing act, access and quiet communion.

For the short walk to the top of the falls, I had the rare pleasure of having the trail to myself. Where the trail reached the creek bank, the only hint that I'd reached the top of the falls was the faint rumble of water to my right, when it flowed over the rocks and disappeared into the undergrowth. This wasn't a place where a canoeist could paddle too close to the falls unawares—the creek was shallow, rocky, and unnavigable, and the noise was warning enough.

The path ended on a narrow section of the creek, where a series of broad, flat stones provided a dry crossing, well back from where the falls made its first drop.

We were apparently the late arrivals, and this hadn't been Lydia's and Frank's first trip from the parking lot. Lydia had supplied folding canvas chairs for the four of us, and the other families had brought their own. The contents of several food baskets crowded a couple of folding tables set side by side. Lydia introduced a tall man with thinning sandy hair as Spencer Munn.

He bent to get a beer from one of several coolers. "Can I get you one?"

"No, thanks," I said.

Lydia had insisted I didn't need to bring anything but myself. I also apparently couldn't offer any assistance in setting up, so I accepted Spencer's offer to introduce me around.

The picnickers seemed to all know each other, but I wasn't going to remember many of the names. Some of them could have appeared at a county bar or a corporate board meeting and passed without question. Others, though, had clearly embraced the free-wheeling boundary-lessness of the academic life, as evidenced by their outdated clothes and well-worn Birkenstocks.

Clemson University, where Frank taught, was twenty miles and a world away from Dacus. He and Lydia had bought a rambling farmhouse on the outskirts of Dacus, and he commuted. The distance— mostly a perceptual barrier—had proven sufficient to let Lydia decide when she wanted to engage as a faculty wife and when she just wanted to strip wood floors and paint bead board and go to church circle meetings.

Spencer Munn introduced me to a tall fellow with skeletal facial bones and a gray rattail hanging past his shoulders, an English literature professor. Eden Rand, a soft-featured woman with a halo of orange hair and wearing billowing acres of mauve and orange gauze, taught sociology. Fred, a buff sixty-year-old, who looked great in his Levi jeans and boots, was a mechanical engineer.

"Fred here has done some expert witness work, haven't you?" Spencer said by way of a conversation starter. "Avery's a trial lawyer."

Fred shrugged. "A couple of grain auger accidents a few years back, that's all." His blue eyes met mine and held. He'd be good with a jury. Real good. I wondered that he wasn't wearing a wedding ring. His gaze seemed a bit forward, hinting he might be unattached with good reason.

"Rog!" Spencer waved over a middle-aged man with pale skin, pale eyes, and a pale shirt with faint wrinkles. "Do you know Lydia's sister, Avery?"

Rog offered me a warm, slightly moist handshake. His eyes were pale crystal blue and searched me as if he genuinely wanted to remember me.

"I don't think we've met. I'm Rog Reimann."

"Thought you might have run into each other. Rog's wife is a hometown girl. Maybe you know Rinda?"

"Ye-es." The unusual name triggered my memory. "She finished high school with Lydia. She was a cheerleader."

Rog's wide mouth softened in a gentle smile. "She was." He looked pleased that I knew.

"Rog and Rinda moved here, when? Two years ago? Rog is one of the university's top grant winners. Some obscure science field I don't understand but should probably invest in."

Rog ducked his head. His work must be extraordinary because I couldn't see him pulling in corporate or government grants on what I could see of his personal sales skills.

"It's nice to meet you. Is Rinda here?"

"Somewhere." He looked around absently.

"Great." As we continued to circulate among the groups, I studied my host. He wasn't quite what I'd expected when he introduced himself as an economist. He didn't look like he fit with the other professors. Instead of ragged cargo shorts and sandals, or jeans and hiking boots, or a cape, his picnic ensemble featured a silk Hawaiian shirt he hadn't gotten off the discount rack. The front pictured a buff surfer dude and a bathing beauty on Waikiki, with a massive pink building in the background.

"The Royal Hawaiian Hotel," he said, catching my stare and pointing to his chest. "That's supposed to be the Duke himself. The surfer movie star, not John Wayne, the movie star." He grinned, taking nothing seriously.

Two canvas chairs stood waiting for us, tucked on either side of a flat boulder that made the perfect side table for his beer.

"So you're a trial lawyer," he said.

"Used to be. Not much call for that in Dacus."

"Lydia said you'd moved back recently. You like being back home?"

"Yeah, I do." I couldn't have said that six months ago and meant it. It wasn't what I'd planned for my life, but every time I thought about what I'd planned, I could hear God chuckling in the background.

"How about you?" I asked. "Where did you grow up?"

"Norfolk, mostly."

"You like it here? It's a long way from the coast."

"I must like it. Been here fifteen years."

"You teach with Frank and the others?"

"Used to, long time ago. I left the big state school

world. Too rigid for me. I'm over at Ramble College, have been for ten years."

I nodded. Ramble was a small liberal arts college in the neighboring county, but it had never been much on my radar screen.

"These guys still keep me in the fold," he said. "Hope they warned you. Once you party with this crowd, they adopt you for life."

I smiled. I didn't point out I already had family in the group.

"So you teach economics?"

"Mostly. Ramble doesn't, of course, have a formal business program. That would carry too much the taint of mammon to suit its liberal arts calling. But they do allow us to introduce the little dears to the realities of the world, disguised as economic theory, and they allow me to do my consulting and investment work on the side, so it's been a good home base."

"Investment work?"

"Yeah. Sure I can't get you something to drink?" He gestured with his almost full beer bottle, dripping with condensation in the muggy air.

"Not just yet. Thanks. My office mate in Dacus is an investment adviser or wealth manager or some such. Melvin Bertram?"

The essential Southern exercise—casting about for degrees of separation, looking for the thread that will unravel how we are related.

"Bertram. I've heard of him. Wasn't he messed up in some murder investigation a few months ago?"

He must have seen a warning signal in my expression.

"Sorry. Was that rude? I sometimes just say what comes first to mind. He's your partner?"

"No, no. We just share office space." I never explain about also sharing the apartment spaces upstairs. That always got too complicated. And I wasn't about to talk about Melvin's wife's death. That was old news long settled. "What kind of investment work do you do?"

All I knew about investment advisers was my mental picture of Melvin staring at his computer screen in his dimly lit office and taking trips—fly-fishing in Canada, deep-sea fishing off Fort Lauderdale, canopy runs in Costa Rica—to see his far-flung and obviously well-to-do clients.

Spence gave a mild chuckle and settled back in his chair, his ankle resting on his knee. "Never meant for it to turn into work, exactly." His shoes were woven leather and linen, not the scruffy sneakers several of the other men were wearing.

"I started out just investing for myself. Developed a system that worked, other people wanted me to help them make the most of their nest eggs. Took me a while to see life beyond the classroom, but now I have the best of both worlds."

"That's nice." I studied him. He was probably six or eight years older than I. Would I someday reach that settled, happy place, certain of what I wanted to be when I grew up? This lanky man with the beaming moon face seemed to have reached it, and was happy to be there.

"Oh, Lord. Don't tell me Spence is over here lecturing you on the time value of money and the wonders of high-yield debentures." The billowy woman floating in swirls of gauze—what was her name?—joined us, a sweating can of Diet Pepsi in her hand.

"Did you see that beautiful little flower over there? I have no idea what it is. Where's a botanist when you need one? I should've brought my camera."

"Have a seat, Eden." Spence wrestled his way out of the embrace of the canvas chair and took a seat on the boulder. "I'll get my camera for you. I left it in the car. But first, explain to us the social dynamic we see about us, as observed by your trained sociologist's eye."

"Better yet," Eden said, "why don't you give us a hot stock tip? Much more useful."

"Oh, I don't know about that. For instance, explain what's with Rinda Reimann and her attachment to that cell phone."

He nodded toward a woman in form-fitting, stark white pants as she strolled away from the group, both hands cradling her phone to her ear. She hadn't changed much in the fifteen years since I'd last seen her.

"I'd have to be a psychologist—or a marriage counselor—to explain that one, my dear. I'm only good at exploring why we eat ground pig parts rather than fried ants to celebrate our political holidays, or why we insist on maintaining the marriage construct when it leaves one looking as miserable as Rog Reimann does right now."

Over Eden's shoulder, I saw Rog approaching, though he didn't seem to have heard her comments.

"Or," Eden continued, "why, in the name of chivalry, you would offer me this ass-grabbing chair from which I'll never be able to extricate myself while you run for the open freedom of your rock."

Spence gave her a mock salute with his beer bottle.

"Spence, old man." Rog joined us, his posture apologetic. "Could I have a word with you?"

"Rog. Sure. Can I get you something to drink?"

Rog blinked, as if just realizing he stood in the center of our gathering. "Sorry to interrupt," he said. Spence stood to join him. Even if Rog stood up straight, he'd still only come to Spence's shoulder. The way Spence's summer-weight silk slacks draped along his long legs made Rog's round-legged, rumpled khakis look even more forlorn. I wondered what Rog taught and where Rinda, the slender cheerleader, had met him.

Rog had to be a professor. The only groups I knew who ignored clothes when measuring a person's worth were members of the academy and street people. Rog fit in too well with the others here to be a street person. It didn't take a sociologist to be intrigued by the wardrobe choices, ranging from Rog's street-worn chic to Eden's and Spence's costumes. My jeans, white oxford shirt, and sneakers put me firmly outside the norm in this crowd.

Emma came running up and grabbed the armrest on my chair, hailing me with the pet name only she uses. "Aunt Bree, Mama says we can walk up the trail if you'll go with us."

"Sure." I nodded to Eden as I extricated myself from my chair. "Can we bring you another Diet Pepsi?"

I was glad of an excuse to avoid more small talk right now, but I could still be polite.

"No, thanks. I'm going to rest in the shade and pretend it's not sweltering."

Emma and Jack ran ahead and around a quick crook in the narrow path with an exuberance that seemed too far past in my memory. On this far side of the creek, the undergrowth crowded the path closely, blocking any hint of a breeze.

I reached the bend in time to see Jack scramble up and run along the top of a storm-felled tree. The thickness of the trunk more than equaled Jack's height.

He paused at the end where the toppled trunk had been sawed in half to free it from its half-buried knot of roots. He held the edges of his cape, ready to launch himself off the edge and down a twenty-foot drop.

Before I could get warning words out of my mouth, Emma gave a sharp command. "Stop that, Jack! You'll kill yourself!"

From his perch above her, his fists still gripping the edges of his cape, he studied the end of the log jutting into space and looked down at her. "Wouldn't be worth that," he said.

Before I could deal with my amazement that a boy had backed down willingly from a brainless stunt, the sound of panicked yells rose behind us.

Jack spun, startled. I stepped up to give him a hand down from the log before he tumbled off without intending to. Gathered in a close knot, the three of us headed back down the path. The screams were compelling and chilling at the same time.

Within a few steps, we came into range and could make out the words. "She fell! Help! She fell! Oh, my God, please, God! She fell!"

I kept Emma and Jack behind me, which offered only symbolic shelter. The screams jolted me with their terror.

Lydia swooped in without warning on Emma and Jack like a protective mother bear, ushering them back up the path and away from the scene.

Rog Reimann stood in the center of a wide, loose circle of faces frozen in shock. He stumbled as if blind, his voice raw with pain and fear. No one moved.

I covered the ground between us in three strides and took him by the shoulders. He wasn't a large man.

"Rog." I leaned close and tried to get him to focus on my face. "Rog."

I gave him a soft shake and kept my tone steady. "Where is she?"

It didn't matter who "she" was. "Tell me where."

He started blubbering. Snot and saliva wet his face. "The falls. She went over the falls. Rinda . . ."

His knees buckled and he sank at my feet.

FOUR

Friday Morning

I left Rog to the others' ministrations and wasted no time hitting the wide trail to the creek and the falls.

Frank split off from the crowd and joined me. A fifty-yard jog took us to the deceptively smooth water and the stepping-stone ford. The insistent, muted roar of the falls rose from twenty yards downstream and the jumble of rocks where the river disappeared from view.

"Rinda!" Frank called. His baritone carried well. I joined him, yelling, "Rinda!" We paused after each call to listen.

I scouted the edges of the water, deciding whether the best path was to the near or far side of the creek.

Spencer Munn startled us by appearing out of the trees on the opposite bank.

He called over the rush of the water. "I heard yelling. What happened?" His outstretched hands conveyed the question.

"Rinda Reimann." Frank cupped his hands around his mouth and yelled. "Have you seen her?" He pointed to the top of the falls. "Rog said she went over."

Spence shook his head. His face blanched, notice-ably pale under his tan, his eyes darting as if trying to put together an unfathomable puzzle.

"When did you cross the creek?"

"A few minutes ago," he called. "I was headed back to the car for my camera. I heard someone yell-ing." He shrugged as if he could offer nothing more.

Talking wasn't finding Rinda. I crossed the creek on the exposed stones and landed a few feet down-stream from where Spence stood. The undergrowth crowding the bank offered no footpath. Animals had no reason to wear a trail along this part of the creek; it led nowhere but over the steep mountainside, and the creek provided easier drinking spots at and above the trail crossing, where the creek banks were rock-edged and open.

The water was flowing higher than normal, though judging from the grass combed smooth and brushed with silt, it was lower than it had been just after the recent rain. Had she been wading in the creek? That was the only way she could have fallen.

I pushed through the thick undergrowth to where the steep hillside began to fall away. I grabbed a sap-ling and tugged gently to test whether its roots had a good hold.

On the other side of the creek, Frank interrupted his calls for Rinda to yell at me, "Be careful!"

I listened intently, hoping to hear Rinda's voice calling from some safe spot.

Others came down the path from the picnic site, but they all hung back from the creek edge, as if fearful the gentle water would reach out and grab them one by one. When I glanced back, I didn't see Lydia in the group. Best to keep Emma and Jack away from this. I didn't see Rog, either. Judging from his near-hysteria, I doubted he would've been much help, though I wished he'd told us more about where he'd last seen her.

I wanted to find a spot where I could look over the edge. I feared she was stuck on a ledge or holding on to a shrub or vine somewhere below. I didn't want to look and not see her, though, because that could mean she'd found no safe purchase.

I glanced over my shoulder. Spence stood alone about twenty yards from me, on my side of the creek. He looked completely out of his element in his brightly colored shirt. Frank and the others were scattered near the crossing stones on the opposite side of the creek.

"Spence," I called, rousing him from his troubled reverie. I held an imaginary phone to my ear. "Call 911. Get the Rescue Squad up here."

Better get them on the road. It took thirty minutes to drive up here, plus the time needed to roll out their climbing gear and walk to the falls—or make their way down the mountainside. Best call for help before I spotted her. If I could spot her.

Spence nodded and reached in his pocket, moving on autopilot now that he had a familiar task to perform.

I picked my way around a thick patch of brambles growing right where I thought I would have the best view over the drop-off. I was glad I'd worn jeans, and I tried not to think about the snakes the warm rocks and thick blackberry hedges would attract. I'd be picking ticks out of my hair for days.

Frank, on the opposite bank, called again, "Be careful." I was glad he hadn't decided to be all macho about who took on the stupid task of trying to peer over the edge. Frank was athletic, a long-distance runner, but he hadn't spent as much time climbing these hills as I had.

Frank couldn't go any farther on his side, but I could edge down a few feet more on my side without turning myself into another Rescue Squad project.

"Keep calling," I said. "If she's on a ledge, maybe we can locate her."

"Ohmigawd! Don't let her fall!" Some woman from the picnic gathering shrieked. She startled me and I almost slipped.

For some reason, I flashed to the hot-air balloon at the fair. Why did that height, tethered to a sturdy rope, bother me and this didn't? Maybe because here I had my feet on the ground—unless they slipped out from under me or my sapling lost its hold. Height was relative and fear—or lack of fear—could be irrational.

"Hush," Frank said, coming to my rescue. "She knows what she's doing."

I tuned out the rest of their chatter, focusing on the spray of cold water that now coated me and the thick green undergrowth and stray brambles in which I found a foothold.

I held my position, straining over as far as I dared and praying the sapling had deep roots. I wrapped a vine around the palm of my other hand, in case it didn't.

Inch by inch, squinting to see through the mist, I studied the solid green and the mottled dark boulders for any sign of movement alien to the amazing volume of water flowing from the gentle creek and the misty waving plants caught in the perpetual breeze from the cascade.

What had she been wearing? I remembered the white pants. What else? Orange top and orange shoes.

Orange. Was there a spot of orange among the greens and blues and frothy white?

I took one more baby step down and leaned as far as I dared, the tree bending its last. My foot slipped and I stopped.

Did I see a bit of orange? Was it a shoe?

Could be. I couldn't tell. It lay below, slightly to the side of the heaviest cascade, where the water foamed white. From this perspective, though, I could see no sign of a ledge tucked back behind the water, no place where she might be clinging to a branch. No sign of movement.

I pulled myself back up along the bent length of the sapling. My right foot slipped on the wet ground and I caught my breath. I had turned my back to the drop-off, but the thunder of the water pounded the vision of the sheer drop into my mind.

Inching slowly, I climbed to where I stood on level ground. I bent over, my hands on my knees, gasping for breath. Adrenaline had burned up all the energy reserves in my body and left me shaking.

Spencer Munn still held the phone to his ear, probably listening to the comforting reassurances and gentle questioning of the 911 dispatcher. I idly wondered who was on duty today.

Frank took me by the arm. I hadn't noticed him cross the creek.

"You okay?" He talked close to my ear, genuinely concerned. I was touched. Frank and I don't know each other well. That he'd married my only sister provided our only real bond. Until I'd moved back to Dacus in November, we'd never had reason to spend time together except at noisy family gatherings. Most of our individual interactions had been when Frank registered disapproval at some of the things I'd introduced to his daughter—beating a best-time run down the mountain in the Mustang, watching an impromptu tobacco-spitting contest at the mountain grocery, target practice with my .38 Police Special, all the words to the moonshine song.

Today, Frank had been the one guy among the bunch who stepped up. The fact that he held my elbow until my legs quit wobbling was another plus in his favor.

"I might have seen her shoe, or something," I told him. "Nothing else." No one could hear our conversation.

He nodded. "Let's go get you something to drink."

"They're on their way," Spence said as we approached him, pointing to his cell phone. "Yes, ma'am," he said to the phone.

Frank and I crossed the stream to a deluge of questions.

"Did you see her?"

"Are you sure she went off? Maybe she's just wandering in the woods."

"Maybe Rog made a mistake."

"Somebody call her cell phone. She's always got that blasted phone to her ear. See if she answers."

That wasn't a bad idea. "Frank, you got your cell phone?"

He still hovered at my side as if he feared I might topple over and he'd have to explain to Lydia how I hit my head on a rock.

He fished it out of his pocket. "Anybody know her number?"

They all looked at each other.

"Wait, I've got it programmed in," a woman in a yellow sundress and strappy sandals said. "It's on the table with the food."

She headed down the path, the skirt of her sundress swaying.

"Why don't some of you take turns calling her name?" Frank said. "The rest listen. If she's just gone for a walk or if she's stumbled onto a ledge or something, maybe we can find her."

That gave them something important to do while we followed the sunny yellow sundress back to the now almost deserted picnic spot.

Rog sat on a boulder, holding a plastic sandwich bag filled with ice to the back of his head.

Lydia, who'd probably fixed the makeshift ice pack, had Jack smearing together peanut butter and jelly sandwiches and Emma stacking lunch meat on mayonnaise bread. Didn't matter who'd eat the sandwiches. Keeping the right people occupied was the real goal.

"You want some tea?"

I nodded, taking a seat in one of the folding chairs near where Lydia and her galley slaves were hard at work.

Answering Lydia's questioning gaze, I shook my head. "Spence has called for the Rescue Squad." I took a long draw on the sweet tea.

Rog's eyes grew large and I thought I saw tears well up, but he didn't say anything, whether from shock or from respect for the little ears, I wasn't sure.

Until that moment, I hadn't thought what calling the Rescue Squad meant: Pudd Pardee and his merry band of misfits, guys who signed up so they'd have an excuse to clamp mail-order emergency lights to the roofs of their pickups and go racing around the county performing daring feats—or ogling blood-and-guts accident scenes so they'd have stories to tell at Tap's Pool Room while waiting for the next call.

The sundress lady flipped her phone shut and joined us. "No answer. I'll keep trying, though."

She disappeared back down the path. I noticed that Jack's parents weren't around. I hadn't noticed them in the crowd at the falls, but I hadn't paid much attention to individual faces.

"Rog," I said, keeping my tone gentle. "You feel like walking with me for a minute?"

I didn't want to upset him or tire him, especially if he'd gotten a concussion or something when he fainted. But if he could pinpoint the spot where she went off, it might help the rescue guys narrow their search area.

He took the dripping plastic bag from his head and stood, looking around as though he didn't quite know what to do.

I took the bag from his hand, the ice almost melted in the thick July heat, and tossed it in a garbage bag someone—likely Lydia—had clipped to the edge of one of the folding tables.

I led him into the trees, just out of Jack's and Emma's earshot.

"Rog. I know this is difficult, but we need to know what happened. The Rescue Squad is on its way. Anything you can do to help locate her . . ."

Tears welled on cue and his bottom lip quivered, slight but unmistakable.

This was going to require leading questions. "She fell off the top of the waterfall?"

He nodded.

"Where was she standing? As you face the falls, was she on the right bank of the creek or the left?" I spoke slowly and simply, as if to a none-too-bright child.

He looked puzzled and shook his head.

I repeated the question. "Where was she standing?"

"In the creek."

"She was in the creek?"

That had looked like the only way the accident could have happened, but why would she do that?

"Why was she in the creek?"

He shrugged. "I don't know. But that must be what happened."

I moved so that we stood face to face. Rog was at least half a head taller than my five-foot-three inches, but he'd slumped into himself. He seemed to have trouble focusing. I blamed shock because I couldn't smell alcohol.

"Did you see where she was standing?"

He shook his head, more tears welling up.

"You didn't see her?"

Another shake.

"Where were you?"

"On the path, farther up the creek. A little glade there, quite peaceful, with the water on the rocks. I heard her scream. Just once."

"So you didn't see her fall?"

"No." His chest deflated like a balloon with air escaping.

"How do you know she fell?"

He looked at me with a blank expression. I needed to slap some sense into him. "That scream. One scream . . ."

"Where was she standing when you last saw her?"

"Near the top of the falls."

"On which side? The side closest to the parking lot path or to the picnic area?"

"On a rock. In the creek."

"Near the path? Or closer to the waterfall?"

He thought for a blink or two. "In between."

"What was she doing?"

"Talking on the phone."

"With whom?" She must have been closer to the trail crossing than to the falls, else the noise would have drowned out her conversation. Who the heck comes to a peaceful place like this with her ear glued to a cell phone? Maybe she was one of those moms who can't bear to leave her kids. Did she have kids?

An expression I didn't quite understand crossed Rog's face, but he didn't answer with anything more than a shrug.

"Did she say anything to you?" I was trying to find a gentle way to ask about her state of mind. Was she angry, out of control? Happily unaware of where she was? What was going on with her?

He just shook his head.

"What happened next?"

"I walked up the stream to the glade. Waiting for her to quit talking."

"You don't know who she was talking to?"

His brow creased as though he'd had a painful cramp somewhere, and he shook his head. He stared off into the trees, where the green closed in thick around us.

"So you didn't see her fall?"

His head slumped forward. "No."

I patted his upper arm, the spot where I'd earlier grabbed him to get his attention. "I'm so sorry. They'll find her. They're very good at this kind of thing."

I walked him back to the picnic spot. "Do you need another ice pack?"

He hesitated before he answered, everything on a slight time-delay for him. "No."

Lydia took charge. "Rog, you need to sit down. Let me get you some tea."

She led him away, and I turned back toward the faint roar of the falls, feeling helpless. The rescuers would be searching in a very tall, very wet and slippery haystack—and they'd need to search in a hurry.

FIVE

Friday Afternoon

The Rescue Squad arrived in their individual pickup trucks, followed closely by the idle members of the Ghouly Boys—the guys who have nothing better to do on a Friday afternoon than jump in their trucks as soon as a dispatch comes over their radio receivers. Some of the Ghouly Boys, spurred only by ghoulish but leisurely curiosity, managed to get there before the last of the rescuers arrived.

Setting up the search and rescue was a painfully slow, methodical operation. I wanted to jump in and start barking orders because it looked as if too many of them were just standing around with no clear purpose. Pudd Pardee, his belly straining his khaki shirt and the few remaining hairs on his head standing as if electrified, had the judicious good sense to defer to a somber, stick-built man who looked the part of a rappeller and swift-water rescue expert. Pudd, on the other hand, looked like a redneck jabber box, good for bellying up to a bar. The only purpose he could serve, in a water rescue, was if they needed a large, round float for some reason.

The picnic food would've gone to waste but for

Lydia offering the sandwiches and potato salad and homemade cookies to Pudd and the guys. The potential tragedy had no discernible effect on the appetites of the Rescue Squad members who hadn't been assigned a task or any of the Ghouly Boys. True, they didn't know Rinda Reimann personally. Her friends and acquaintances, anxiously awaiting word that she was safe, could do little more than sip tea or beer.

Three of the rescuers left to drive down the mountain and make the demanding hike up the falls from the bottom, two others were scouting how to rappel down either side, and Pudd was on the phone seeing if a helicopter could approach the falls and provide "aerial reconnaissance," as he called it.

I sat on the flat boulder we'd used as a side table when the picnic began, bent over trying to pick a blackberry briar out of my sock. A pair of leather and linen loafers stopped within my low field of vision.

"You okay?" Spence asked, his voice soft.

"You have a tear in your pants." I sat at eye level with the inch-long rip in the beige silk near his knee.

He glanced down. "If that's the worst that happened. You didn't answer my question. You okay?"

"Yeah." I looked up. His eyebrows were knotted in concern. "You?"

He nodded.

I dusted my hands on my knees and stood. "I think Lydia's all packed up."

"I'll see you later?" He presented it as a question, not as a casual farewell. And I swear he shuffled his feet.

"Um, sure," I said.

He smiled and ducked his head, making me think of a shy third-grader as he turned and joined the mechanical engineer on the path to the parking lot. He stopped to speak to Lydia, apparently offering to carry something. She shook her head and gave him a pat on the arm.

As he left, I joined Lydia, and we stayed just long enough to make sure we couldn't do more to help. We crossed the creek one last time carrying a final load to the car, making sure Emma and Jack were in tow.

Rather than acting either panicked or fixated on what had happened, Emma and Jack asked a few questions before discussing whether they'd play two-person soccer or have a club meeting in the tree house. I credited Lydia's calm vibes for that.

"Wow, Jack," said Emma as I checked their seat belts. "You made it through the whole picnic without spilling anything on yourself. That's good." Her tone implied *for you,* but carried no malice or meanness.

Jack fixed her with a round-eyed stare. "Not quite," he said. He tugged at the hem of his T-shirt, uncovering a jelly stain that had been hidden in a fold.

Emma studied it with a solemn expression. "Still, that's good. You can't hardly see it."

He nodded, accepting the compliment.

Lydia returned from giving Frank instructions about the rest of the picnic supplies and checked that both kids were settled in the back of the van. Emma waved at me, and Jack solemnly followed suit with a cocked open hand.

I drove off alone. As soon as I slipped in the clutch and shifted into reverse, my legs started shaking. I hoped the search and rescue went quickly and would not have had reason to become a recovery operation.

Friday afternoon before Fourth of July week felt like a holiday in Dacus. I'd given myself and Shamanique, my new assistant, today and all next week off.

Melvin was out of town. I had no appointments, nothing to prepare for, nothing pending next week. Dacus is an old cotton-textile mill town and, years after most of the nineteenth-century plants were shuttered and replaced by high-tech jobs, many in the county still took off the first two weeks in July, just like they and their grandparents did when the big textile mills closed for summer vacation.

The junk shops dotted along Main Street were full of tourists, the folks who'd headed to the hills to escape the heat in the low-lying parts of Georgia and South Carolina as well as those who'd come home to visit family but who'd already enjoyed enough of being cooped up together. My usual haunts, though, are not on the tourists' paths and seldom suffer from crowds.

When I walked in, I was surprised to find the light on my office answering machine blinking. Surely it was too early in the day for calls from celebrants who'd found their way to the Law Enforcement Center intake.

"Miz Andrews? This here's Pinner Pliny. Could you call me as quick as you can? I'm in a steaming pile of trouble and all I hear is you're a good one to call."

Pinner Pliny? The voice, though husky, sounded female.

"Oh, I'm with the carnival in town. The sheriff's shut us down, which leaves me in a world of hurt. And my husband. Please call me soon as you get this." She repeated the phone number for good measure.

I dialed Pinner Pliny's number and, on the second ring, got the same smoky voice.

"Thank gawd. We're in a pure nervous fidget here, let me tell you. Nothing like this has ever happened.

Well, not since the peep shows, says E.Z. My husband. Can you hear him in the background? Says they used to have to pay off the sher'ffs in the little towns, to keep the girlie shows open, but nobody runs those no more anyhow."

"Just go to the movies for an eye full now." A voice in the background carried over Pinner Pliny's end of the line.

"We'd offer to pay 'em off on this, but something tells me that wouldn't work. They're acting like we kilt somebody. Which we didn't."

"Yes, ma'am," I said, more to break the flow than to agree. "What exactly would you like me to do for you?"

"Get us opened back up. We're gonna starve to death otherwise. Miss this whole stop, the whole Fourth of July. We can't rebook the date. It's already too late. Even if we could, the sher'ff made noises like she might hold us here anyway. As some kind of witness or something. E.Z. said he didn't think she could do that but, to me, she didn't look like somebody I'd want to mess with."

Mrs. Pliny had that figured right. I wouldn't mess with Sheriff L. J. Peters. I'd known L.J.—Lucinda Jane—since grade school, but familiarity had not bred fondness. Wariness, but not fondness.

"Tell me about—what you know." I'd never had a client who'd been carting a dead body around in a carnival attraction. I didn't offer that I was the one who'd reported the body.

"We don't know nothing. They say that was human, not a mannequin. How the hell were we supposed to know that?"

"Where'd you get the mannequin?"

"In with a bunch of props we bought from this guy when he died. We knew him in Gibtown. Decided a one-off would be easier to operate than some of the center joints we'd been running. So we bought it off his daughter, refurbed the trailer, added the automation. Pretty tame before E.Z. got hold of it. We've been doing good with it, though. This'll kill us."

"What's the sheriff told you?"

"She ain't told us nothing. Mostly she's just eyed us all squinty, with her hand fondling that gun of hers like she was itching to use it. She ain't told us nothing except we couldn't run our show. Until further word, she said. E.Z. threatened to open anyway. Told her he had a right to earn a living. He hadn't done nothing wrong. She said that'd be contempt and she'd arrest him. Can she do that? E.Z. can't go to jail. That wouldn't be good for him at'tall."

"Been in worst jails than this," came the background voice. "And faced down better sheriffs than that towering tub of lard. I'll show her what E. Z. Pliny's made of."

"E.Z., calm yourself. You're gonna flip yourself right outta that wheelchair, you ain't careful. And I ain't coming over there to pick you up off the floor."

"You have no idea who the—mannequin was?"

"Not a bit. How would we know that? Who in their right mind would drive around the country to-tin' a dead man?"

I cut in and didn't wait for her to catch a breath to start another diatribe. "Who'd you say you bought the show from?"

"The joint's ours. E.Z. put it all together. Got a guy to paint the canvases for the banner line, everything.

But we got that mannequin—whoever he is—and some other props from Con Plotnik."

"You said he lived where? Gibtown?"

"Permanently." She snorted. "He retired to Gibsonton, Florida. Lots of carnies live there. Not so upscale as Sarasota, where Ringling used to winter, but we like it. Con Plotnick's there for good now. He died pretty soon after he parked his trailer."

"Which is exactly why I ain't never quitting," said the male voice. "Too damned easy to die, you stop moving."

"E.Z. don't understand why anybody'd quit, until you just can't go no more."

"Any idea where Mr. Plotnik got the body?"

"Nope. Not a clue."

"Does Mr. Plotnick have any family?"

"Everybody's got family, though some would just as soon pretend they didn't. Nobody knew much about Con, except what we knew on the road. That's the way most of us like it."

"All anybody needs to know about somebody else," finished the Greek chorus.

"Miz Pliny, I can talk to the sheriff for you, find out what's going on."

The business reality hit me about then. Collecting a fee might be difficult. As far as I knew, Shamanique was still in town. I could send her over to get a fee agreement signed and collect an hour's fee up front. My new assistant lacked my qualms about talking money with clients. In fact, she was just the opposite. With her talents, we'd do better to hire ourselves out as a collection agency.

I explained about the contract for representation, hung up, got hold of Shamanique, who was planning to go to the festival with her cousin anyway, then called Deputy Rudy Mellin. I was surprised to catch him.

"Danged dead body in the fright house means somebody's got work to do. Since somebody couldn't leave well enough alone and just had to report what looked like a human leg bone . . ."

"Knew you'd rather work than goof around," I said. "Glad I could help you out. Keep you from getting bored. What have you found out?"

"Any reason why I'd be telling you?"

"I can think of lots." For one, he didn't mind talking to me when something weighed on his mind and he needed a sounding board. For another, we shared a table and plenty of gossip at Maylene's several times a week, so why was this any different?

"So far, we know it's human. That what you wanted to know? That surprise you?"

"What I really need to know is when can the Plinys reopen their business?"

"The Plinys?"

"They run the fright house. They're losing business. Every day they're closed is money."

"What's that to you?"

"They hired me to represent them."

He sighed. My being the lawyer newly returned to Dacus is fine with Rudy, right up until I'm the one pushing for something he'd rather not fool with.

"No need for them to go lawyer up."

"That's a bit harsh. They just wanted somebody on their side. I'm sure, in their business, they've run into plenty of inhospitable police officers and public officials."

"And with good reason, given the number of ex-cons, fresh fugitives, and crooks that travel that circuit."

I didn't know anything about the Plinys, hadn't even eyeballed them, so I didn't offer a hollow defense of their character. For all I knew, Mr. Pliny, with his running voice-over commentary, might have just the rap sheet Rudy alluded to.

"We know they need to be back in business," he said, "but we've got other concerns, too."

"Such as?"

"Adrienne Campbell, for one."

"What's she—"

"Madam Festival President insisted we shut that venue down. She didn't think it seemly that curiosity-seekers would jam that attraction, making lots of money for what might well be a couple of cold-blooded murderers."

"That's ridiculous." I knew Rudy was mimicking Adrienne. I just couldn't quite figure her logic.

"L.J. agreed to keep 'em closed until the autopsy was complete. Then they can reopen. Hopefully, we'll know better what we're dealing with."

"Any idea who the guy is? Or how he ended up as part of the display?"

"Nope. Gotta admit, though, it adds to the draw for that stupid fright house."

I hadn't thought about it, but people would flock to the scene of the crime, at several dollars a ticket, in hopes of seeing a dot of blood or a bone fragment, something the cops overlooked. Or just to say they'd been on the scene. Even though the Plinys had missed out on the Friday ticket sales, they'd more than make up for it on Saturday, provided they could reopen.

"Yep, it would be a draw. Rudy, if Adrienne and the festival committee are okay with reopening the fright house, would L.J. go along with that? Is that the only reason L.J. closed it?"

"It's probably best to let things die down a bit, give it at least a day. Might seem disrespectful otherwise."

"L.J.'s all about being respectful," I said with no attempt to disguise my sarcasm.

"Yeah, well, she'll be up for reelection, come November. She's become kinder and gentler lately."

I didn't snort, though I was tempted.

"Besides, we do have to process it as a secondary scene until we know otherwise. Should something end up in court, you know how you lawyers love to insist on i–dotting."

He was right. Just in case, no need to make the target larger for a defense attorney.

"Rudy, what do you hear from up at the falls? Have they—I keep hoping they'll find Rinda and she'll be okay."

"Yeah, well, that's not likely. How'd you know about that?"

"I was up there this morning. At the picnic. When she fell."

"Oh." He was quiet for a moment. "I'm sorry."

"I just can't quite believe it. I mean, how many times has one of us been there, or hiking somewhere else? You just don't think about going out to have fun and it being—permanent."

"In my job, you do."

"Yeah." Couldn't say much to that.

"Wow, Counselor. You're on the scene for two incidents in two days. Maybe you ought to stay home for a while. Having you around isn't going to improve our holiday weekend crime and accident statistics. The Chamber of Commerce ain't gonna like that."

"Thanks, Rudy." He was constitutionally incapable of being serious for long. "Talk to you later."

No wonder I felt beaten. It had been an adrenaline-draining two days.

I dialed Adrienne Campbell's cell phone. I knew she'd be marching around the festival, flicking her wrist first one direction, then another, issuing orders and obsessing over details. No point being festival president if you couldn't stir up a cyclone with yourself at the center of the whirling activity and attention.

"Avery! I'm sure you've heard. What a disaster."

"When—"

"We've called an emergency meeting of the committee. For tomorrow morning. Eight A.M. We need to get this under control."

"Okay." I didn't ask when she'd planned on letting me know about the meeting. "Is that when we'll decide to reopen the horror house?"

"Reopen? I wanted that thing hauled off the lot. They can't get it out, though. I can just see the complaints, the lawsuits. People traumatized simply by seeing it there."

"Adrienne, don't you think that's a bit—" She cut me off before I could say *melodramatic*.

"I'm here monitoring the crowd as we speak. Seems to me everyone on the committee charged with the success of this event would feel the need to be here, too."

I hadn't really known Adrienne before Mom had talked me into joining the festival committee, but it hadn't taken long for me to understand how much she enjoyed a crisis, even if she had to first whip it up herself so she could rise to save the day. Far be it from me to interrupt her glory, but don't ask me to come witness the drama unfold. None of her other manufactured crises had been that entertaining.

"Finding the body yesterday kind of tired me out," I said. "I'm sure you understand."

She gave that a long pause, probably wanting to find a way to blame me for the tragic effect on her festival. "I'll bring the information on how this has affected the gate receipts to the meeting. We need to kick into crisis control here. I fully anticipate a huge drop-off in attendance. We need to decide how to handle that. That Mr. Letts of the carnival midway company and L. J. Peters arrived at some compromise, which suited them but doesn't suit me in the least. After all, they aren't the ones who are responsible. We'll be seeing what we can do about that."

"See you tomorrow, Adrienne. Don't eat too many sausage dogs." I'd meant to lighten the mood with a joke. Not until I clicked off did I remember Adrienne was a vegetarian.

I couldn't think of anyone on the committee to call who'd be willing to make a wager on what effect this would have on the gate receipts. Adrienne was probably the only one who thought a dead body would keep people away, but she wasn't the sort to enter into a friendly bet.

The more I thought about it, the more I felt for the Plinys. They stood to lose the most—not just their regular take, which couldn't be much when kids put on better haunted houses in church basements at Halloween. What really hurt was losing the boost in business from the cachet of having a fright house that once held a real dead body. They couldn't find a bigger crowd pleaser, and no one in the next town was likely to know or care. This was their best chance to make the most of it.

My phone rang, jolting me from my musings.

"Avery? Spence Munn. From the picnic today?"

"Sure. How are you?"

"Not sure. I was wondering if you'd—heard anything? About . . ." He didn't finish his question.

"No. I keep hoping someone will call and say they found her safe. That she's fine."

"That would be good news."

Neither of us sounded as though we'd convinced ourselves, much less each other.

"Avery, I hope this isn't bad timing, but—well, my condo feels a bit quiet, after what happened this morning. I was wondering if you'd care to have dinner tomorrow night? Maybe go dancing? There's a place in Greenville, a colleague owns it. An evening in good company would be welcome."

"Oh. Well." That certainly wasn't what I expected. "Um. Sure. That would be nice."

As soon as the words were out of my mouth, I couldn't believe I'd agreed. A date would be a decided change of pace, but not one I was sure I welcomed. Maybe it had been the lure of dancing. I'd always loved dancing, but these days, what guy invites you to go dancing? Does that happen, outside a Nick and Nora Charles movie?

"Leave about six? That suit you? I'll pick you up at your place."

"Um, sure."

Soon as I hung up, I started wondering if, buried upstairs in a box I'd had no reason to unpack, I had something suitable to wear. Did Spence Munn wear Hawaiian shirts to dinner and dancing, or was that just his picnic attire? What had I been thinking, saying yes? At least this might keep me off Adrienne

Campbell's civic improvement project list. If she made another of her lame attempts to fix me up with Todd David tomorrow, it would be convenient indeed to actually have a date.

SIX

Saturday Morning

The next morning, Adrienne was, as usual, the last to arrive for the emergency meeting she'd called. The best way to make a grand entrance, after all, but a lost opportunity to till the soil, plant seeds, get others to see her point of view.

Adrienne had, of course, used her phone calls yesterday to alert everyone to the danger and let them know what the committee's course of action would be.

I hadn't talked to anyone before the meeting, but I did arrive early, with two boxes of assorted doughnuts—still warm—and enough coffee to float a bar exam review. I'd been there in time to unlock the church meeting room, using a key borrowed from Mom, and to chat with everyone about what keeping the Plinys' attraction closed could be costing the festival.

With any good trial, the jurors should hear from both sides. They'd heard an earful from Adrienne yesterday in her phone calls reporting directly from the scene of the disaster. She had, of course, been the only committee member who'd seen a need to be on site last night, though she'd shamed Todd David, the city attorney, into driving over to join her. Dacus is so small that the city attorney's job is only part-time, but Adrienne wanted to get her tax money's worth from her public servants.

Today, before Adrienne arrived, the committee members licked doughnut glaze off their fingers while I told them the other side—with full disclosure about the Plinys' plea for help.

When Adrienne arrived, she refused a doughnut and launched into her meeting agenda. Mr. Wink, seeing there would be plenty, reached for another— chocolate-iced. Mr. Wink was ninety if he was a day and didn't look the least worried about saturated fat.

"Todd, you're the city attorney," Adrienne said. "Surely there's some precedent to protect us. I'm envisioning lawsuits for emotional distress. This could ruin us."

I couldn't help but snort when she said *emotional distress*. One of the most naïvely feared lawsuits. I stuck another bite in my mouth and tried to look innocent, as though perhaps a crumb had lodged in my throat, nothing more.

"Well, we certainly wouldn't want to be sued," said Todd, an accommodating fellow who dealt with the law safely ensconced in his law office, never venturing close to the courthouse if he could possibly avoid it.

"Let's be realistic," I said. "If someone is worried about psychological scars from being too close to where a dead body was found, she'll probably stay home. If you're really worried about a lawsuit, worry about the Plinys as the operators and about the midway company. We contracted with them. They have an expectation of a profitable week. If there isn't a clause in the contract to require us not to hamper their efforts, never fear. A judge could—and probably would—find that to be a reasonable expectation, given their exclusive contract, the expenses they've incurred traveling here, and the other July Fourth engagements they've given up in order to meet their contractual obligations with us."

The look on Todd David's face told me the contract probably did provide such a clause. When you need a contract with the correct clauses, I suspected Todd was the lawyer you wanted.

"Avery Andrews!" Adrienne braced both hands on the tabletop. "Do you mean to tell me you intend to bring suit against the town of Dacus and the members of this committee? That's bound to be—criminal!"

"Of course not, Adrienne. It's not criminal, but it would be a conflict of interest. I am telling you that they could sue—and would probably win. Lawsuits aside, what's the problem with letting the Plinys open their attraction?"

"Well! I never! It's—it's unseemly." Adrienne overflowed with indignation. "For all we know, these—people are cold-blooded murderers."

"And dumb enough to haul the body from town to town?" I didn't point out that they would also have to be schooled in the art of mummification if they'd created what Emma and I had found.

Mr. Wink wiped his skeletal fingers on a napkin. "I don't see a problem with reopening it. As long as the sheriff has finished doing whatever they do, then we don't really have a good reason to keep it closed."

Mr. Wink's father had owned a store on Main Street. Mr. Wink had built the Camden County equivalent of a real estate empire that his grandson now ran. He'd lived in Dacus his whole life, and he knew what made money and what didn't. "Shutting that fright house is losing money, for us as well as for the people who count on it for their living."

"No one is going to want to go in that place," Adrienne said.

"Oh, I don't know about that," said Luke Deep, the new pastor at Dacus Baptist, his resonant baritone a contrast with his boyish face. "My children were bugging me all yesterday afternoon about going to the festival just so they could stand and look at the outside of the trailer."

Adrienne drew herself up as though she'd sniffed a foul odor. No one else looked shocked. I suspected Pastor Luke and Mr. Wink would be in line for a tour of the fright house themselves.

"What's the harm in letting them open?" I said. "If, by some remote chance, the investigation shows they were responsible, we can always close it down again."

I noticed no one had asked if there'd been a precipitous plunge in gate receipts yesterday, and Adrienne offered no evidence to support what she'd most feared. I bet the absence of her proffer of evidence, as we lawyers called it, was good evidence to the contrary.

"When will the sheriff finish with her investigation?" asked Pastor Luke.

Adrienne gave a toss of her head at his mention of L.J., but let a derisive sniff serve as her only comment.

They turned to me for a more detailed answer.

"I don't know for sure," I said. "I'd expect the autopsy back by Monday, though."

"We can't let the Plinys miss the rest of this weekend," said Mr. Wink. "This'll be a big-money weekend, what with the holiday. If I was them, I'd sue us for taking that away—or come huntin' who to whale the tar out of. I move we let 'em open back up."

"Can we do that?" Pastor Luke asked me. "I mean, does the sheriff have any objection?"

"If she does, she has the power to keep it shut," I said. "But from what I understand, it's closed at our request."

Adrienne's lips drew into a thin line. She shot dagger looks at me but said nothing. Everyone around the table knew she'd acted unilaterally in the committee's name, but no one felt it worth spending breath to challenge her actions.

"All in favor, then," said Mr. Wink, his brown jacket sleeve falling away from his bony wrist as he raised his right hand.

Pastor Luke and I raised ours. Todd David threw an anxious glance at Adrienne before he eased his hand to half-mast. Adrienne's lips stayed tight, a little smirk that said she was biding her time until she could come back and tell us all, *I told you so*.

I couldn't help but notice this was the first meeting I'd attended where she hadn't hinted, suggested, or insisted that Todd David and I should work as an ad hoc committee on something or join her and her husband for dinner. Here I was with an actual, honest-to-goodness date lined up, and no call to use it as a defensive measure.

"I've got to see Rudy Mellin about something else this morning," I said. "I'll let him know what we decided." That wasn't entirely true. I didn't *have* to see Rudy, but asking Adrienne to bear news she didn't welcome wasn't the smartest or kindest idea.

We scooted back our chairs and gathered our notepads and pens, those shuffling movements that signal when a group is breaking up. Mr. Wink said, "Anybody hear anything more about what happened up at the falls yesterday?"

"Wasn't that sad?" said Pastor Luke. "So tragic."

No one looked at me, so I didn't volunteer any on-the-scene reporting.

"What exactly happened?" asked Todd. "I just heard somebody went off the falls."

"Rinda Reimann," said Adrienne. "She finished high school here. Just recently moved back."

"Usually it's college students who don't have sense enough not to wade in the creek," said Mr. Wink with a *tut-tut* in his voice.

"What a scary accident," said Todd, whose pale skin and soft hands hinted that walking from his office to his car was his only outdoor activity.

"I hope they aren't too quick in terming it an accident," said Adrienne. "Though our sheriff usually wants to take the easy way."

We all stared at her. She took that as the prompt she wanted.

"Everyone knows Rinda and Rog were having problems. She was seeing someone." The emphasis made it clear she knew who but was being discreet. "Wouldn't be the first time someone found a cheaper solution than divorce."

"Oh, my." Pastor Luke's tone carried a mild rebuke.

"Oh, come on." Adrienne challenged the frowns and raised eyebrows. "Facing reality is better than hiding from it. Always look at the spouse, isn't that what they say? Of course, given the crack law enforcement we have around here, it must be frightfully easy to get away with murder."

No one graced her pronouncement with a response, even though that left her thinking she'd won.

Given Adrienne's self-absorption, rebuttals would've been wasted.

Everyone had somewhere they'd rather be on a bright Saturday morning, especially before the heat set in. At my encouragement, Pastor Luke took the remaining doughnuts to his three children. Mr. Wink and I had eaten our fill.

As I locked up the basement, I wondered whether other people were as ready as Adrienne to blame Rog Reimann for Rinda's death. Why hadn't I stepped to his defense? Because I didn't know enough to defend him. Rog was in a dangerous spot, especially if Adrienne wasn't the only one who was ready to accuse him.

I wasn't willing yet to admit Rinda was dead. When the facts were in, the myths would be easier to dispel.

I wasted no time calling Rudy and the Plinys. Given the Plinys' business, I should have realized they probably weren't early risers even before I heard the slurry sound of Pinner Pliny's voice. Despite being awakened at nine o'clock in the morning, she was thrilled to know they could once again entice unsuspecting patrons into their tame but now irresistibly interesting fright house.

"We can't thank you enough," she said over and over. Mr. Pliny offered no commentary. Maybe he was still asleep.

"I didn't do much, Miz Pliny." I'd stop by later and return part of her retainer.

The rest of the day, I puttered around the house, pulling weeds from the foundation shrubs and watering the impatiens I'd set out around my angel statue. I'd gotten advice on how to check the electrical wiring, to make sure we didn't have any problems that required expert attention, but I was putting that off until a cool, rainy day. On a day like today, the attic would be sweltering, while spiders and who knew what else would be taking refuge in the basement. That could wait.

As the sun rose higher, I finished my few outdoor chores and went upstairs to my sitting room. I slit open the tape on one of the packed boxes stacked neatly against the wall. The black dress I found inside just needed to be freshened up and would do fine for dinner and dancing.

I had to admit—to myself, but to no one else—that I had butterflies. Why had I agreed to go out? Spence Munn was a nice enough fellow. He was very tall, but not as athletic as I usually prefer. We didn't know each other, so this fell solidly in the almost-blind-date category, full of pauses and stumbling attempts at conversation and the exploratory examinations that must be both performed and endured.

Over the years, I'd gotten quite adept at saying no to dates. For much of my adult life, I'd simply been too busy, too focused on the next trial, on making partner, and, since leaving the law firm, on putting my life back together in Dacus. Once you're out of the habit, it's just—well, scary.

Upon analysis, I attributed my moment of weakness to two motives. One, I loved dancing, but I hadn't done much dancing since college. When he'd suggested it, I'd flashed to those romantic movie musical dance scenes that always popped into my head, even though the reality was usually an awkward lurch and jerk within a proscribed square on a postage-stamp, rough parquet dance floor. Reality never quite measures up to a movie dream sequence.

The movies never showed the hours of rehearsal—or mentioned the fact that even accomplished dancers didn't look like the movies if they're dancing with a new partner. Dancing is truly a well-rehearsed team sport. Maybe I could just focus on the dream and quit fretting over the inevitable reality.

The other motive for accepting was so I could truthfully say to Todd David that I was busy Saturday night. Of course, today Adrienne hadn't even bothered trying to fix us up. I could've been busy on Saturday night, even without the date, but somehow dinner and dancing would've sounded more legitimate than "I'm building my niece a new clubhouse."

Despite the reasons for saying yes, my brain now flooded with all the reasons why I should've said no.

Even though the temperature had climbed to a muggy ninety degrees, I went for a long afternoon walk during which I stopped by my parents' house. Mom and Dad gave me a paper sack full of yellow squash she'd gotten on her morning trip to the farmer's market. I knew how to cook squash, but the question was, Would I? When was Melvin coming home? Maybe the squash would keep until he got back. He made a killer squash casserole.

By the time I showered, made an emergency run to the drugstore for panty hose, and fussed with my dress and hair, it was six o'clock.

My old-fashioned doorbell—the kind that must be twisted to ring—jangled promptly at six. I charged down the stairs, tugging to make sure my dress fell straight. Even through the beveled window glass, I could see that Spence Munn was not wearing a Hawaiian shirt.

SEVEN

Saturday Night

Spence Munn's shirt was starched, so free of wrinkles I wasn't sure he could bend. His suit, a dark silk blend, flowed as only an expensive fabric can.

He took my elbow as we went down the stairs, and he opened the car door for me. His actions stirred faint memories of other first dates. I knew the courtliness never lasted, but I could enjoy it while it did.

He'd parked in the on-street parallel parking in front of my office, right on Main Street. Convenient. Maybe Adrienne or someone would drive by, and word would get out that I'd been on a date. Why my love life—or total lack of one—engendered such interest was a mystery. Judging from the marriages of some of the most active busybodies, misery might love company.

As I perched on the stiff, beige leather seat in Spence's BMW, waiting while he circled to the driver's side, I also had a moment to remember why I avoided dates, especially dates with guys I don't know well. Number one, how did I know he could drive? He might be a terror. Number two, why had I agreed to go all the way to Greenville? An hour each way, plus dinner and dancing, required a lot of conversation.

Avery, it's only an evening. I could've been sitting at home reading, or watching a movie with Emma, neither of which sounded like a bad idea.

Playing the "do you know" game and giving personal history summaries took up most of the drive to the restaurant.

Spence had mostly grown up in Norfolk, Virginia, had come farther south to attend Appalachian State University and had decided to stay.

"My family moved around a lot," he said. "Dad was career Navy. He'd had a stint in Charleston, but they settled in Norfolk, where he'd been stationed early in his career. It felt as much like home to them as anywhere. Even though I finished high school there, I didn't really feel tied to that place."

"Just a rolling stone, huh?"

"I guess. Got to admit, though, I envy your closeness with your family, having everybody here. Or does it get claustrophobic?"

I chuckled. "No, my family's a live-and-let-live bunch. There when you need them, for sure. But not big on messing in your business."

"Dacus is awfully small, though. Was it hard to come back?"

That had a complicated answer. I'd never planned on coming back—but losing my temper with a lying witness and then losing my job had pushed me to reassess what I really wanted. I'd fought moving home and considered my return last November as a personal failure and only temporary. The cases and the lives I'd gotten involved with over the last few months had eroded my resolve. I'd quickly found myself in a new office, a new apartment, with a new and unexpected life, as if the soil itself had set about planting me here.

I didn't offer any of that. I simply said, "No."

"Is it weird having people who knew you when you were a little girl?"

"As Aunt Letha—actually, she's my great-aunt Aletha—says, once you've powdered and diapered a baby's butt in the church nursery, it's hard to ever imagine them as grown-ups."

"There's a picture."

I couldn't tell if he was embarrassed or bemused by the mental picture.

"Now you're back, you can see how some of your high school buddies turned out. Any surprises?"

Other than the way I turned out? I didn't say that out loud. "A few."

"For some reason, Bill Gates comes to mind. Wasn't he supposed to have said be nice to the nerd in your class, one day he'll be your boss?"

Was he calling me a nerd? Or talking about himself? "Can't tell how some folks are going to turn out," I said.

"Best be careful whose butt you diaper or whose head you dunk in the junior high toilet, huh?"

His memories had turned the conversation somewhere different. I wondered if he had been the dunker or the dunkee. Spence was at least six foot two, but he might have gotten his height too late to save him in junior high. Unlike with me and now-sheriff L. J. Peters, who had been bigger than everyone in elementary school. Good thing I'd relied on pure anger and not waited for a growth spurt to get her to quit punching me, or I might not have made it to junior high.

The drive passed quickly. Spence handed his keys

to the valet, and we entered the restaurant—once an outsized mansion near downtown, with grounds expanded to park cars and accommodate patrons with a discreet air of red brick and ivy charm.

The woman in the black mandarin dress didn't even pause to check for Spence's name in the reservation book.

"Hello, Mr. Munn. Your table is ready."

We followed her swaying hips up the lush staircase flanked by massive oak railings on one side and flickering gaslight sconces on the other.

The table nested in its own alcove. The velvet curtains could have pushed it too much toward a Victorian bordello, but the jewel green color and the table lamp avoided the gaudy with touches of elegance.

"How do you like your steak?" he asked as I studied the menu.

"Medium plus," I said.

"Blue cheese dressing? It's excellent here."

"Sure."

"Allow me, then." The waitress appeared and he rattled off our order—filet, lettuce wedge, mashed potatoes, creamed spinach, and some sort of red wine. The name of the wine went too quickly for me to know—or care.

It had been years since a man had ordered for me. I couldn't complain about his choices, but I had to admit I was—what? Surprised? Was it the presumed familiarity? The hint of machismo? A gallant memory?

"You come here a lot," I said.

"Good place to take clients. Quiet. Good wait staff." As if he could read my mind, he said, "Not something a faculty salary would allow on a regular basis." He chuckled, with a pleasant, self-deprecating grin.

I'd wondered about the BMW. Added to the expensive wardrobe and his favorite restaurant, his lifestyle quickly exceeded what I knew to be the limits of Lydia's and Frank's faculty salary. True, Spence didn't have a wife and child—at least as far as I knew. But I did know how much it cost to live this life. I'd once lived it myself.

"I enjoy teaching, and the faculty salary provides a nice base, but the investment work provides the perks."

I smiled but didn't comment. From the looks of things, Melvin Bertram had some competition in the investment-advice neighborhood. Some successful competition. Melvin didn't spend money like this. He might make it, I didn't know, but he sure didn't spend it like this.

"That dress suits you," Spence said. His approving gaze lingered to the point I had to look away.

"Thank you." Self-conscious about whether the V-neck dress was cut too low, I fought the urge to reach for my necklace—pieces of red art glass arranged in a free-form gold wire by an artist friend.

"Have you heard anything more about Rinda?" His voice was somber.

"No, nothing new as far as I know."

"Do those search guys know what they're doing? I mean—I'm sorry, that was rude. It's just that Dacus is very small, and those guys who came to search for her yesterday . . ."

"Don't worry. Their fan club looks scruffy, but the guys doing the work know what they're doing when it comes to search and rescue. They live for that."

"Sorry." He held up his hands in truce. "It's arrogant for an outsider to come rolling in like he has all the answers. It's just—of course I'm concerned."

"We all are."

"I don't live in Camden County, so I don't know all the players. What's this sheriff like?"

"L.J.?" I shrugged. "She's pretty good. Why?"

L. J. Peters had gone from grammar school bully to county sheriff, an unlikely career trajectory—or maybe not. I grudgingly admitted she'd turned out to be a good sheriff, even though she was still a bully at times.

"She questioned Rog Reimann, yesterday and today. Seemed a bit—jackbooted. Talking to his friends, asking about his and Rinda's marriage. Shouldn't they be trying to find her? Couldn't she still be alive?"

I hesitated, choosing my words. I doubted Rinda could have survived, if she'd gone over the falls. I had never heard of anyone who survived it, but I wasn't sure how close Spence was to Rinda or Rog, and truth might not be what he wanted to hear right now. L.J. was nothing if not thorough, and she was just doing her job, though I could see how it might seem harsh to a friend of Rog's.

"They need to cover all the bases," I said. "If somehow it turned out not to be an accident, people would be upset that the sheriff hadn't followed that angle more aggressively."

"I guess." He took the sip of wine offered by the sommelier, nodded his approval, and waited for the pouring ritual to be completed.

When we were alone again, Spence asked, "Does Rog need to get a lawyer, do you think?"

That question took me by surprise. "Um, I don't know." I've done only a little criminal defense work and always small-time stuff: breaking and entering, minor drug offenses, always at the procedural level. Setting bond or doing pleas had been the limit of my criminal court experience so far, no full trials or big stakes. With criminal work, I'd started small and didn't intend to develop much taste or aptitude for it.

"At the very least," Spence said, "I told him he didn't need to be talking to the sheriff if she was threatening him. I had a lawyer friend tell me once that's where most criminals mess up, they talk to the police. Keep your mouth shut, he said. You like the wine?"

Did Spence realize he was lumping his friend Rog in with "most criminals"? I reached for my glass. I hadn't even taken a sip.

"Which Kennedy was it in that rape trial in Florida?" he asked. "My friend always cited that case. Said the first time the cops heard—William Kennedy Smith, that was his name. First time they heard his story was when he took the witness stand—after the prosecution had rolled out its entire case to the jury. The defendant could then explain it neatly away. The police have to prove their case. He doesn't have to help them."

"That's true. You think Rog had something to do with Rinda's fall?" My tone was gentle, but the question startled him.

"No! No, of course not. It's just—small-town sheriffs might rush to judgment, especially with an outsider. Somebody said she's up for reelection this year."

"She's just doing her job. But if Rog is uncomfortable, he should talk to a lawyer, somebody who does criminal work." Whether that would convince L.J. he had something to hide would be a question for someone with more experience in that arena than I had. I had my guess, though, knowing L.J. as I did. Still, Rog was safer getting good legal advice.

"Is there any way to get the sheriff to just back off? I mean, the guy's in torment right now." He took another sip of wine before he continued. "You know her pretty well, don't you? Somebody said . . ."

"We've known each other a long time, but I wouldn't say we're friends."

"Could you talk to her? Find out what's going on?"

"Might be best if Rog did that himself, or got a lawyer to represent him and make those inquiries for him."

"I don't mean to be insulting. It's just that, well, there are all those stereotypes of small-town Southern sheriffs, and she fills most of them."

"Except that she's female."

"You sure? No offense, but that's one bruiser big woman."

L.J. was six feet tall to the top of her black bowl-cut hair, without the steel-toed brogans she wore, but I felt an unexpected flash of protectiveness toward her.

"Spence, old buddy." The man's greeting reached us a split second before he ducked into our green velvet cocoon. "How are you?"

The new arrival studied me as Spence half-rose to shake his hand.

"Eliot, this is Avery Andrews. She's a lawyer. Eliot Easton. He owns this place."

"I won't hold that lawyer thing against you. Ha!" Easton's short bark of a laugh didn't touch the corners of his eyes. "Keeping this reprobate out of trouble?"

I just stared at him with what I hoped was a civil smile. He was a perfectly ordinary-looking business-man, average height, with a thinning hairline, somewhere in his late forties, with that soft face and build that usually comes from rich food and no treadmill time. He didn't speak as though he were from around here, something I increasingly notice in people now that I'm back home in the Upstate. I tried to ignore the lawyer reference, but if he tried to tell any stale lawyer jokes—and they were all stale—all attempts at civility were off.

"Hope everything's going well?" he said to Spence. "Still rolling in the dough, old man?"

Spence smiled but with his bottom lip curled in, as if he was trying to bite off a reply.

"We do need to talk. Tomorrow?" Easton's jocular tone turned serious but only for a moment. "When you're not with a lovely lady lawyer, though. Attorney-client privilege, right? Make sure you give her a retainer. Ha! Tomorrow?" He took Spence's hand in a farewell clasp and ducked away from our table.

"Eliot's quite the business genius," Spence said. "This restaurant was his brainchild, but he's into lots of other ventures. Very successful."

Not an excuse for being a boor, but I didn't say that out loud.

"Did you help make him successful?" I asked.

"Hardly." He slid his hands, palms down, around the stem of his wineglass. "Easton pointed me toward a couple of good investment opportunities—and the best steaks and wine cellar between Atlanta and Charlotte."

"So you're in business with him?"

"No, nothing like that. I'm an investor, not someone who wants to actually run a business."

"What kinds of things do you invest in? Is that something you can talk about?"

"Without having you sign a nondisclosure agreement or boring you to death?" He shrugged. "It really is kind of boring. I've worked out a mathematical model that helps anticipate changes and—more important— rates of change in the markets. The model itself is complicated, but the theory isn't. I just buy low and sell high."

"I see." Sharing an office with Melvin had whetted my appetite for understanding the arcane world of venture capital and high finance, but all the talk seemed either obscure or clichéd or dull.

"You invest for other people? Besides just yourself?"

"I make recommendations, introduce people to some small, intrastate offerings, things they wouldn't know about otherwise. The offerings operate under state law only and avoid the burdensome reporting requirements the federal government forces on publicly traded securities through the SEC."

"Um-hm."

"Kind of nerdy, I know. Not nearly so glamorous as life as a high-powered trial attorney. I understand you were quite the golden girl."

"I don't know about that." I played with my napkin. Talking about my irrational response to an ethical dilemma—and the opportunity a few months ago to see the liar who'd precipitated it hoist on his own petard—was too complicated and too fresh to share over dinner with a new acquaintance.

"You're too modest. You were the go-to lawyer for complex corporate defense. Thorough and determined. You'd win or kill someone, according to my sources. And they're impeccable."

I wasn't surprised that he'd checked me out, but I

did wonder who he'd used as sources. I wasn't going to ask, though.

"Why'd you come back to Dacus?"

"It's home," I said. Nothing in those two words indicated the mighty battle that had raged in me over that decision. Income, prestige, a sense of accomplishment—those hadn't been easy to give up. Spence was implying a question: *What're you doing, sitting in a hick-town backwater with no future?* I didn't have an answer he'd understand.

He gave me an appraising stare. Maybe he was calculating my investment potential in his mathematical model.

"If we'd gone to high school together," he said, "you'd have been the girl who wouldn't have gone out with me."

That took me by surprise. "What makes you say that?"

He focused on his wineglass as he slid it to a new spot. "I don't know. Just remembering who I was, and imagining who you were."

You don't have any idea who I was. Aloud, I said, "Who were you in high school?"

"A nerd. A kid nobody noticed. Not the best at anything, really."

"But not the worst, either."

"No, not the worst."

"Oldest child?"

"No," he said. "Middle. Older brother, younger sister. All the striving and angst that implies. You?"

"Oldest. You know Lydia, my sister. Why do you say you were a nerd?"

"I don't know, never seemed to quite fit in. Okay in sports, baseball mostly. Grew too late to consider basketball, not that I would've been any good. Okay in school. Just, you know, average."

"That describes most everybody, doesn't it? Even the popular kids don't think of themselves as popular—except in Disney TV movies."

"That doesn't mean they aren't. Popular, I mean."

"I don't know," I said. "One of the prettiest girls in my class never invited anybody home with her. Lots of us knew where she lived, but we never said anything. Living in that ramshackle house didn't make her any less pretty or any less popular, but it made her feel awkward. In other words, just like every teenager."

"So you would've gone out with me?"

"Don't know. Would've depended on what kind of dancer you were."

"So the pressure's on, huh? Not sure what my dancing skills now will tell you about how a younger, less experienced little Spencer Munn might have measured up."

Our salads arrived, followed by steaming steaks drizzled with garlic butter and charred to perfection.

I wasn't too shy to ask for a to-go bag; I couldn't eat all the steak, but no way I'd let it go to waste out of false daintiness.

By the time the waitress returned his credit card, we'd sat long enough for the dinner to settle and agreed to delay dessert until we'd danced some. He slid out of the booth and pulled the table away from my bench so I could stand out gracefully.

The pressure really was on. I'd tossed down a challenge, in jest though it was. Could I measure up? I hadn't danced in years. I also hadn't felt a wave of silly insecurity, reminiscent of those high school insecurities, in at least that long. Not a pleasant trip down memory lane. Spence ushered me down the stairs, through a double door wide enough to accommodate a passenger bus, and into a gold and mahogany ballroom.

EIGHT

Sunday Morning

No matter that dancing and the drive home had pushed into early Sunday morning, I still had to make it to church. An unwritten, but long-standing family rule. Nothing on Saturday night excuses you from church on Sunday.

For that reason and no other, I was dressed and downstairs drinking hot tea in the kitchen when the front door chime rang.

As I came down the hall from the back of the house, I was certain the redheaded kid standing on the porch with a spray of flowers must have confused his delivery address and arrived at the old funeral home by mistake.

"Miz Andrews?" he asked cheerfully when I opened the door. "For you."

Before I could check the card for any mistake or offer him a tip, he bounded down the steps to his florist delivery van, probably loaded with the last of his Sunday sanctuary arrangements.

The note read, *What's the verdict? Would you have danced with me at the prom if I'd been lucky enough to attend Dacus High?*

The massive round table in the entry hall, usually barren, begged for just such a generous explosion of colors. I smiled as I centered the vase carefully on the table.

Spence Munn was quite a dancer. As we danced set after set, we quickly learned each others' rhythms and quirks. My own rusty awkwardness had melted.

He knew how to lead and he wasn't afraid to risk looking foolish, which good dancing demands. I gave the flowers a gentle fluff and smiled.

Great-aunts Aletha, Hattie, and Vinnia were lined up in their usual pew, center aisle, about two-thirds of the way back. They'd saved me a seat on the end, next to Vinnia.

Mom, Dad, Lydia, and Frank were in the choir, among the few other stalwarts. The Fourth of July holiday took lots of families out of town. The visitors it brought to town seldom included church in their plans, unlike at Easter or Christmas.

Luke Deep, the pastor who'd been called to Dacus Baptist only four or five weeks earlier, brought his usual upbeat energy to the service. He had the children waving their miniature American flags during the children's sermon, and the hymns were a patriotic medley from the back of the hymnal, the special occasion section.

His sermon, though, didn't mine God-bless-America themes. Baptists aren't required to use a lectionary or a prescribed annual list of sermon topics. Baptist churches typically let each pastor do his own thing, and we espouse the "priesthood of the believer," a sort of organized chaos that can provide fertile ground for some extreme views. However, Dacus Baptist, for all its cloistered small-townness, maintained a moderation and inclusiveness that I appreciated.

Pastor Luke, as everyone called him—though I did like the image cast by the name Pastor Deep—picked Christ's temptations for the sermon. He tried to get us to feel Jesus' hunger and fatigue after forty days in the wilderness, even though we sat in air-conditioned comfort and most of us had eaten breakfast and slept at least a little the night before. He took us to the mountaintop and tried to show us how enticing the offer of sustenance, of power, of fame must have been, given what Jesus had endured, what he came to accomplish, and how terribly painful it would be to achieve. Here was the easy way, all worked out. All you have to do is take it. Still awfully tempting, even when we're well fed and rested and secure.

I didn't notice Aunt Letha using the stubby pew pencil a single time to scribble notes to Hattie, which was a good sign. Her notes, as I knew as a past recipient, were usually indictments of someone's behavior, critiques of the pastor's academic preparation or delivery style, or a reminder of something the recipient had been responsible for and failed to do.

No scribbles meant peace reigned in her land. Always good. Aletha—Letha for short—was the eldest of my grandfather's septuagenarian and octogenarian surviving sisters, and she'd assumed the matriarchal mantle a decade earlier when Granddad died. She'd actually run things before that, so the transition had been seamless.

After the final chords of the organ sounded, the three sisters bustled toward home, with Hattie driving the big sedan and Letha in back, as befitted royalty.

They had some dishes to bring to Lydia's house

for our family's holiday gathering, and they had to change clothes, though I knew I wouldn't see much difference between their church dresses and their picnic dresses. Vinnia especially, though, was quite particular about not ruining her nice church clothes.

I hurried home to change into shorts so I could arrive at Lydia's ahead of the crowd and help her set up. She insists that hosting parties is no strain on her, but she has a Superwoman complex. To help out, on my trip to the grocery on Saturday morning to get doughnuts for the festival meeting, I'd picked up a chest of ice and grocery bags full of soft drinks, hamburger and hot-dog buns, chips, and whatever else had looked good as I'd cruised the aisles.

Lydia perpetuates the myth that I can't fix Brown 'n' Serve Rolls without ruining them. That's not entirely true, but why set yourself in the competition with fine cooks like Lydia, Mom, and the great-aunts? I'm happy to do the mundane, the uninspired but necessary tasks, as long as I earn my place at the table.

When the guests began to arrive, some on the guest list surprised me. In addition to Mom and Dad, who also came early, and the great-aunts, the party included my parents' neighbors, Pastor Luke and his wife, and a couple of choir members—semiregulars at our frequent family cookouts, and no surprises there.

The first surprise came when Eden Rand led a shell-shocked Rog Reimann into the backyard.

"Rog really needed to get out of the house." Eden swept her frizzy hair off the nape of her neck and reached for a paper napkin to daub at her forehead as she confided that to Lydia. Frank had led Rog to the table loaded with soft drinks and tea. "You wouldn't believe what it's been like."

"I can't imagine," said Lydia.

"That sheriff of yours as been hounding him with questions but refuses to tell him when the body will be released so he can make funeral arrangements."

My head snapped up from my assigned task of setting the serving table. "They found her?"

"Yesterday," Eden said. "But they won't answer any of Rog's questions. They just keep after him with questions. I told him to just quit talking to them. He doesn't have to say anything. Does he?"

The sociology professor shot her question at me, as if she'd suddenly remembered what I did for a living.

"No, but—"

"He doesn't want them to stop talking to him, of course. He wants to know what's going on, but I say hey, they aren't telling you anything anyway, so why're you bothering? I say he needs a lawyer."

Lydia looked in my direction, but I wasn't about to volunteer. Besides, Rog was the one who needed legal advice, not his colleague Eden. In any event, she didn't want any advice; she was too busy giving it.

"When did they—find her?" Lydia asked.

"Yesterday afternoon, late. Said they needed to do an autopsy, so she was shipped off somewhere."

"I'm sure, as soon as they know something, they'll talk to Rog."

Eden snorted. "That sheriff's on a power trip. I hear she's up for reelection. I'm not going to stand by and let her turn Rog into some publicity stunt to get votes."

Lydia and I kept ripping open bags of chips, setting containers of dip into bowls of ice water, arranging napkins, and the myriad other tasks required to make a picnic look casual and spontaneous. This annual gathering was usually reserved for family and close friends. I admired Lydia, who came by her Miss Fix-It tendencies from a long line of Howe women, for inviting the wounded birds, but I selfishly wished the picnic was just family. Then I felt guilty for being selfish.

Rather than offering to help with the preparations, Eden said, "I'd better go check on Rog." She floated off in a waft of gauze and unfettered frizzy hair.

"She sure has taken him on as a project," I said.

"She'd done that long before Rinda's accident," said Lydia. "Rog has just been too clueless to see the net tightening around him. Then again, brilliant but clueless might be Rog's middle name."

She used a chip to taste test her crab dip.

"A typical absentminded professor?" I asked.

"I don't know about typical," Lydia said. She wasn't about to acknowledge her professor-husband's space cadet qualities. "Everybody but Rog had been watching as Rinda renewed her old high school friendship."

"With who?"

"Whom." The correction was pure reflex, which is why Emma talks like a pocket-sized encyclopedia. "Ken Tharp. They dated in high school. When Rog took the teaching position at the university and they moved back to Camden County, Rinda and Ken picked up where they left off a decade ago. Well, maybe not in the back of his mom's minivan, but . . ."

"Ken Tharp from the city council? That Ken Tharp?"

"You don't think there's more than one, do you? That's why he and his wife Weesa weren't up at the picnic on Friday, though everyone knew that's who Rinda was jabbering on the phone with."

Not everyone knew, since I hadn't a clue that scandal seethed around me.

"You'd think that, after being married, having

kids, all the rest, they'd stop acting like dogs in heat," Lydia said. She may have Mom's huge heart, but she'd also grown up with Aunt Letha's judgmental pronouncements.

I didn't point out that, biologically speaking, only one dog was in heat, and the other just followed along.

"I tried to introduce Rinda around, get her involved. I feel bad now that I didn't do more. We never were close. She was always— Well, she spent all her time chasing boys. Never outgrew it. I'm sorry she's dead, but—I don't know. I'm not a very nice person."

"That's not true." I knew what she couldn't say. Stirring up false grief was, well, false. "Nice of you to invite Rog."

Her mouth pressed tight in a look of mild disgust. "Yet again, he doesn't have a clue. The lady sociologist has not chosen him as a random research subject."

Before I could mine her gossip reserves further, Mom joined us.

"Is that Peg and Matt's son-in-law over there? Rinda's husband?" She nodded toward Rog.

"Um-hm," Lydia said.

"Bless his heart. He must be devastated. I know Peg and Matt both are. I stopped by there yesterday evening. I can't imagine losing a daughter." She spoke as if daughters were an abstract concept rather than standing on either side of her.

"Rinda was their only child. Peg was talking about how thrilled they'd been when she'd moved back to Dacus, after living away for so long, then she just broke down. It just ripped at my heart. I realized how lucky I was."

She patted Lydia and me each on the arm, the extent of her Calvinist closeness. She loved us, no doubt, but no one in our family allows themselves to let mushiness run amok.

Emma walked up, bringing Spence Munn out of the house as if she was leading a dog who wouldn't obey her.

"He was ringing the front door bell," she said. She rolled her eyes as if to say, *Who doesn't know how to find our backyard?*

"Hi." I didn't control the squeak in my voice. He hadn't mentioned being on Lydia's guest list. "Um. Get you something to drink?"

I could feel Lydia's radar receptors on full alert. I turned toward the drink table, which stood under a tree at the side of the patio. If she couldn't see my eyes, she couldn't shoot her mind-reading probe into my brain.

I waited until we were out of earshot before I said, "Thanks for the flowers. They're lovely."

"Don't know when I've had so much fun. I'm sure we're the talk of the dance club crowd wherever they gather today. Who was that extraordinarily talented couple, they're all asking."

"Right." I handed him a cup of Diet Pepsi full of fizz and ice.

"Aunt Bree." Emma marched up to us. "Can you play horseshoes with me? Grandpa says he won't play me anymore."

"What'd you do? Lay a leaner up against his shin with a horseshoe?"

"I beat him." She stared up at me, matter-of-fact.

"I—uh, really need to finish helping your mom." I hated to let her down, even though I knew I would go quickly down in defeat. I'd just noticed she was the only kid at the picnic.

"Can I play?" offered Spence.

Emma turned an appraising eye on him, from his slipper-soft loafers and sand-colored slacks all the way up his long, brightly flowered Hawaiian shirt to his smiling hazel eyes.

I knew what she was thinking as clearly as if she'd said it out loud. *Dumb shirt. Dumb shoes.* Out loud, she said, "Sure," and led him away with an expression that said she expected this to be quick and merciless.

Spence smiled at me over his shoulder and followed Emma to what I knew was certain humiliation. Emma's grandpa—my dad—hadn't let her win. He'd been beaten. Beating the ringer queen at her own game would be the only way Spence could redeem himself and his wardrobe choices in her eyes. I didn't hold out much hope. I went back to get orders from Lydia.

"Who is that?" Aunt Vinnia joined us, carrying a bowl of her famous potato salad.

"A friend of Frank's," Lydia said. "He and Avery have been seeing each other." The teasing in her voice was faint but embarrassing nonetheless.

"We had dinner last night," I said, the defensiveness in my voice hard to miss. Do we ever outgrow our childhoods?

"You two spent a lot of time together at Bow Falls on Friday, too," Lydia said.

Before someone was swept off the falls, which changed the tone of the day. Neither of us mentioned that.

Aunt Letha joined us with a loud *harrumph.* "I always had gumption enough to pick out my own beaux. None of this nonsense getting fixed up with somebody." She set down a crock of baked beans. I bent over to let the brown sugar smell fill my nose so they couldn't see my face coloring red.

Growing up, Lydia and I—and sometimes Mom

and Dad—had speculated about Aunt Letha's beaux. She'd never married, we knew, and we couldn't imagine the man who could have withstood her gale-force personality. Maybe in her younger years, she'd been sweet and gentle. Doubtful, but reality hadn't stopped us from making up outrageous pairings and laughing ourselves silly.

Vinnia, the short, soft, plump youngest sister, had married. She'd raised five children—none of whom had stayed in Dacus—and buried a husband before I'd been born. Hattie, rangy, slab-sided, and shorter than her older sister Aletha, had also stayed single and taught high school biology, while Aletha force-fed generations of pupils the value of knowing and thereby choosing what parts of history to repeat. In their late seventies and early eighties now, my great-aunts offered constant lessons in how to live a life, some by example, some by scathing, outspoken indictment of stupid choices, the latter mostly from Aunt Letha.

When I stopped to consider their contemporaries, the avant-garde quality of their lives was evident. Even among my own contemporaries, few had the "gumption" to live single by choice. Hattie's boyfriend had been killed in the Second World War. She'd never dated again, as far as my mom knew. All three sisters lived in the rambling white clapboard house on Main Street that my grandfather—their brother—had bought. He'd married late in life, and his much-loved wife had died soon after she'd given birth to my mother.

Granddad, oldest of the siblings by more than a decade and the only male, had been a lawyer, a judge, and my idol. He'd died while I was in law school, and I still missed his wisdom, his dry humor, and the sweet dusty smell of his pipe tobacco.

In my reverie, I missed a shift in the conversation

away from critiquing my dating choices to the telling of family stories. The great-aunts had all three taken seats in the padded chairs around the long patio table.

"Lordy day, I was ready to tan every one of you that day," said Vinnia, laughing, her face pink as a cherub's.

"Right up until the moment Old Man MacEntyre stomped over there threatening us," said Lydia, "then you turned into an overprotective banty hen ready to peck his eyes out."

"You young'uns had no business shooting BBs off the sleeping porch anyway," Aunt Letha said, her glare alternately pinning me and Lydia as intensely as if it had happened yesterday afternoon instead of twenty years ago.

"We weren't shooting at Mr. MacEntyre's house," Lydia said, laughing but still needing to explain, no matter how many times the story had been rehashed.

"I don't remember you shooting anything," I said.

"Don't go trying to blame your cousin Aaron," said Vinnia, smiling. "That was your BB gun, Avery Andrews."

"She's not the one who decided to shoot at the squirrels in the tree." Lydia came to my defense.

"No, but she was always the first one to climb out on the sleeping porch roof, no matter how many times I threatened to tan your hides."

"My feats of derring-do can't change the fact that your grandson Aaron was the big-game hunter who wanted to see if he could hit a squirrel." Later that summer, when he finally killed a squirrel, he'd cried like a girl. I'd reverently scooped it up and carried it to our nanny, who'd taken it to her house and made stew.

I could still hear the dry rustle of the BBs snapping through the oak leaves and the sharp claws of the squirrels—who were never in any danger from our marksmanship—as they scratched for purchase on the rough bark. And I could hear Mr. MacEntyre's high-pitched screech as he danced across the side street, calling a halt to the barrage of pellets pinging dents in his second-floor siding and nicking holes in his window screens.

"Just lucky you kids didn't slide off that roof and kill yourselves," said Mom, shaking her head in mock dismay.

Everybody laughed, enjoying the tale's reprise, funnier with distance and repetition than it had been at the time, removed now from the real risk of the slippery slope of the roof.

"Avery." Eden Rand floated over to take my elbow, breaking the family circle as she drew me away from the table. "I want you to talk to Rog."

I waited for her to explain her wait-till-your-father-gets-home tone. With her face close to mine in a conspiratorial huddle, I could see that the orange frizz had been aided by a bottle to cover some gray now shining at the roots. Her mascara clumped thick to bring depth to pale, stubby lashes, and her lipstick migrated into the tiny cracks of late middle age ringing her mouth.

"He's just not tending to business," she said. "I know he's probably in shock, but that's no reason to let that sheriff push him around, and it's no reason to let his own financial interests just fall by the wayside. He doesn't seem to understand he'll have expenses."

"I'm afraid I'm not—"

"He won't even talk about contacting the insurance company to notify them of her death. I'm sure processing a claim takes time. Shouldn't he get started with that?"

I managed not to let my mouth hang open in disbelief, but I couldn't manage to find the words to respond.

"Spence." Eden waved him over to our huddle. I couldn't tell from Spencer Munn's expression whether he'd been successful at horseshoes, but seeing him here and Emma still over at the pit starting a game with her dad gave me a hint.

"We were just talking about helping Rog out. I've been trying to tell him what you're always preaching, Spence, that there's a time value of money. That he doesn't need to let the insurance company keep his money a minute longer than necessary, that he'll have expenses. Funerals aren't cheap, these days."

The look on Spence's face probably mirrored mine, shock covered quickly with a polite veneer. "Um—"

"He needs to get that money invested. Get it busy working for him instead of for those greedy corporate shills. Right?"

Something in Spence's expression changed. "Ye-es. That's a good idea." He glanced at me. For support? To see whether I agreed with her or whether we agreed in our shock? "I doubt he wants to rush too fast. He doesn't want to look disrespectful."

Spence turned to me, but this really wasn't any of my business. At the same time, it didn't take reading many accounts of spousal homicide to realize how closely cops watch those left behind, to see how desperate they are to get their hands on the insurance proceeds. Setting his grief aside too quickly, before he'd held a funeral service, even before an autopsy had been completed, might make Rinda's death look more convenient than sad.

"Rog will be the best judge of that," I said. "After all, he's just learned she died. He needs some time to grieve."

"But he's also got to pay for the funeral. I know for a fact those funeral homes want their money up front, so they don't get stiffed." She registered no recognition that her last comment made an awkward pun. "Spence, you could invest the proceeds for him, couldn't you? What's left over?"

Spence again glanced at me, perhaps looking to form an alliance but not sure how far he could push his crazy colleague.

"Sure I could invest it, but there'll be time enough for all that. We need to get Rog through the funeral first."

The corners of her mouth crinkled in frustration at failing to find allies among the business-minded members of Rog's circle.

"He's in shock. Somebody's going to have to take him by the hand," she said. "You're a lawyer, Avery. Will you at least talk to him?"

"If he has attorney questions, he can call tomorrow for an appointment."

I'm sure my careful emphasis that he needed to call was lost on her. She heard something that was close enough to what she wanted to hear that it satisfied her.

"Good." She spun around, the loose ends of her scarf and skirt sailing behind her.

Spence Munn and I shared a resigned look and a shrug, but neither of us offered a comment. We had heard in each other's words what Eden had chosen to ignore.

We turned to the picnic tables. The food was great. The July heat, even under the canopy cover of trees in the shaded backyard, put a damper on some of the games, but the horseshoe pit stayed busy with a changing array of challengers and champs. Emma's dogs—two black Labs and a miniature Schnauzer who ruled the pack with an officious toss of its salt-and-pepper head—didn't mind the heat. After most of the guests had left and Emma finally persuaded her mom to let the dogs out of the house, they happily chased the Frisbee and each other as Emma and I played keep-away with them.

When we finally collapsed in the grass from full bellies and too much activity, I knew this afternoon should merit one of those entries in the social columns of the *Dacus Clarion*. A good time was had by all—at least so far today.

NINE

Sunday Evening

On Sunday evening, I decided to wander over to the festival grounds to check in with the Plinys. Nothing wrong with a corn dog for supper, since the picnic food had had plenty of time to settle. After all, the carnival wouldn't be in town after this week. Might as well take advantage of it.

The festival grounds weren't crowded. Too many Baptists attending Sunday evening church activities, though I'd hoped more tourists would be out enjoying their Fourth of July vacations.

The entrance to the House of Horrors was quiet, the lights over the banner line hung dark.

A matronly woman in a faded orange T-shirt and wavy hair gone gray years ago hunched behind the plywood podium that served as the ticket stand, sweeping with a bent–bristled broom.

"Miz Pliny?"

She eyed me, studying a moment before she gave a curt nod.

"I'm Avery Andrews."

That loosened up what might have been a smile,

but her eyes kept reviewing me, as she seemed to study everything in her vicinity.

"We gave your girl a check," she said, her husky voice full of old cigarette smoke.

"Yes'm, I know. I need to return part of that to you. Getting things sorted out didn't take that much time. Wanted you to know I'd bring it by tomorrow." I didn't mention that I planned to make sure their check cleared before I delivered any refunds. I may at times have trouble charging people for what seems a simple task, but I'm not a complete business idiot.

She pursed her lips and kept studying me.

"Have you heard anything more from the sheriff yet?" I asked.

"Nope."

"They should get the autopsy results by tomorrow."

"Good." Her lips disappeared, as if she were mulling a deep puzzle. "You got a minute?"

"Sure," I said, with a wry thought about whether I should deduct that minute from her refund.

After she stowed the broom under the battered ticket stand, she signaled to someone across the lot behind me. A boy, maybe twelve years old, appeared as if by magic.

"I'll be back in a bit to open up. You keep an eye on things."

He settled on the top step, worn smooth by years of shoe soles, happy with the stature he gained from his new task, eying the passersby who were waiting for the fright house to spring to life.

Pinner Pliny was even shorter than I was, and she stretched her turquoise polyester slacks and T-shirt to their limits. She also moved at an agile, quick pace.

"Thinks he wants to run away and be a carnie," she

said, jerking her thumb over her shoulder as we ducked past a canvas banner and picked our way through snakes of electric cables. "He's filled in for us some since we got here. Nice kid, nicer than most."

"He's from Dacus?" I hoped the concern didn't sound in my voice. Surely she had road sense enough to avoid a kidnapping charge.

"Reckon his momma or daddy will stir out of a drunken stupor before long and come drag him back home by his collar. Or what passes for home. Tried to talk those stars out of his eyes, but I seen 'em before. Shoot, I had 'em myself."

Pinner Pliny used the handle mounted beside a travel trailer door to pull herself up the foldout steps. I don't know much about motor homes, but this one was nice. Longer than most of the others gathered tightly out of sight behind the midway, it nestled beyond the bright glare but not far enough away from the rumble of the rides, the pumping rock music, the pings and calls from the games.

"E.Z.! You decent?" she yelled in the door. "That lawyer lady, Avery Andrews, is here." To me, she said, "Why the heck they want to lay around in their undershorts is beyond me."

Fortunately for us all, E. Z. Pliny appeared to be fully clothed, sitting in the tiniest sport wheelchair I'd ever seen. He didn't act as though he recognized me, though he was the same man who'd been taking tickets the night I'd called Rudy to report finding Prune Man. E. Z. Pliny hadn't been in a wheelchair that evening, and I wondered what the story was.

E.Z. himself, like his wife, wasn't very tall. He sat in the center of a remarkably well-ordered living space, with plenty of maneuvering room for his chair on the polished oak floor.

Hanging in the galley kitchen to the right of the entry and on built-in cabinets over the banquette were lines of photos in black frames, screwed into the cabinet doors in orderly rows.

"The good ol' days," said Pinner as she followed my gaze.

I took that as an invitation to step closer. "This is you?"

"And friends." E.Z.'s voice was raspy, Mickey Rooney on a bad day. He also sported Mickey's haircut, a stiff, short halo of ginger fuzz all over his large skull.

"That's me," Pinner said, "when somebody'd still pay to see me balance on knives."

Pinner pointed to a photo where a young blond with curls swirled down her back stood on a stepladder, her legs shown to good advantage in a short cheerleader skirt. On closer inspection, I saw the ladder's rungs were upturned saber blades.

"Simple weight distribution," she said. "And less weight to distribute." She patted the belly of her tight T-shirt.

"They'd still line up to see you, punkin." The way E.Z. looked at his wife said, to his eyes, his wife was still the girl in the picture. "You just don't need to work like that no more."

"That's E.Z." In another photo, he stood on a stage surrounded by upturned heads, all watching him slide a sword down his throat. In the first of two separate shots, the sword looked impossibly long.

"How do you do that?" I asked, then wondered if I'd violated some unwritten code of silence.

He shrugged. "Teach yourself not to gag. About anybody can do it."

I tried not to gag thinking about it.

"Not the way you could," said Pinner. "E.Z. could build a tip better'n anybody. He'd call 'em in, tease 'em with a couple of stunts, and promise better inside. They couldn't hand over their money fast enough."

"Ancient history," E.Z. said, a sharp edge in his rasp. "Gotta be so danged politically correct now, it's no fun."

"What's this?" I pointed to a photo of a trailer topped with a string of giant banners, the images too small to make out what each said.

"Our ten-in-one," said Pinner.

One look at my puzzled expression and she continued. "A series of attractions for one admission price. You know, a three-legged chicken or a snake charmer. Most were gaffs—something made up to look like a freak, like the living half-lady."

E.Z laughed. "The banners were better'n the show."

"Now, not always. Gorilla girl was good."

"Yeah," he said with a grin full of memory.

"A beautiful girl would transform into a raving gorilla right before your eyes," she said. "Before anybody could study on the gorilla too long, though, he'd go berserk, shaking the cage until the bars broke open."

"Which sent the crowd screaming for the exit," said E.Z. with a snort. "They knew they'd gotten their money's worth."

"Which of course built the tip—the crowd—for the next show. A'course it was all done with mirrors and a monkey suit."

"Those were the days," said E.Z. "Everybody wants to protect the freaks now. That's what they called themselves, you know. Can't put them on display, it's not kind. What I want to know is what kind of life does a kid with flippers for feet and claws for hands have these days? Or some kid with no arms or legs at all? I ask you. Least as carnies, they had family. People who treated them like they'uz real people. They could earn their own keep. Where are they now? Hidden away somewhere, living on the dole, without knowing there's others like 'em. Sad, if you ask me."

"Now, E.Z., they have ways to fix stuff now so they don't have those problems, and maybe some of them don't want to be freaks, they want to be normal."

"Hmph. Show me normal next time you spot it. I'd pay to see that. I liked a world where freaks could find a home with their own. That was a kinder place, you better believe it. Some a'those families some of them came out of, makes you ask who the normal ones were."

Pinner glanced at me to see how their well-worn argument was sitting with me.

E.Z. didn't care how it sat with me, but he was the one who changed the subject. "Is old man Letts going to cut us any break on the nut?"

"Our rent for the space," Pinner explained. "Folks are interested. We'll open shortly."

"Sure hope that's soon enough. Usually like to make the nut by the end of the first weekend, for a longer run like this," said E.Z. "Get that put behind us and earn us something to eat."

"We like to earn it by the first weekend," said Pinner, "but usually don't." Her tone hinted that she was the realist.

He just shook his head with the routine melancholy I've seen on an apple farmer's face any time somebody asks about the weather or the crop. No matter how good it is, it's always bad.

"Thanks to Avery, we'll make the nut," she said. "The crowds outside are fair, especially for a Sunday."

"Hope it holds," he said with cultivated gloom.

"Why's it called the nut?" I asked.

"Always heard it's because the show owner used to take a nut off'a the wagon's wheel so an operator couldn't take a roll before he'd paid off the owner at the end of a gig."

"Avery here stopped by offering to return part of our money," said Pinner.

E.Z. turned from the silent TV screen where cars in a NASCAR race ran on a continuous loop. His right eyebrow raised in a suspicious question.

"I got to thinking," said Pinner, "about what we talked about?"

The question, asked in their secret married short-hand, hung in the air until he offered a relenting shrug and a half-nod, still looking at me.

"Why're you giving our money back?" The question in his voice carried a load of skepticism.

"Because I didn't earn it."

Both his eyebrows shot up. To a man who'd made a living liberating money by scaring people into running from a gorilla suit, that must sound as unbelievable as a real gorilla girl.

"We were thinking . . ." Pinner paused, waiting for him to respond.

We stared at each other, E.Z. sitting in front of his silent stock-car race, Pinner and me standing surrounded by the kitchen cabinet photo gallery.

E.Z. finally spoke. "Would you be willing to do a bit more work for us?"

I didn't answer right away.

"We got to find out who that poor fella was," Pinner

said. "Get him proper buried. Nobody ought to be dumped in a pauper's grave."

"We've been talking it over. That man might have family that's been missing him," said E.Z.

"It ain't right," said Pinner.

"Uh, sure," I said. "I'll do what I can." Shamanique came to mind immediately. A few months ago, Edna Lynch, a private investigator who had proven both invaluable and intractable in a couple of cases, had hauled her young cousin by the ear into my office, frustrated with us both: with me because I wasn't businesslike enough to hire someone to answer my phone and with Shamanique because of her bad choices in boyfriends and a minor brush with the law.

Edna figured that putting the two of us together would solve a world of ills. Surprisingly enough, it had worked. Shamanique was a bulldog when she needed to track somebody down. She would probably call upon the same arcane skills to find a mummy's family that she used to track down dead–beat dads.

"You told me who sold it to you." I fished in my pants pocket and came out with my ticket stub and a pen.

"Con Plotnick."

She spelled it while I wrote in tiny letters on the ticket.

"Any idea where Mr. Plotnick might have family?"

They exchanged questioning glances. "We knew Con in Gibtown," said E.Z. "He didn't have any family there. You remember him talking about where he came from?"

"Nope." Pinner wore a thoughtful frown, but it apparently wasn't conjuring up any remembered connections.

"You mentioned Gibtown before. You live there when you aren't on the road."

E.Z. nodded. "One of these days, we'll retire there. When we build our poke."

Pinner nodded. "When he gets too old to climb the stairs into this trailer," she said. "That's when we park for good. Until then, he's looking for the next mark. Don't kid yourself, old man."

He shook his head but with a wry grin of agreement.

"Let us know what it costs," said Pinner. "We'll pay you up front, if you want."

Her tone carried no irony, no hint that I was their next "mark."

"Let me see what will be involved. If it's very complicated or we hit a quick roadblock, I'll let you know."

Their satisfied looks said the deal was sealed. I bid them both good night. I didn't mention the autopsy again or the need to reassure the sheriff—or, more particularly, to reassure Adrienne Campbell—that the Plinys had nothing to do with the strangely dressed man's demise. We could cross that bridge tomorrow, if it needed to be crossed.

TEN

Monday Morning

I went downstairs to the office earlier than usual, anxious to get started unraveling some tangled knots.

The message light was blinking. Rog Reimann had called late last night, according to the message machine, and he wanted me to call him back if it wasn't convenient for him to drop by at nine o'clock. Presumptuous of him, but not inconvenient. I glanced at my watch and decided I'd have to delay breakfast. I wouldn't have time to make it to Maylene's and get back by nine. This meeting should be interesting—and painful.

I didn't expect to find Rudy Mellin in his office this early, but I called anyway and left an innocuous message: "Hi. Just checking in." No need to tell him what I wanted to know. He knew.

My next call was to Shamanique. I doubted she'd be out of bed, on a vacation day, but I was wrong.

"You mind doing some work this week?"

"Nope. I'm at Auntie Edna's working as we speak."

"I imagine you could work this one like a skip trace, but I don't know. You're the expert. I need to find where the guy in the horror house came from, who his next-of-kin is, that sort of thing."

"The cops know what killed him?"

"Not yet, at least as far as I know. The autopsy should be complete today. I'll let you know when I hear anything."

That was two autopsies I hoped to hear about from Rudy. What a sobering thought, even though the mummy in the trailer didn't carry the same pang for me as wondering what they'd learned about Rinda Reimann. Still, the autopsy results marked two definite, final acts for two lives. Not exactly how I'd expected to fill my summer holiday.

I paused for a moment after I hung up the phone. Should I wait to find out how the mummy man had died before sending Shamanique on his trail? After all, we had no idea what had happened, how he'd earned his slot in the show.

I almost reached for the phone to tell Shamanique to hold off, then decided that was silly. Shamanique did her searches on a computer, safely tucked away in Dacus. She'd be the first to warn me if she found her questions stirring up any trouble. That girl can sniff trouble out from a distance—and then, according to her aunt, get herself into it. No worries there, though. Messing with dead guys wasn't her kind of trouble. She liked them very much alive.

Rog Reimann showed up at my office fifteen minutes early. That was not surprising. People are often anxious about visits to lawyers—or doctors or dentists—and want to get it over with. What was surprising was that he wasn't the first one through the door. Eden Rand, her orange hair, and her diaphanous clothes swirled through the doorway, unmistakably creating the draft that drew Rog along in its wake.

"Avery, it's so good to see you. We can't thank you enough for making time for us."

I'm sure my surprise registered on my face. I wasn't trying to hide it, but Eden was either unaware or unconcerned. My surprise at Eden's presence was a mild reaction compared to Rog's air of befuddlement.

"Come in." I led them from the cavernous entry hall into my front office, where Shamanique would normally be working at what would be a receptionist's desk, if I ever had clients stacked up waiting to see me.

I stopped beside Shamanique's desk and turned, my hand on the corner of the massive antique oak top, blocking the way to my inner sanctum.

"I told Rog he simply had no choice," Eden said. "He had to shake himself out of his lethargy, he has business to attend to." Eden hadn't taken a breath since they had come through the front door.

She linked her arm protectively through his. She may have tried to comb his hair before they arrived, but, if so, she hadn't been any more successful with his than she was with her own. His gray hair stood in greasy spikes, and he wore the same faded expression and what may have been the same pale, slightly wrinkled cotton shirt he'd worn Friday at the picnic. The only thing moving him from one place to another seemed to be his place in Eden Rand's powerful undertow.

The gaze she rested on his face saw nothing out of place, not his crookedly shaved whiskers or his sallow, sagging skin. Her attention wasn't what I would expect from a concerned colleague or even a family friend. It went beyond mere affection to unalloyed adoration.

I'd observed a few funeral home husband-hunters, lonely women who circled around newly available widowers, offering comfort and casseroles. Was that Eden's story? She was, given her tenure at the university, at least a moderately successful academic. She didn't fit the gold-digger stereotype, that was certain.

"Do you want to wait here?" I asked her. "Or we can call you if you'd like to go down the street for some coffee?"

I don't drink coffee, and I wasn't really interested in encouraging her with hospitality. If Rog Reimann needed a lawyer, he'd have to make that choice on his own. I'd prefer he not be influenced by Eden's presence, which, given the persistence of her attentions, might be forceful enough to emanate through the heavy pocket doors into my inner office.

"Oh." Eden looked surprised. "I—I'll wait here." She reluctantly slipped her arm from Rog's but didn't relinquish her gaze so easily. She studied his face with concern. "Can you talk to Avery?"

He blinked. Was he sedated? He had appeared much the same when I met him on Friday. Maybe this was his normal absentminded professor routine, compounded with less sleep and more preoccupation than usual. Maybe Eden was just being a good friend because he really did need a keeper.

"Okay." Eden looked around the front office as if she was being temporarily confined. She choose a well-worn leather club chair in the front window and settled her skirts about her, her oversized striped canvas bag at her feet.

"Mr. Reimann." I ushered him ahead of me and slid the doors shut without another glance at Eden.

Rog Reimann didn't act capable of choosing his own seat, so I indicated one of the two wing chairs in the alcove facing the side porch. The sunlight made it a bright haven in the morning, welcome in the cavernous, dim room.

Rog registered none of the details. He sank into the chair, his gaze fixed on me like a retriever awaiting his handler's signal.

"Mr. Reimann, I'm so sorry about Rinda. I can't imagine how hard this must be for you."

His nod was almost imperceptible, but the sunlight caught the tears welling in his eyes.

"I understand Ms. Rand thinks you need to waste no time pursuing your interests." Why was I talking like a funeral director offering a preplanning discount? Maybe because Reimann looked fragile, unable to deal directly with anything that made his wife's death real. This visit was premature, to say the least.

"Doctor," he said. His first word since he'd arrived.

"I'm sorry?"

"It's Dr. Rand," he said.

"Oh. Dr. Rand." I paused. At least I knew he could speak. "What did you need help with, Dr. Reimann?" I realized I'd failed to use his title as well.

He stared at the bookcases lining the back wall, several feet from my chair.

"Insurance," he said finally. "Eden says I need to do something to collect the—insurance."

The tears threatened to collect and fall.

"And something about the will, the estate. I don't know about these things."

He looked like a sad shadow of a man, rumpled and slightly dirty. Did Eden Rand just like scruffy middle-aged puppies, or did Rog Reimann offer charms I couldn't see buried beneath his grief?

Rather than tell him to come back when he was off tranquilizers and could shower and shave by himself, I decided now was a good time to make use of the "counselor" part of my job description, albeit the skills I had learned from hospice training in a church basement, not in law school. Given Eden's sense of urgency, I couldn't very well tell him to come back when he was farther along in his grief process.

"Tell me about Rinda." I leaned toward him, my gaze fixed on his face.

He blinked. His expression brightened a watt. "I love her very much. We were very happy together."

"I'm sure you were. How long were you married?"

"Over two years."

"Oh, my. You were newlyweds." Odd to think of Rog as a blushing bridegroom.

He stared at the floor.

"Where did you meet?"

"In St. Louis. We both worked there. She was the department secretary. We'd both been married before."

"Mm-hm." I offered an encouraging murmur. He needed to tell his story any way he wanted. Just letting someone talk about a loved one was often the kindest gift.

"One of those things, you know. I'd married too young, then we'd stayed together out of habit. Thought that was the way it was for everyone, you know, before I met Rinda. I certainly hadn't gone looking for love, but there she was. I was just swept away."

He sat for a moment, lost in a memory of unplanned passion.

"Then my wife died."

Whoa, back up. "Your first wife died?" I struggled to keep my voice even, my tone calm.

"A car accident. She was killed." His face crumpled in a remembered pain, even though he recited it in monotone.

"Rinda was already getting a divorce. We've been together ever since." I noticed he left out what happened to Rinda's husband and any children caught in the changing tide.

"When was the accident?"

His gaze rose to study the ceiling as he thought. "This is July? Wow. Three years almost exactly. July Fourth. Some guy had spent the afternoon at a party. He hit her."

"This was in St. Louis?"

"Webster Grove. Just outside St. Louis. Not far from our house."

I jotted notes on the legal pad balanced on the arm of my chair. Shamanique's vacation was about to be further interrupted with another research request.

"The accident really—threw me. I didn't know what to do. If it hadn't been for Rinda . . ."

More tears brimmed and one slid down his cheek. He bit his lower lip as he stared at the floor. He didn't look up to see how I was taking his display of grief. By all evidence, it was genuine.

"When did you and Rinda marry?"

"Just before Christmas that year. Didn't see any real reason to wait."

Some often-dormant Calvinist part of me thought propriety and respect might make good reasons, but if you're already fooling around on your first wife when she dies, who's going to look askance at an abbreviated mourning period?

"When did you move to Dacus?"

"Seneca, actually. Last spring was two years. I got a teaching job at the university because Rinda really wanted to come home."

"Home?" I knew the story, but he needed to tell it.

"Yeah. Rinda grew up in Camden County. Her folks are still here, and she has family and friends here."

He didn't catch himself and move her to the past tense.

"I'm so sorry, Dr. Reimann. I know this is hard. Wouldn't you rather wait until after the funeral?"

He looked confused.

"To attend to the other—matters?"

His almost-invisible sandy eyebrows met in a bewildered frown. "No." He shook his head, looking more like he was trying to clear away the clouds than refuting anything. "Eden said I needed to take care of this . . ."

He looked around my office as if realizing for the first time that Eden Rand hadn't joined us.

"Dr. Reimann, it might be best to wait—"

"No," he said without force. From the pocket of his rumpled short-sleeved buttoned-down shirt, he pulled a long envelope. I hadn't noticed it sticking out of his shirt pocket because it fit so seamlessly with his faded disarray.

He offered the envelope to me.

Inside was a summary sheet of contact information. Someone in the Reimann household paid attention to details. The list had bank accounts, insurance policies, everything I could imagine needing in the event a loved one passed on.

"Rinda left that. She said it had—everything?" he said.

"Looks like it."

"Can you—do whatever needs to be done?"

"Why don't we wait?" I said. "There's nothing that can't wait until—"

He shook his head and wiped his palms along his thighs. "Eden said I shouldn't wait. That it would be better to get things rolling. The sooner I get the money, the sooner I can invest it. Time value of money, you know."

He was parroting a lecture he'd heard more than once. From Eden Rand? I was back to the question, why the rush?

As I studied him, huddled in the wing chair next to mine, I wondered what I was seeing. The more he talked, the more I suspected this was the real Rog Reimann. Not overmedicated, just spacey. Frank or someone who knew him well could give me more insight, but this looked like the real Rog. He was clearly stunned by Rinda's sudden death, but, judging from Rinda's careful list of contacts, he was obviously used to someone else taking charge of life's little details.

Had it always been that way with Rinda? Had she "arranged" their love affair as neatly as she planned their financial affairs? Was Rog content with being led around by the nose—or by something else? I couldn't picture him carried away in a passionate embrace. I could see him led away by someone with a good idea what she wanted from him.

Or could this all be an artful act? Could he be hiding something more sinister behind his flaky helplessness? According to his colleagues, Rog was a respected professional, someone who attracted substantial research grants. Was he also a clever manipulator? Self-absorbed criminals—and they were all self-absorbed—often created plausible decoys, drawing attention away from their real motives. Was the helpless act and his reliance on Eden a decoy? Was he pulling the puppet strings, while making it appear that Eden was?

My mind flashed to the gorilla girl act. What was the costume and where were the mirrors?

"I'll make some calls and be back in touch," I said. My calls would involve finding a lawyer more qualified than I was to handle his estate matters, then I could suggest that Rog contact that lawyer.

Rog didn't look relieved or even aware that he'd convinced me to see things his way. He looked— unfazed.

"Have you finalized plans for the service?" I asked. That was the nicest way I knew to ask, without saying, *Has the ME released her body?*

"Um. Yeah. We're waiting until Friday. For family and friends from out of town."

"I see." I stood, and he followed my lead to the door. Eden was on her feet, staring out the front window. If she'd tried to listen in at the door, she'd have found how solid and well-fitted the pocket doors were.

"I'll be back in touch, Dr. Reimann." I offered my hand. He stared a moment, then took it in his limp grasp.

Eden guided her charge by the elbow into the front hall, glancing every few steps at his face for some clue to his state of mind.

I sure hoped Rog Reimann was ready to have Eden Rand in charge of his life because she'd already appointed herself to the role.

Why hadn't Rudy returned my call? Why couldn't other people be up and working early on Monday morning, the day before the Fourth of July? Heck, was Rudy off this week? He'd said he wasn't taking any time off, but he might have changed his mind. If he was in town, I knew where he'd be—if Maylene's wasn't closed today.

I was disappointed to find that Rudy wasn't inside enjoying the unquaintness of Maylene's. I nodded at Mr. Earnest, my dad's barber, who shared a table with a guy in a seersucker suit eating an omelet and grits. I hadn't brought anything to read, and it felt lonely, staring around at the half-empty restaurant.

The reduced workload did nothing to brighten the attitude of the one waitress who was working the day before the Fourth. She took my order—oatmeal with walnuts and an ice tea—but nothing said she was happy about it.

I studied the scratches on the tabletop, trying to decide whether they formed a Rorschach outline or a meditative maze I could trace with my finger. A flash of blue seersucker appeared at my table.

"Avery? Ken Tharp."

I stared at him with some interest as he offered his hand. An athletic man, he kept his wiry blond hair cut short to control the curls.

He nodded toward the seat across from me. "Mind if I interrupt for a minute?"

"Not at all."

He sat sideways in the booth, not sliding in for a long stay. His dark blue eyes studied me. He had a strong, tanned face, though his summer suit indicated that he worked in an office.

"Can you tell me anything about the investigation into Rinda Reimann's—death?" His voice caught and his eyes glistened. Given the gossip, I could understand his emotion. I just wasn't used to men wearing it quite so close to the surface.

I held up my hand to stop him. "I don't—"

"I understand you can't violate any attorney-client privilege." He said it as if it had a bad taste. "But—"

"Mr. Tharp, I'm not sure why you think I know anything. The sheriff or one of the investigators—"

"They won't talk to me. I'm not family. All Peters wants to do is ask questions and make snide comments. As Rog's lawyer, I—"

"I'm not Rog's lawyer. And if I was, I wouldn't be free to talk about it."

"You're not?" His tumble of words stopped and his mouth hung slack for a moment. "I heard—I—"

I searched for some soothing, innocuous balm I could offer to smooth his hurt and anger.

His mouth tightened and he cut me off. "What I want to know is, when is that worthless excuse for a sheriff going to arrest the murderer? Has he paid her off with the money he made the last time he got away with murder?"

I held up my hand to stop him, but he had to say what had been gnawing at him. The story about the first Mrs. Reimann's car accident wasn't going to answer his anger. Besides, I wouldn't trust the story until Shamanique had worked her magic and confirmed it.

"How can he just wander around free while Rinda is—" The rest of the sentence wouldn't come. He slammed his hand on the table. The scars on the table no longer brought to mind a meditative maze.

"Mr. Tharp, I'm so sorry. I know you and Rinda were—close."

I saw nothing in his red-rimmed eyes that would respond to anything I had to offer. No use arguing that her death could've been an accident.

Was this anger grown from real grief? The anger

was certainly real. It was the grief I couldn't be sure about. Was the anger a mask, for guilt or something else?

Ken hadn't been on the mountain that day—at least, not that any of us saw. That didn't mean he wasn't. It was, after all, a large wilderness area. What were all the whispered phone conversations that day? Plans for a hot rendezvous later that morning? The passionate twitterings that mean nothing except to the two people exchanging them? Or was it a prolonged argument? Was Rinda breaking it off? Was Ken having second thoughts? Had the phone calls not settled the issue and he'd driven to Bow Falls for a face-to-face that had gone horribly wrong?

Could he read any of my wild speculation in my expression? His gaze was fixed on my face, his jaw muscles knotting and working, but he didn't act as though he saw me.

Was I sitting across from a clever killer, someone who'd decided the best defense was an offensive strike on Rog Reimann? That seemed unlikely. His emotion felt too raw to be so calculated. But what did I know? He clearly wasn't rational or in control.

"I'm sorry, Mr. Tharp. I know it's hard to comprehend." I made soothing sounds, just as I'd been taught to do by the gentle ex-nun who'd taught the grief-counseling course I'd taken in law school. It had been something to give me another focus, a few Sunday evenings in a church meeting room away from studying civil procedure and contracts. I'd had no idea how useful it would be in my life as a lawyer, or how difficult it was to look at grief and realize how impotent you really were in the face of it.

I felt guilty turning Ken Tharp into an ideal fantasy suspect. Maybe that was my way of holding his anger at arm's length. He didn't have the luxury or release of grieving openly. She'd been another man's wife. Would an adulterer feel free to call the preacher for a grief-counseling session? He certainly wouldn't be wrapped in the public sympathy a spouse would be offered. Nobody was bringing plates of pound cake and fried chicken to his house. He was out in the cold, alone with an impotent anger. Just alone.

I reached across the table and laid my hand on his knotted fist. He jumped, as if just realizing I was there.

I held his gaze. "I'm so sorry."

He jerked his hand away and began to blink rapidly. Without another word, he rose from the booth and headed for the door, acknowledging no one else in the restaurant.

With "impeccable" timing, the waitress plunked the ironstone bowl of oatmeal in front of me and sashayed off without asking if I wanted more sweet tea.

I sat for a moment, my head bowed. Anybody watching would assume I was praying over my breakfast, but I was numbed by Ken Tharp's visit, by his aloneness.

The booth across from me creaked and I jerked my head up.

"Rudy!"

"You okay?" He looked genuinely worried.

"Uh, yeah. Fine."

"I know the food here itn't great, but it itn't that bad. Tell them to drop it on a hot griddle, it'll be fine."

"Thanks." Rudy's presence was stolid and calming after Ken Tharp's unreachable emotion.

Even though the waitress wasn't doing anything but standing near the coffee machine picking at her cuticles, it still took a minute before Rudy could attract her attention and wave her over to take his order.

"You're later than usual," he said. His thick finger wouldn't fit in the handle, so he wrapped his hand around the battered ceramic mug.

"You, too. Hear anything on those two autopsies?"

"No 'Good morning, Deputy, what kind of gas mileage you getting on that new cruiser the department bought?' No friendly chitchat?"

I gave him an exaggerated frown. "How's the mileage?"

"It sucks eggs."

"The taxpayers will be disappointed to hear that."

It was his turn to give a frown, this one not false or exaggerated.

"Did you get the medical examiner's reports?"

"Preliminary. On both of them."

"And?" He was making this difficult. Had he worked the night shift? Best not to ask. He just needed to drink his coffee and tell me what I wanted to know. "What about the mummy man?"

"He was just that. Mummified," he said, then paused to sip his coffee before he offered the crowning surprise. "With arsenic."

"He was poisoned?"

Rudy, with his impeccable timing, knew the word *arsenic* would startle me, but he remained calm, as if it was all in a typical day.

"No." He drawled it out. "Embalmed with it."

"Embalmed with it? How'd they know that?" That explained Rudy's bored recitation, despite the dramatic news.

"You don't poison somebody with several pounds of arsenic, for starters." He settled back. "How old you think that body was? How long you guess he's been dead?"

"How the heck should I know? He looked fresh, if that's what you mean. Not rotten or anything."

"The ME said they used arsenic to embalm bodies from around the Civil War to about the turn of the century. Some morticians continued using it into the 1930s, before they got concerned about the risks of using it in such quantities. Not healthy having lots of that stuff wandering around loose because it was darn popular for making people dead as well as preserving them afterwards. Not to mention what happens if it leaches from a graveyard into someone's well. So they started using other embalming methods. Maybe not better ones, though, because arsenic preserves really well. As you saw."

"So that guy's been dead what? Seventy plus years?"

"Wish I looked that good now."

The stump of the leg lying on the floor came to mind. Dry, a bit scaly. That hadn't looked so good. Neither had those half-closed eyes.

"What killed him?"

"Remarkably easy to tell, according to the ME, with everything so well preserved. An aneurysm."

"No sign of foul play?"

"Apparently not. Very straightforward cause and manner of death. Unless somebody scared him into having a stroke." Rudy chortled at the thought. "Then put him in a horror house. That's a good one."

"A straightforward cause and manner of death still doesn't explain how he ended up traveling the carnie circuit in a horror house. Could the ME estimate the date of death any closer?"

"Nope. Apparently the state of preservation makes

that difficult. No clues from the clothes or anything, since he'd been dressed in some sort of costume. A couple of layers, actually."

"So now what happens to him?"

Rudy sat back while the waitress thumped his plate—his one, solitary plate of food—in front of him.

"On a diet?" I asked, eyeing the two eggs, steaming sea of buttered grits, four strips of bacon, and two pieces of buttered toast sliced into triangles.

"Cutting back some," he said, snappishly.

I stirred a dollop of syrup into my oatmeal and returned to the topic.

"Any idea who the guy is?"

"Not a clue. Reckon they'll keep him for a while. Depends on how backed up the cooler is. My guess would be he's headed for potter's field."

That was sad. After a life on display, to be relegated to a life of anonymity. I observed a moment of silence with my mouth full of oatmeal.

Rudy finished chopping his runny egg yolks into his grits. As he used his fork to scoop the mess onto a piece of toast, I asked, "What about Rinda? Anything unusual?"

He stopped, toast poised. "Lots of questions around that one."

"What do you mean?"

He shrugged. "Autopsies don't tell the whole tale. Sometimes you got to get to the real story other ways."

"Meaning what?"

"Meaning I got people to talk to."

"About what?"

He shoved a bite of dripping toast and grits into his mouth.

"You're not going to say?"

He chewed and swallowed, slow and deliberate. "Not at liberty to divulge at this time, Counselor."

"Fine," I said. Not much I could threaten or cajole him with and not much point. He'd talk when he could—or when he wanted to. We ate in a companionable quiet, though I felt a sense of unease thinking back on my meeting with Rog Reimann. Maybe Rudy's secret really was none of my business. Maybe it was safely unrelated to my potential new client. Somehow I doubted it.

I sat with Rudy while he finished off his diet breakfast and wiped his plate clean with the last bite of buttery toast.

We said goodbye at the cash register. "See you later, A–vry," he drawled as I left him hitching his pants up at the cash register and reaching for a toothpick.

ELEVEN

Monday Morning

After I got back to my office, I studied the list of contact numbers Rog Reimann had given me. I'd never handled an estate before, didn't really know where to begin, and doubted it was something I wanted to learn to do.

I'd have to check with another lawyer, probably Carlton Barner. Carlton had been my unofficial mentor since I'd returned to Dacus, when I found myself having to learn how much law I didn't know. Working in a specialized trial practice had left a lot of holes in what I knew about nitty-gritty law—the kind of stuff clients really need their lawyer to know.

I still wanted to make sure Rog Reimann was in his right mind—or at least his usual mind—which was why I hadn't bothered having him sign a fee agreement. Being unable to collect a fee from him was the least of my worries.

Rog had been so insistent on starting the insurance collection process. The rush seemed in poor taste, but he was getting a lot of pressure from Eden. Maybe paying for the funeral was a financial stretch for him. I could also see how focusing on getting something done might serve to distract him, in some small measure, from his grief. It wouldn't hurt to get the ball rolling, if it made him feel better. I could introduce him to Carlton or someone more experienced later in the week, or next week after the funeral, after some of his shock had worn off.

I called the number listed beside Life Insurance on Rinda's neat list, then punched my way through the computerized prompts until I got a female voice asking for policy numbers and other information, which I read from Rinda's careful list. I listened to several minutes of Muzak until a rich, slow male voice said, "Hello? Miz Andrews?"

"Yes."

"You are calling in reference to . . . ?" He left the question hanging.

"Rinda Reimann." I gave him the policy number so he could confirm I wasn't a random drive-by caller.

"You phoned this weekend?" His drawl was honey-smooth. I pictured him as a black man, probably because his rich voice sounded like the singer Barry White.

"Um, no. No, I didn't."

The line was quiet for a moment. "You didn't call to notify us that the insured was deceased?"

"No."

"Do you know who did call?"

"No, I don't." How strange. "Didn't you get the caller's name?"

"She left a message, but no name."

"Dr. Reimann has asked if I would handle some of the details of his wife's estate."

"Are you a member of the deceased's immediate family?"

"No, I'm an attorney."

Another pause. "I see. Perhaps you can give me some of the information I'll need to begin processing this claim. Do you have a death certificate?"

"No-o. Not yet. I understand the medical examiner has completed the autopsy, so the certificate should be available shortly."

"Mm-hm. So you don't know the cause and manner of death."

"Not officially, no. I do know she fell off a waterfall."

"And how were you made aware of that?"

"Because I was there when she fell," I said.

Something about his hypnotically rich voice made me think of a spider weaving a seductive web.

"You were present at the death?" He had the good grace to sound shocked.

"Not exactly present. We were attending a large picnic near a waterfall. Mrs. Reimann was wading in the creek at the top of the falls when someone heard a scream. The rocks are extremely slippery. The Rescue Squad recovered her body from the falls the next day."

"I see." He paused, taking notes, I assumed. "The date on which this occurred?"

"Last Friday. June 30."

"You don't know who called this office on Saturday to report the death?"

"No, I told you I didn't." I myself wondered who it could have been. He had said "she" had left a message. Who would call a corporate office on Saturday? Who was in such a rush to collect the insurance? Eden Rand's name popped immediately to mind.

"Dr. Reimann is shocked and a bit overwhelmed, as you can imagine," I said. "His friends have rallied around to support him, so perhaps one of them called for information."

"Um-hm."

"If you could let me know what documents and information you'll need, I'll pass that along to Dr. Reimann."

"We'll need a signed copy of the death certificate."

I was surprised he didn't ask for a copy of the autopsy report, after I'd mentioned a postmortem had been done. If I'd been him, I'd have been asking for all kinds of information. Given my proximity to the death, the mysterious weekend call only a day after the death, and the odd way Rinda had died, anybody would have lots of questions. Maybe he was being gentle out of respect for the newly grieved—even though the newly grieved did, under the circumstances, seem oddly anxious to get the money wheels turning.

I knew, from years of representing insurance companies in medical and corporate defense work, that insurance companies make money from investments. They know they'll have to pay out eventually, but they prefer to hold on to premiums and delay those payouts as long as they can, within reason, because more time is more money.

I also knew insurance company claims people are, by nature or nurture, a suspicious lot. If they aren't when they start in the job, they soon learn to be as they gather wild tales and questionable "accidents" in their daily reports.

The sorghum-voiced claims guy on the other end of the line couldn't know about Spence Munn's lectures on investing early and often. He couldn't know that Rog Reimann's cluelessness seemed to call out a fierce protectiveness in the women in his life. He couldn't know about the shock of Rinda's fall. Given what he did know, though, I'd be suspicious, if I were him.

"I'll get that to you as soon as I can, Mr. . . . ?"

"Jacobs."

"Mr. Jacobs. Thanks for your time."

I had fulfilled Rog's request and gotten things started. I winced, thinking about the scrutiny the insurance company would give that file now, especially with not one but two phone calls before Rinda was even mourned and buried. I felt as though I'd stepped in a cow pie. The calls to the insurance company looked overanxious, but Rog Reimann couldn't be the only person in need of money when faced with a spouse's death. That's why people buy life insurance.

That Saturday phone call was very strange. And it was even stranger that neither Rog nor Eden had mentioned it. I suspected Eden as the mysterious caller, but Rog could have other helpful females hovering about, watching over him.

I needed a cup of tea, steaming dark tea. Even more, I needed the full ritual of steeping it in my favorite ceramic pot with the insulated cover that kept my second cup hot.

In the front hall, I smiled as soon as I saw the crystal vase brimming with flowers. They would need some fresh water.

I hadn't gotten flowers since—forever. Dear Lord, since law school. Some of the flush of pleasure evaporated. I stared at the flowers. With a jolt, I realized that Tappson G. Roderick had been the last guy who'd sent me flowers.

Tapp and I had met in torts class the first day of law school and had built a not-always-friendly rivalry over who could best argue the subtle intersections of law and fact on which plaintiff's cases are won or lost. Within weeks of our first study group meeting, he'd begun insisting on driving me home from the late-night sessions, the first of many courtly gestures that eventually swept me off my feet.

Even now, I wasn't exactly sure when things shifted from courtly to controlling. Not that I haven't tried to figure it out, because not knowing when it happened, that I hadn't seen it coming, still scared me. If I'd let it happen once, what would keep me from being blind a second time? I wouldn't ever open myself to that chance again.

Memories of my slow-dawning realization were as fresh as yesterday, returning with a wave of prickly emotion. In the middle of the night, a Sunday night, my phone rang. I'd spent the day at a horse show watching a friend compete. It had been a golden, crisp late autumn day, and I'd fallen into bed exhausted.

"Where the hell have you been?"

The clock by my bedside blinked 1:15 A.M.

"Tapp?"

"I've been calling you all day. Who were you with?" He was screaming accusations in a tone I'd never heard from him before. I felt groggy from being awakened, and confused. And angry.

He was beyond reason; I hung up. When the phone rang again, I stretched to reach behind the nightstand and unplugged it from the wall. Had he been drinking? Not really like him. In any case, better to give him a chance to calm down and come to his senses.

By an odd coincidence, early that same morning I was scheduled to meet with a woman at the law clinic office. Law students get experience working with real clients by spending a certain number of hours working in a clinical setting. After law school, when I began practicing law, defending hospitals and doctors,

I learned what a poor imitation this was of the rotation system used in medical schools. Doctors leave their training with a much better idea of their real world than lawyers do, which may explain why so many lawyers are unhappy and looking for ways to escape the profession.

Even though their clinical training may not adequately prepare lawyers for the real world, my client interview that day was the most powerful learning experience of my career.

The legal clinic was where I learned why they called us "counselors" and that the most valuable thing I'd ever give some of my clients was a sympathetic ear.

At the clinic, my job was to take client histories and outline what I thought the next steps should be. The clinical supervisor would then review my recommendations with me and refer the client, usually to a third-year student or to an external agency or sometimes to a district attorney to initiate a criminal prosecution.

I was twenty-two years old and green as a gourd, though I thought myself quite worldly wise. That morning, a woman in her early thirties sat across from me. She didn't look as though life had cut her many breaks. With most of the client histories, we had to listen to a lot of chaff before we got to the few kernels of necessary information. That, of course, was the purpose. We had to learn to listen. We had to learn to pick out what was important and, eventually, to direct the conversation where we needed it to go.

In a rambling tale that I struggled to summarize in my notes, the attractive woman with water-pale blue eyes and teeth too small for her wide smile laid out what I came to know as a classic domestic abuse story. Prince Charming had charged in, driving a red Blazer, had swept her into his arms promising to adore and protect her always. He called her constantly, showered her with attention, didn't want to let her out of his sight.

After they were married, his constant phone calls eventually caused her boss to fire her. Her husband started writing down the mileage on her car before he left for work. Eventually she'd lost her car when she couldn't make the payments, and with it, she lost her last vestige of freedom. The final straw, she said, had been last Thursday. He came home drunk and hit her for the first time.

The slap wasn't hard enough to leave much of a mark. I took a photo of it anyway. The slap was hard enough, though, to wake her up.

"Afterward, he tried to be all lovey and apologize," she said. "I just smiled and said I understood. As soon as he left for work the next day, I called a cab."

She started crying at that point. One lone little tear streaked straight down her smooth cheek. "I didn't know where to go, but I knew where I wasn't going, ever again." Her voice was ragged but set.

I remembered staring at her dark blond hair framing her pale skin. She had no job, no car, no friends. He'd alienated her family, left her in control of only enough money for a modest week's groceries, if she budgeted well. But she had enough courage to risk whatever was outside her narrow prison—and, without intending to, smacked me with a painful truth.

I never heard how things turned out for her, but seeing the determined set of her jaw that morning, I knew she would be fine. Bruised, but fine. She knew what she had to do, even though at that moment she was swinging without a net.

As soon as that morning interview ended, I skipped medicolegal jurisprudence class and took a long walk. Down Main Street in Columbia, back along busy Assembly Street, over the hill to Five Points, circling back up through the main campus. I walked and walked, replaying in my head all the vignettes. The things that had seemed chivalrous now were ominous, threatening. My face stung with chill air and perspiration and some odd mixture of anger and embarrassment. As my mother was fond of saying when Lydia and I were kids, "And you're some of the smart ones." How could I have missed it?

By the time I got back to the law school, I knew I would waste no time settling things. Tapp was always in his library carrel by ten-thirty. He didn't expect what was about to hit him.

I knocked on his carrel door. Through the skinny window, I saw his face light with a smile as he turned in his chair to open the door. He reached for my waist, to pull me close. I stepped back, just out of reach.

"Avery, I'm so—"

I cut off the apology. "Nobody cusses me, you son of a bitch. I don't know what part of me you thought you owned, but you can consider that phone call last night as your quit-claim deed."

Law students spend three years trying out legal jargon, sometimes in the oddest places.

"Leave me the hell alone," I said. "Is that clear?" From somewhere, I was channeling Aunt Aletha, even while I was certain she'd never found herself suckered in and manipulated.

I closed his carrel door for him. He had the good sense—or the arrogance—not to follow me.

We knew each other's habits well enough to avoid each other. I dropped out of the study group and moved to the front row in the tiered lecture halls, where we shared classes.

He sent flowers, then cards with sappy sentiments. I ignored them. After a week of Mr. Nice Guy, I met the real Tapp in a torrent of prank phone calls, flat tires, and a gossip campaign that most of the other students tried to avoid, embarrassed at seeing Tapp's private self exposed.

I got a concealed carry permit and hoped the Christmas holidays would bring the space he needed to set himself on an even keel. Instead, it gave him time to get more creative—and meaner.

I had time to get angrier. I walked out of my garage apartment one frosty January morning to head to class and found all four tires flat, all four stems cut. The friend I called for a ride was horrified and wanted to take me straight to the police station. I declined.

That evening, I went to a dance club near Fort Jackson and, with my sad story, propositioned a fellow who worked there as a bouncer and bartender. I assured him all he would have to do was stand behind me with his arms crossed. He volunteered the scowl without my having to ask.

Later that night, we waited in the law library parking lot. I knew Tapp would leave the library around midnight.

I'm sure two figures stepping out of the dark in the empty parking lot got Tapp's adrenaline pumping, which only added to the stage effect. I didn't raise my voice. I just leaned in close and lied. I told him I had photo and line-tap evidence of his nonsense with my car and phone and, if he didn't cease and desist, I would see to it that he never sat for the bar exam. That would be after somebody scraped him off a dirty sidewalk and hauled what was left of him to the ER.

My bouncer friend just leaned against the light pole without saying a word. His silence kept him from committing an indictable offense and also worked better than I'd hoped. It worked so well, I was often tempted to suggest the tactic to some of the women who sought help at the legal clinic. If the lawyering thing didn't work out, I figured I could hire myself out as muscle.

I stared at the flowers on the hall table, the sunlight slanting through the leaded glass door. I shook myself. It was time I remembered that nice guys send flowers, too. *Get some perspective, Avery, and enjoy the ride.*

I brewed a small pot of tea, carried it to my office, and called Shamanique.

"Ye–uh," she answered.

"Sorry to bother you."

"No bother. Sittin' at Auntie's computer. What else."

"Thought you were taking a few days off."

"So did I. Sumbody"—I could feel her cut her eyes, even though I couldn't see her—"thinks she got to keep me outta trouble."

In the background, I heard the reply: "You got that right." Edna Lynch kept her young cousin on a short leash. Whether Shamanique's behavior was questionable enough to warrant it, I couldn't say. In my office, she was a hardworking young woman with a sassy tongue, not unlike lots of others her age. She seemed to have a penchant for bad boyfriends who had skated her at least once too close to the line of legality. I took that as youthful indiscretion. Aunt Edna took it as a harbinger of a life doomed unless drastic, life-altering measures were applied. Edna applied them with a heavy hand.

Edna had gotten me to hire Shamanique about a month ago, while Shamanique was on work release after a bad check charge. Before I'd known what hit me, Edna had the giraffe-legged girl with giant hoop earrings and ever-changing hair-dos sitting at my reception desk. When I'd found out what she could do with a computer and a phone, I was happy for her to become a permanent fixture—even if she did tend to disapprove of my circumspect love life.

I hoped the flowers would die before she got back to the office. She wouldn't mind asking questions that I'd rather not answer.

"Would you have time to run down one more thing in the next day or two?" I outlined what I knew about Rog Reimann's first wife and her death.

"You thinking he killed her before he killed this'un?"

"I don't think he killed anybody. I just want to make sure I have the facts."

"Mm-hm." Shamanique is quick to assume the worst, not unlike her aunt Edna. "This other'un supposed to've died in a car wreck? Not a fall?"

"That's what he said. There ought to be a record."

"Yeah, no problem. I can probably get this today. Anything else?"

"That'll do for now."

"I'm 'specting something back on that dead guy at the carnival. That's one creepy thing you got yourself mixed up in there."

I didn't explain I hadn't involved myself in it, exactly. Just no point in trying to explain. "Talk to you later."

It was too early for lunch. I carried my tea upstairs, piled clothes in a hamper to wash at Mom's later, and wandered back downstairs to catch up on reading the advance sheets from the South Carolina appellate courts.

I couldn't concentrate, so I decided to stroll down to Maylene's for the early lunch crowd. Chances were good I could catch Rudy Mellin there, even though I'd just seen him for breakfast. Chances were also good that he'd had time to digest the preliminary autopsy reports and might have a better idea what he could safely share.

Something had left me feeling unsettled—and melancholy? Was it the tone in the insurance agent's voice? My uncomfortable flashbacks? Or did I just need some physical activity? Option three, I decided, as I locked the door behind me.

TWELVE

Monday Lunch

Rudy wasn't in Maylene's, but I didn't have to wait long. He knew what I wanted as soon as he saw me, but he didn't abandon lunch or choose another booth.

"Let me order first and catch my breath, how 'bout it? Before you launch into me. Why don't you find yourself a new best friend?"

"Ouch. And abandon you? I don't see anybody else standing in line to eat lunch with you."

"I feel so cheap, so used," he said with exaggerated drama. "It's not really me you're interested in."

"How'd you know? Okay, I confess, it's the uniform," I said, then snorted. "What makes you think I come here looking for you? It's lunchtime, you know. Half the courthouse is usually here."

"Yeah, but you're the only one with your eye on the door waiting for me to bring you news about dead people. Some appetizer."

I didn't point out that nothing ruined his appetite. He sounded touchy today.

When he ordered baked chicken and steamed squash, I made no comment. I'd ordered a cold tuna salad plate just because it was too hot outside to eat much. I suspected some kind of diet, rather than the heat, was putting Rudy off his feed. If he wanted to tell me about it, he would.

"Anything new on the guy at the carnival?"

"Nope. He's still in the cooler at the ME's, still loaded with arsenic and beautifully preserved. Maybe after the holiday, we can spend some time trying to ID him. Until then . . ." He shrugged and took a long draw on his sweet ice tea.

"The Plinys asked me to see if I could track him down, find out who he was."

"The who?"

"The Plinys. E.Z. and Pinner Pliny. They own the fright house."

"They paying you?"

"That's how it works," I said. "The state pays you. Clients pay me. The world goes 'round."

"Why they doing that?"

"They want his family to know what happened to him, want him to get a proper burial."

"That's nice." His voice dripped with cop skepticism.

"Shamanique's working on it," I said. "If she turns up anything, I'll let you know."

He didn't reply. He turned sideways in the booth, his back against the wall, so he could eye the people coming in the front door. Rudy hates it when I beat him to Maylene's because he hates sitting in the booth with his back to the door. If we're both late and have to take one of the tables in the middle of the room, then he can choose his position. Knowing he hates it was one of the reasons I try to grab the booth first. Just because.

"Has the ME sent a report on Rinda Reimann?"

Rudy turned his gaze directly on me. "Interesting

you should ask that. You the one who called her life insurance carrier?"

"How'd you know about that?" Heck, that had been only a short time before I left for lunch.

Rudy read my mind. "The adjuster called me as soon as you hung up. Seems he's more than a little suspicious about that accidental death. Especially when you're calling before the body's even found."

"That wasn't me."

His eyes narrowed. "You didn't call on Saturday?"

"Nope. I told Mr. Insurance that, too."

"So who did?"

I shook my head. I had my suspicions about Rog's overzealous guardian angel, but nothing more than suspicions.

"But you called this morning."

I nodded. "Just to see what documents Rog needed to supply to put the process in motion."

"Cheesh, A–vry. Didn't your mama raise you any better than that? Show some respect. She's barely cold."

Underneath his mocking tone was a vein of suspicion, the natural state of mind for a cop as well as for life insurance claims guys.

"Funerals cost money," I said. "A friend of Rog Reimann's is concerned that he might need the money. I can assure you it wasn't Rog's idea to call."

"But Rog hired you."

Rudy didn't need an answer to his rhetorical question, so I didn't bother supplying one. Remembering Rog's fey, perhaps drugged state, I wondered what Rog even remembered about our meeting.

"So," I said, "this insurance guy called you this morning?"

Rudy turned in the booth to face me, his back

squarely to the door, his forearms propped along the table's edge.

"Twice."

My turn to stare until he elaborated.

"He called first thing this morning to report the weekend call," he said, then waited until I responded.

"He told me he'd gotten that call," I said.

"But he didn't tell you he'd gotten the preliminary autopsy report?"

I didn't try to hide my surprise. "No. He acted like he hadn't seen it."

"I assume his fax machine was working," Rudy said. "In any event, he knew the important part."

"Which is?"

"That Rinda Reimann had bruises on her arms."

She fell several hundred feet down a rock cliff face, battered by a cascade of water. I would expect she had lots of bruises, but Rudy's sly tone hinted at something unexpected.

"And?" I prompted.

He studied me a moment, either to build the tension or to assure himself that I wasn't playing dumb.

"The ME found bruises on her upper arms. Finger bruises. As if somebody stood behind her and grabbed her. Hard."

He studied my face for a reaction, some indication that his bombshell news combined with something I'd learned from Rog or another source to yield a telling connection. He got no such revelation from me, just shock. And questions.

"She had to have a lot of bruises. Didn't she? I mean, how can they be so specific about what caused certain bruises in a situation like that?"

"Of course she had a lot of bruises. Almost every

inch had an abrasion or a contusion, plus the broken bones."

I suddenly wasn't interested in the tuna salad scooped onto the lettuce leaf that the waitress plopped in front of me.

The visions in Rudy's head didn't tamp down his appetite. He picked up a knife and fork and started sawing away at his clammy white chicken.

"I just saw the digital photos attached to the report," he said. "The fingertip bruises on her arms really stood out. Remarkable, considering what the rest of her looked like."

Rudy eyed me as he took a bite and chewed slowly. He knows I don't keep things from him unless I'm protecting a client confidence. It had taken a while after I'd come home to stay, as we renewed our high school acquaintance, for me to stop getting defensive under his suspicious probing. It's what cops do, I realized. Some instinct they were probably born with and refined to a sharp point as cops. Without that skepticism, they didn't make very good officers. Knowing that didn't make it any less offensive.

He finished chewing. "Most of the other bruises were part of large scrapes. These particular bruises were small and dark. Four on the front." He pointed to where his beefy bicep strained his uniform shirt. "And one on the back of each arm."

I pushed my plate away and took a sip of tea. My mouth felt dry as white flour.

"How do they know when she got those bruises?" I asked. Could they somehow time-date bruises? I had a dim memory from research or reading that they couldn't accurately date bruises, but the state medical examiner's office had some smart people on staff.

The corner of Rudy's mouth tightened, then relaxed, the tenseness passing in a second. I'd hit a soft spot.

"The time element is something we'll be asking questions about. Somebody left those bruises on her. Clear ones, from a tight grip."

"Who are you going to be talking to?" I hoped Rog would have sense enough to call me—or somebody—before he sat down for a chat. How embroiled did I want to get in this?

Rudy shrugged. "Don't know yet. Haven't got all our questions together."

I stared at the chopped egg white glistening in the brown tuna, the lettuce limp in the humidity.

"You gonna eat that?" Rudy pointed his fork at my plate.

I pushed it in his direction and he shoveled up a mouthful.

"Too hot to eat," I said.

Maylene's was air-conditioned, but during the heat of the day and the height of the lunch rush, the system couldn't handle both the kitchen and the crowd. Rudy's forehead glistened along the fringe of his short-cropped sandy hair while he ate his lunch and mine.

"So that guy at the insurance company, he knew about the bruises?" I asked.

Rudy nodded. "I'd just finished reading the report this morning when he called."

No wonder Mr. Jacobs had been so antagonistic. He'd had more reason for his suspicion that I could've guessed.

We sat in silence while Rudy worked his way through both plates of food and occasionally raised his fork and nodded a greeting as someone passed our booth.

I sipped my tea and kept him company until he was ready to leave. I paid for my half of Rudy's lunch, of course.

Perspiration popped from every pore as soon as I stepped out on the sidewalk. The humid air wrapped around my head, and I had that summer-familiar sensation of swimming in hot Jell-O. I dragged myself down the sidewalk back to the office.

Shamanique surprised me, sitting at her desk fanning herself with an advertising brochure from the fresh stack of mail.

"Nice flowers," she said. "A special occasion?"

I ignored her question. "You just get here?" It didn't take Sherlockian skills to observe the glistening line of perspiration along her carefully shellacked hairline. The office, with its twelve-foot ceilings and deep porches, was designed to stay cool. The air-conditioning served to hold the clamminess at bay and keep the books, furniture, and rugs safe from the high humidity.

"Auntie Edna was using her computer, so no point hanging around there. Besides, got a lot of stuff for you."

I slumped into the leather chair across the room from her desk. "Great. Let's hear it." Neither of us bothered turning on a light. Somehow the dimness, lit only by sunlight shaded by the deep porch, protected the illusion of coolness.

"First off, did you know accidental falls are a leading cause of death in the national parks?"

"Makes sense, when you stop to think about it." I'd just never thought about it. What else would you die from? Bad potato salad? Bear attacks? Only rarely and not around here.

"Which could raise some eyebrows about whether the cops're trying to bust some guy just for the hey."

She had a point. An accident made at least as much sense as a murder—if you could ignore those bruises. Those could've happened days before her fall. Maybe that's why they stood out so clearly.

I knew how our county solicitor thought. Josiah Thames wouldn't waste taxpayer money trying to find some hired gun to testify that he could time-date the bruises and tell exactly when they were inflicted. Defense attorneys with rich clients and big budgets might try a junk science route, but scant few prosecutors can afford to—and Josiah would never even consider it. No, instead Josiah would artfully use the finger bruises to point to the most likely culprit—Rinda's husband Rog. No matter when he'd grabbed her, Josiah would argue, he'd grabbed her in anger.

To my mind, the most logical explanation was that Rinda's fall was an accident. The idea that Rog Reimann could face the vagaries of a murder trial for what was most likely an accident was starting to scare me. Those bruises stuck out in my mind, just as they must on her pale, bloodless arms—ten mute but powerful witnesses. Witnesses to what, though?

Shamanique finished shuffling through some typed pages and continued her recitation without prompting.

"Reimann's first wife died in an accident three years ago. Smashed by a semitrucker driving drunk. Killed instantly. She had a hundred-thousand-dollar accidental death policy from her employer, which paid out to her husband. He also sued the trucking company."

She paused to read directly from one of her print-outs. "The case was settled for an undisclosed amount. I couldn't shake loose how much it settled for."

"No," I said, "you probably can't. Likely a sealed settlement, which is negotiated by the parties. The defendant agrees to pay money, the plaintiff agrees not to tell anyone how much, and they both avoid the risk of a trial."

"How much you reckon he got?"

"Hard to say. The amount of damages would depend on the financial loss her family suffered from her death, usually the present value of her future income. Was it a large trucking company or a small local operation?"

"I didn't recognize the name," she said.

"A small operation doing local hauls might carry a half to a million in insurance. A big outfit would easily have over a million. If the driver was drunk, the defense would've been worried about punitive damages at trial, so a settlement could've exceeded the insurance limits."

"No shit? That mean her ol' man's a millionaire?"

"Probably not. The lawyer and the case expenses would've taken a chunk, probably forty percent or more."

"Still," she said, "he would've gotten a chunk of cash, huh?"

"Any indication how he's doing financially?" I asked.

"Haven't checked that yet. I'll see what I can find."

My mind flashed to Eden Rand and her urgency over getting the insurance proceeds invested and her insistence on Spence Munn's advice about the time value of money.

"I might have a lead on that," I said. Not that Spence

would betray any confidences, but no harm in asking if Rog had any money invested with him.

I continued with my questions. "So no sign that the first wife's car accident was anything but that, a drunk driving accident?"

"No sign. All the reports seemed pretty straight-forward. Truck crossed the center line and hit her head on. She died instantly. The other driver was treated and released, later sentenced for vehicular homicide. He got a deal in exchange for a guilty plea."

For Rog, that created a bad coincidence, having two wives die in accidents, even with evidence that each was nothing more than an accident.

"Any mention how much life insurance the latest Miz Reimann had?" I asked.

"Nope. Want me to find out?"

"No, no." I flagged her with both hands. "We'll wait on that." No need rattling the insurance claims adjuster's cage again, and I was certain any periph-eral inquiry would make its way back to him.

"To change the subject, any word on our carnival guy?"

"Not yet. Got some leads, though. I'll make some more calls today. Most everybody who would know seems to live in Florida, but I'm having trouble get-ting anyone on the phone." She grinned and cocked her head. "Might just be cheaper for you to send me down that way."

"Hm." I responded with a shake of my head and a smile. "The Plinys said that's where lots of carnival folks live when they're off the road." I hadn't thought about it, but Gibsonton and the carnival world sounded like just another small town—one whose residents happen to be widely traveled. That small-town quality could make it easier to find people who know people who know something.

"More than likely, they're on the road, working the Fourth of July holiday fairs," I said. "Keep trying."

The bell on the outside door jangled. From her vantage point, Shamanique could see the front hall. She sat up straight, so I knew we had a visitor. By the way she pressed her lips together and cocked her head, I knew she was wondering who this was daring to enter without an appointment.

Eden Rand floated into view, her thick waist and middle-aged heavy hips and breasts once again trying to seek disguise in a series of jagged-edged scarves and skirts. This afternoon, the outfit was sea-foam green with baby-blue beaded flats and a thin scarf tied through her frizzy hair.

She stopped in the doorway, pinned by Shamanique's frown. When she spotted me, Eden brightened.

"Avery, I'm so glad you're here. Do you have time? Could we have a word?"

Shamanique didn't tell her we were closed. Maybe I should have, but it was hot outside, so it wasn't as though I had anywhere else to go.

"Come on back." I pulled myself out of my deep slump and gestured toward my office. I paused in the doorway to tell Shamanique, "Don't work too long. You're supposed to be taking some time off."

Shamanique cocked her head. Lord, how she reminded me of her forbidding aunt Edna, who also hated being told what to do.

"I'm just biding my time. Got to go get my hair done today."

That, I knew, was an hours-long operation.

"Going to the carnival tonight," she said. "All this talk got me curious."

Knowing Shamanique, she'd have some hunk in a tight T-shirt buying ride tickets and cotton candy for her. She has powers.

"Hate I missed seeing our famous man in the flesh, though." Shamanique shook her head in mock mourning.

I grinned and slid the pocket doors shut. Eden Rand had claimed one of the wing chairs in the window nook rather than one of the wooden armchairs in front of my desk. Might as well make ourselves at home.

"Avery, I'm worried sick about Rog. That stupid sheriff seems to have made up her mind that there's something fishy about Rinda's accident. How the people in this county could elect such an oaf to office is beyond me."

"Has Rog talked to the sheriff?" I tried to keep my tone even, but I hoped he had better sense than to go into what likely would be a hostile interrogation without counsel.

"He has refused."

I knew from her tone that she had been the one to put her foot down. Rog—at least the way he'd presented himself this morning—was in no shape to exert himself with anyone.

"I'm not sure completely shutting down on the sheriff is wise," I said.

Her eyebrows shot up under her frizzy orange bangs in surprise.

I wasn't being contrary just for the heck of it. "Cops assume people want to find out what happened to their loved ones. Innocent people do, anyway. The deputies might draw some unfortunate conclusions if Rog refuses to talk to them."

"But they'll just try to trap him into some sort of admission. You saw him. He's in shock. He barely knows his own name. I just told them he wasn't able."

Just as I'd suspected. I didn't push it any further for now.

"I thought you could talk to them," she said. "There's some things they should know. About Rinda. Things that would change everything. But I'm not the one to tell them."

"What sorts of things?" My caution flags raised.

"For one thing, Rinda had a lover. I don't know if that's why she wanted to move back to Camden County or if that's something that started after they moved, but she took up with an old boyfriend almost as soon as the boxes were unloaded into the house."

"Who?" For once, I might be ahead on the small-town gossip, unless Rinda was a lot more active than my sister Lydia knew.

"Ken Tharp. They knew each other when she was growing up here. I don't know if they kept in touch over the years or what, but everybody knows they're together now. I don't know if you noticed her talking endlessly on the phone at the picnic, but that's who she was talking to."

"How do you know?" I'd assumed Rinda was checking on her kids or something. How many others beside Eden and Lydia had leapt to the assumption she was talking to her lover—and had a name for him?

Eden rolled her eyes in dramatic fashion. "Who else? And so compulsively? It's typical for someone to be so consumed by another person in the first passionate blush of an affair. Rog knew, for certain."

I didn't argue with the sociologist, even though I doubted any judge would recognize her as an expert on the effects of the first passionate blush of an affair, based solely on her academic credentials.

"Rog knew she was having an affair? You're certain?"

Eden had the graciousness to pause for a minute, acknowledgment that she might not know everything about Rog. "He knew that's who she was talking to. I don't know if he knew about the affair. Men can be so gullible. Especially Rog. He didn't necessarily want this move. He took this new job to appease her, to bring her back home. He was focused on his job, on making the transition. Universities can be highly political and treacherous. He needed to get himself positioned appropriately. That was his focus."

I'd hate to take notes in Eden Rand's class, given how peripatetic her path. "Were the Reimanns happily married?" I was more interested in Eden's response than in the reality.

She started shaking her head immediately. "Oh no. I don't think so. They weren't terribly compatible. Rog is cerebral, devoted to his research. I think Rinda swept in when he was vulnerable, in distress over his first wife's death. Rinda was married at the time, you know, to someone else. That didn't stop her from insinuating herself into Rog's life."

I bit the inside of my lip. We do tend to hold up mirrors that reflect ourselves, and we so seldom realize it.

"So Rog had an affair with Rinda while she was married?"

With no more than a wave of her hand, she brushed aside the implication that his actions had been less than chivalrous. "Marriage is an artificial construct. Rinda's first marriage had no meaning for her. Why should it have meaning for Rog? Besides, he was hardly the aggressor. That's not in his nature."

What in his nature brought out this passion and protectiveness in women? I'd spent time with Rog. I hadn't seen anything magnetic or alluring. Maybe it only worked on women who longed to have someone to care for.

"Was Rog still in love with Rinda?"

"Ah." She sounded almost exasperated. "What is love? A series of chemical reactions, with marriage as a social convenience, no more than a formal contract to protect the procreative result. I doubt he was ever in love with her. It was convenient, a way to process his grief over his first wife's death."

I pictured Rog's hollow-eyed stare as he'd sat in my office this morning. His grief looked real enough. Or was it shock? Shock at Rinda's death? Or shock at something else?

I studied Eden. Her face and arms carried the puffy paleness of someone who spent too much time indoors. She wore no makeup, and her clothing, her scarves, her reading glasses buried on top of her head all spoke of a created carelessness.

"You have some interesting views on marriage," I said in what I hoped sounded like an intellectually curious tone rather than a cross-examination. "Are you married?"

"No." Again, the dismissing wave of the hand. "I don't need the state's permission for how I choose to gratify myself."

I nodded. Was Rog Reimann her one shot at matrimony? I might believe the free-floating spirit act from somebody else, but I'd watched Eden dance attendance on an oblivious Rog Reimann. Her attendance sent a different message than her words did.

If I was Sheriff L. J. Peters, my suspicion meter would be pointing at Eden Rand. She seemed in much better control than Rog, much more deliberate. She obviously had him under her control. She might know he already had money and obviously knew he had more insurance money coming. Eden wasn't a large or athletic woman, but neither was Rinda, in her pencil-thin white pants.

Eden's hands nestled in the folds of her tiered peasant skirt and its layers of faded cotton. She wore no rings. Was protecting—or winning—Rog a powerful enough motive? Could those fingers have grabbed hold of Rinda Reimann's thin arms with enough force to leave bruises, with enough force to send her over the edge?

At that thought, I had trouble meeting Eden's gaze.

"So you think Rinda's boyfriend—Mr. Tharp— had something to do with her death?"

"I don't know. Maybe they were having some kind of argument, with all those phone calls that day. She kept going off by herself, so no one could overhear. Maybe in despair, she threw herself off the mountain."

Or maybe her husband found out about the affair. Maybe he overheard sweet nothings or plans for an assignation, or maybe someone told him. Someone who had her own agenda. Maybe a hurt and enraged Rog had grabbed his wife and flung her off the top of Bow Falls, her slender, white pants legs flailing as she fell.

"Did Rog care that she'd renewed her friendship with Ken Tharp?" Asking the question in different ways sometimes yields more telling answers.

She gave a deep shrug. "He didn't really love her. They had nothing in common. She caught him at a weak moment, when his first wife died. That was all they had. I think they both realized it was a mistake. Rog missed his old job. He'd earned the kind of comfortable perks that come from surviving the battles in an academic institution. Of course, he's in a better position now, more opportunity for national visibility. He'll come to see that."

Was it easier for her if she convinced herself that Rog hadn't loved his wife, that he was a sort of renewable virgin? I didn't know him well enough to draw a conclusion, but from this morning's visit, I would judge he was either on drugs, in deep grief, or a permanent space cadet. To what lengths would Eden Rand go to protect the sad puppy? Had she already gotten him to follow her home? For Rog's sake, I hoped not. It wouldn't do him any good for L. J. Peters—or anyone else, for that matter—to find out he'd already taken up with another woman.

"I appreciate you letting me know all this." I stood to draw our little chat to a close. For a smart woman, Eden seemed particularly clueless about the implications of the gossipy tidbits she'd carried in.

"It would be best if Rog avoided any appearance of impropriety, especially while the sheriff is asking questions." I fixed her with a stern eye. "It's a small town, you know. A very conventional little place."

She drew herself upright, stiffened by a touch of indignation. "Don't I know that."

I cut her off before she could launch into another of her lectures. "It would be best to give Rog some space right now. I know you want to help, but the appearance that you're too close to him could complicate matters."

She blinked and drew back. A range of reactions danced across her guileless face: disbelief, hurt, anger, sadness. Embarrassment?

"I—"

"I'm sure you understand. It would also be best to

keep what you know about Rinda to yourself. No need to stir up any small-town suspicions."

As her mouth pulled at the corners, I knew I'd struck the right tone with her. Perhaps her disdain for the plebian small-town minds could help her sublimate her sexual energy. She needed to steer clear of Rog for a while. She could entice the clueless one into her little love web later. Right now, she didn't need to be wrapping him in a cocoon and delivering him into L. J. Peters' not-so-tender embrace.

THIRTEEN

Monday Afternoon

After I escorted Eden Rand to the front door, I noticed the light on in Melvin Bertram's inner sanctum. I hadn't heard him come home.

"Yoo-hoo." I peeked in the French door to his outer office to make sure he wasn't on the phone.

"Greetings," he called.

"Welcome home," I said as I entered the doorway to his sanctum.

He leaned back in his desk chair and stretched his arms over his head as if he'd been hunched over his computer too long.

"When'd you get back?"

"Late last night. Heard you all've had a bit of excitement this week. Made the national news, you know."

"Which story?"

"The dead guy in the traveling show. Don't tell me you got something that tops that."

"Rinda Reimann fell off Bow Falls on Saturday." The regional television stations had mentioned it, but an accidental fall lacks the drama that television scandal news craves. The story was taking too much time to unfold and couldn't be captured neatly in a sound bite.

"Oh, gosh. I'm sorry to hear that."

Melvin had lived away from Dacus a lot of years, and Rinda would've been too many years behind him in school for him to remember her.

He paused for a respectful moment before asking, "So what's the local chatter on the traveling mummy? Has he set the town on its ear?"

"Parts of it," I said, picturing Madam President Adrienne Campbell's dramatic hissy fit. "Most folks find it a curiosity."

Melvin chuckled. "Well, sure. It's not like he's from around here."

"So what's the gossip?"

"Guess the news reports didn't mention who discovered the body."

"No." He paused, reading the expression on my face. "No-o. Not you. You're kidding."

"'Twas me. And Emma."

"They said some kid bumped into it and the leg fell off."

"That wasn't Emma. She just happened to be the one to have it land at her feet."

"Your sister still letting you see your niece?" He was only half-teasing.

"Amazingly enough, she is. Come to think of it, though, we've had only supervised visits lately."

"I can understand that. I've long wondered why they would turn you loose with an impressionable child . . ."

I snorted. "Impressionable. Emma?"

"Seriously, is she okay?"

"No signs of residual psychological damage, which is good. I do worry about that. I can't quite believe we're the adults in her life. Somehow, the adults in my life seemd so much more, what? Serious? Mature?"

"Responsibly adult?"

"Something like that."

"Yeah, but the adults in your life included Miss Aletha Howe, and Miss Vinnia, and Miss Hattie. Those are formidable role models."

"Yeah." Somehow it was reassuring to realize that Emma may have an Aunt Bree who doesn't always think through the long-term effects for a child, but she also has the same greater-aunts who'd watched over me. I'd been aware, growing up, of the high standards they set, of how formidable they were, but I later realized how protective they'd been, avenging and punishing angels as required.

I needed to change the subject before I got sloppy and sentimental. "Do you know Spencer Munn? He's a professor over at Ramble College, but he also—I don't know how you'd put it—gives investment advice to people."

Melvin pursed his lips as he shook his head. "No, that name doesn't ring a bell. Is he with a firm?"

"I get the impression he's a one-man show."

"How do you know him?"

"Frank and Lydia. He used to teach at the university. He and Frank were in separate departments, of course. Spence—Dr. Munn, I guess he is—teaches economics."

I didn't mention dinner and dancing. Melvin and I keep our office-sharing and our private lives very separate.

"I don't really know that many people around here," Melvin said.

Melvin had left Dacus and built his investment-advising business in Atlanta. With clients spread all over the country, he had decided he could sit at his computer in Dacus just as easily as he could in Atlanta. As he said, all he needed was Internet access and a way to get to an airport.

"Well, just wanted you to know you've got some competition in town. His clients rave about him."

Melvin gave the same tight smile I would offer him if he were to rib me about how good some unknown attorney was. Not that Melvin would do that. He tends toward gentlemanliness.

"Twelve percent is a really good rate of return right now, isn't it?" I asked.

"Well, that depends."

"That's a lawyerly answer," I said. "I'd expect better from you."

He leaned back in his chair, prepared to lecture. "What sort of risk does it carry?"

"Not much." I didn't say *guaranteed*. I knew that was ridiculous and leaned heavily toward another good lawyerly term: puffery, as in an expression of opinion designed to aid a sale, rather than a statement of fact.

Melvin's brow knotted downward. "This Dr. Munn is offering that?"

"Getting that, according to his satisfied clients."

Melvin shrugged. "That's a great rate. Probably fairly volatile right now, though. I wouldn't count on returns like that being steady—and certainly not long term."

I didn't rib him about how serious his competitive threat was, if he was giving his clients gloomy forecasts like that.

Melvin stared at me a beat too long. "You have anything invested with this guy?" He kept his tone casual, but I could hear the effort that took.

"Naw. I don't know anything about what he's doing, just some snatches of conversation."

The differences between Spence Munn and Melvin Bertram struck me. One was Brooks Brothers, the other Armani. One was Atlanta, fly-fishing for mountain trout, and a good square dancer. The other was Las Vegas, with no clue how to dress for a picnic in the woods, though he sure knew how to wine, dine, and dance. To be fair in balancing the scales, Melvin might be a good ballroom dancer, I just hadn't seen him in action.

One made a great friend and office mate. The other was a fun date—and did I mention? A really good dancer.

I would keep my money in my balanced selection of mutual funds and let the investment gurus battle it out for the high-flying risk takers.

"Glad you're back," I said, and I meant it. "Guess if I leave, we can both get back to work." I pushed myself up from the antique corner chair he kept in front of his desk for the times when I came to distract him from his work. He didn't have to contend with pesky clients dropping in—just with me.

I had one other friend to bug before I declared a holiday of the remainder of the day.

From the phone at my desk, I called Rudy, not sure even as I punched in the numbers how I would raise the topic.

He answered with a bark on the second ring.

"Recognized your number and started not to answer. Trying to get out of here."

"I feel the love way over here. I'm touched."

He snorted.

"Just one question." With any other cop, I wouldn't dare offer up a possible motive for someone who was

a quasi-client. Rog had consulted me for help on collecting his dead wife's life insurance, but he hadn't
asked me to represent him in a criminal investigation. With Rudy, I didn't have to split ethical hairs
about whether my question stepped over a shadowy
line. Rudy was a play-fair investigator. He wouldn't
take a question and turn it into an indictment. On the
other hand, if he had solid evidence, he wouldn't
back away, either. For my peace of mind, though, I
needed to see in which direction the investigation
was heading.

"Yes?" He sounded tired.

"Have you heard any rumors about Rinda Reimann?"

Rudy gave my open-ended question a long silence.
When he spoke, he didn't dangle me along. He must
be on serious overtime now.

"You talking about Ken Tharp?"

"Guess you have heard. Anything to that?"

"You mean were they having an affair? Unless
they were carrying on a long-running clandestine
chess match up at his lake cabin, where the neighbors saw her car at all hours, I'd say there was something to it."

Rudy probably didn't know it, but South Carolina
divorce courts would tend to agree with his presump-
tion of guilt. In one case, the judge talked about the
conclusions drawn from "the extraordinarily ordinary
or, perhaps more accurately stated, uncommonly common" evidence when a husband parked at night in a
graveyard with another woman.

I had committed the judge's poetic opinion in Prevatte v Prevatte to memory: "When two people, a man
and a woman, park by themselves at night in lonely
places and purposely sit very close together, unless

some other reason appears for their behavior, even the most dispassionate observer may very well infer that they are romantically disposed toward each other. Such is life."

Such is life, indeed.

Rudy said, "Adultery might make a good motive for a jealous husband to shove her off a cliff. It looks especially bad if the husband's hell-bent on collecting the insurance money and refuses to even talk to the investigators."

"Yeah, but what about Tharp?" I did feel a twinge of guilt, sitting here in Maylene's where Tharp had bared his soul. He'd meant to attack Rog, but that wasn't what stuck hardest in my mind from our conversation.

"You mean could Tharp have killed her? You were at Bow Falls that day. You tell me. Was he there? Could he have used a remote control device?"

"No, not that I saw." I was sure Rudy knew where Tharp was that morning, as well as where he wasn't. No need to get snide. "But what about Tharp leaving the bruises?"

"Possible," Rudy drawled out. "If he grabbed her from behind. For what? Now that you mention it, guess there's no telling what went on in that cabin."

Rudy was baiting me now.

So my revelation about Ken Tharp's relationship with Rinda was not news to Rudy. Around the sheriff's office, they may even have dissected the various positions in which those bruises could have been made.

"Who you been talking to, Counselor?"

"Just somebody with some gossip." Despite my respect for Rudy's judgment, drawing attention to Eden could only strengthen the suspicions about Rog. Eden's friendship with Rog was already destined to cause him problems. That fire didn't need any more fuel. Besides, Eden's attentions were so overbearing and obvious, Rudy would be developing his own suspicions without my help, if he hadn't already.

I changed the subject. "You need to get some rest, Rudy. You sound beat."

"No shit, Sherlock. First, traffic control around that danged festival, then your little friend in the fun house and that header off the falls, then some drunk goes airborne in a Camaro off the side of the mountain, and some guys here actually want to spend some vacation time with their families. Can't imagine why I'm tired."

"Go home, Rudy." I hung up. I too planned to leave the office, head up to the cabin, and paddle my little johnboat out onto the muggy, still lake.

FOURTEEN

Tuesday Morning

I'd driven up to the lake Wednesday evening, then driven straight back to town. The endless buzz of Jet Skis and the squeals of laughter and the constant chatter of picnic preparations at almost every cabin drove me back down the mountain before sunset. I hadn't gone to the lake during the Fourth of July week in years and had forgotten that my restful lake haven exists only in November or January, when I'm the lone figure on the lake braving the chill breeze. The lake is anything but a haven in the summer.

Tuesday morning, I wandered downstairs for my morning cup of tea, only partially awake but mostly dressed. Through the beveled glass doors, Main Street looked serene and calm, waiting for the day's festivities.

In response to the staircase's creaking announcement of my descent, Shamanique called from her office, "Good morning."

"What are you doing here? It's the Fourth of July!"

Shamanique looked up as I poked my head around the corner. I'd done nothing more than run a comb through my hair and let it fall to my shoulders. I had also managed to pull on a pair of shorts, but I still wore the T-shirt I'd slept in and I hadn't bothered with a bra, so I kept my arms crossed, looking rumpled and unfriendly.

Shamanique couldn't have run a comb through her hair if she'd wanted to. Today, it was curled in loops on her head, bringing to mind a bow on a package, shiny black bands of hair arranged in precise chaos.

"Had a few things to leave for you," she said. Didn't know you were sleeping in." Her tone was far from approving. She had a sternness no twenty-year-old should possess.

I didn't point out it was a holiday. After all, I was the one who'd repeatedly interrupted her over the first few days of her vacation with all sorts of questions.

"Want some tea?" I asked.

She nodded toward her half-full cup and stayed on task.

I settled into the chair in front of her desk. "So, what'cha got?"

"First off, this Rogert guy has punked off a lot of money."

"Reimann? What do you mean?" *Rogert? That's his name?*

"I mean he ain't got none, least none he's paying his bills with. He's got thirty thousand dollars stacked up on his credit cards, he's paying just the minimum each month, and he's late most months with that."

"So he's got penalties to keep all that interest company."

"No kidding."

"Any sign what he spent his first wife's insurance money on?"

"Not anything I can find. He's got a mortgage on

his house. He pays, but it's sometimes late. His car is leased."

"A big house?"

"No, not expensive. Neither is his SUV."

"Lots of trips? Jewelry? What?"

She shook her head. Her curls were unmoved. "Not that I could find."

"What's he bought with the credit cards? Can you get that detail?"

She flicked a look across the desk at me that warned *Don't doubt me.* Her head bent toward the computer screen. "The usual stuff. Man eats at Mickey D's a lot, I gotta say."

It'd take a lot of hamburgers to burn through thousands in insurance and lawsuit settlement money.

"Trips to Atlantic City or Vegas?"

"Nope. No hotel bills or plane tickets, not since his first wife's death. Just a couple of flights between here and St. Louis, just before he moved here."

"A hotel in Cherokee? He could've driven over there." Harrah's Casino on the reservation of the eastern band of the Cherokees lacked the glitz that drew the high rollers to the big-name gambling resorts, but a dedicated man could still lose a pile if he set his mind to it.

"Nope, not even a gas receipt. He didn't get out much."

We sat a moment before she shrugged and turned from the screen. "A'course, he could've gambled himself into a hole before his first wife died and paid it off with the proceeds. I don't have stuff going back that far. And there's always private games."

"Yeah." I dragged the word out, along a slow-developing thread of thought. "Wouldn't he still be gambling, though, if he'd been doing it before he moved here? Or whatever he did to waste his money, wouldn't he keep doing it?"

"Most folks like their bad habits."

"Was he in financial trouble when they moved here?"

"Not from what I see." She turned and scrolled up the computer screen. "His payments were on time, and, at that time, he didn't have any credit card balances. He paid them off every month."

"Hm." I slumped in the wooden arm chair, my legs stretched out straight. "Guess we'll put that in the interesting but unhelpful column for now. Anything else?"

She looked at me over her shoulder. "Not quite yet. I'm on to something, but let me finish checking some things before I tell you."

"Okay."

Her tone had an edge of excitement, as though she had her eye on the perfect present but was having trouble waiting until time for the birthday girl to open it.

I pulled myself out of the chair. "I've got to head to the festival planning meeting."

Shamanique could tell from my tone how thrilled I was by that prospect, but she sensibly refrained from asking how I'd gotten mixed up with the planning bunch in the first place. I intended to remember how much fun this committee had been next time Mom insists a community group might need my help.

By the time I dressed and sauntered down the street to the church basement meeting room, everybody else had arrived and Adrienne, in her place at the head of the table, was holding forth.

The topic was far afield from festival business.

"I'm just being realistic," she said. Her hand rose

to cover the mother-of-pearl pendant at her throat. "Far be it from me to leap to conclusions, but you have to admit it's suspicious."

"The police haven't arrested him," said Luke Deep in his pastoral baritone.

"But they are focusing on him," said Tina, the past-president of the Parent-Teacher Organization. She usually spoke only when outlining tasks, her thick calendar binder always placed squarely in front of her, the bottom parallel to the table edge.

"And who wouldn't focus on him," said Adrienne. "He was carrying on an affair when his first wife died a suspicious death, he collected a pile of insurance money, and took off with his paramour. Then she betrayed him by taking up with an old boyfriend. That's just too much lined up."

Where did the gossip mill gather its fodder? As was typical in Dacus, the gossip was amazingly accurate—and often missing only the redemptive detail.

"Actually," I said, "his first wife was hit and killed by a drunk driver. There really wasn't anything suspicious about that."

Adrienne pinned me with a dagger look, disappointed that I would challenge her much more dramatic version of the story. Only days ago, around this very table, the tongues had been united in support of Rog and against the jackbooted enforcers of the law. Now the gossip tide had turned, and Rog was caught in the undertow.

"Don't know why it would surprise him that his new wife would fool around on him," chimed in ancient Mr. Wink. "After all, she apparently thought nothing of being married and fooling around with a married man when she first took up with him in St. Louis. It shouldn't surprise people that someone who

has been unfaithful will do it again. Seems he'd
know he ought to keep a close eye on that one."

Mr. Wink's tone lacked the venom of Adrienne's.
He merely observed life in all its kaleidoscopic idio-
syncrasy and reported with faint bemusement.

"Well, from what I hear, he's expecting another
big insurance check," said Adrienne. "I pity the next
woman who falls into his clutches."

Word of Eden Rand's tender ministrations hadn't
reached Adrienne's ears. Then again, Adrienne didn't
travel in the intellectual crowd and Eden didn't serve
on charity gala committees. From my observation,
Rog wasn't the one with the "clutches." He looked
like the unsuspecting victim about to be clutched.
Maybe that was his deadly charm. Maybe his hope-
lessly lost act was irresistible to women. I shouldn't be
amazed at how quickly town gossip could shift, turning him from victim to monster. I'd wager Adrienne
didn't even know Rog. Opinions became more subtle
and more difficult when mixed with knowledge and
friendship rather than mere speculation.

"We really should get started," said Pastor Luke.
His years of managing church committees showed in
both his tone and his timing.

"Yes," said Adrienne, "now that Avery's joined us.
The most important item of business is to make sure
today's parade goes off without a hitch. Mr. Wink,
you'll be in the viewing stand with me. That way, you'll
be in a central location should anyone have anything to
report and you can reach the appropriate personnel by
phone or pager. We'll have police officers and medics
on hand, in case of emergency."

She consulted her agenda, handwritten on color-
coded notebook paper in her official festival-planning
binder.

"Pastor, if you and Tina would station yourselves at the end of the route. Make sure the floats pull into the church parking lot and away from the street. Make sure they come to a complete stop before any riders disembark. We don't want someone injured and trying to sue us."

She glanced in my direction. I didn't know if she suspected I might file the lawsuit or if she expected me to rescue the city in case someone else sued. No, that would be Todd David's job. He was the city attorney.

"Todd and Avery, you'll be working together today." She gave us a sly smile and I could've sworn she winked. Her nonstop plans for fixing us up had moved into high gear. She'd just arranged our first "date" for us.

"You'll line up everyone at the start of the parade route. You have the list of rules. All registered entrants have also received copies of the rules, so no one can claim ignorance when you enforce those rules. No scantily clad participants, no reckless driving or stunts. Remind the Shriners. The horses must remain at the end of the parade line-up. They certainly shouldn't be surprised by that. Everyone on the floats must remain seated at all times, and no tossing candy to the crowds."

"No candy?" I said. I looked around the table to see if anyone else was as surprised as I was at the news.

"It's in the parade rules," Adrienne said.

"That's the most fun part about the parade. While you're waiting on the bands and seeing if you know anybody on the floats, you chase cheap wrapped candy you usually wouldn't eat on a bet and pick it out of the gutter."

Adrienne gave me an imperious frown. "It's a safety risk. It has been decided and it's in the rules. All the participants have been informed."

I looked around at the others. Pastor Luke shrugged. Mr. Wink offered a conspiratorial raised eyebrow and a half-smile. No point arguing. Thanks to the passive voice, "it has been decided" and it wouldn't be changed by something foolishly collective, like a committee.

I sure wasn't enforcing any no-candy-throwing rule. That was for certain.

"If there's no further discussion, those working the parade line-up should proceed to the Broad Street checkpoint. You have the line-up sheets in your packets, along with cell phone numbers if you have questions or need assistance."

Walkie-talkies would have made more sense—and been more fun, but we were too low-budget. We'd programmed everyone's cell phone number into our phones at a meeting a few weeks ago. We could almost yell from one end of Main Street to the other. True, that wouldn't really work, especially with the street crowded with parade-goers and booming music from every float and band. Still, Adrienne's military precision seemed laughable, given the hodge-podge of parade entries.

For Adrienne, my dissent over the candy and correcting the rumor about Rog took some of the bloom off her matchmaking efforts. She didn't hover over me and Todd, smirking with her usual proprietary *you'll-thank-me* air. We were left to make our own way out of the church basement.

I figured it was easier to walk the eight blocks to the other end of the street, but Todd insisted on driving his miniature Mercedes sedan.

"I need to stop by my office," I said. "I forgot—

something. I'll be right behind you." I left him standing beside the open door of his car, watching me over the roof.

Sure enough, by the time he navigated the detour barricades and the first trickle of the crowds searching for parking on the back streets, I'd beaten him by fifteen minutes. Of course, I hadn't really stopped by the office.

The "command center" was two lawn chairs and a folding card table set up under one of the Bradford pear trees that lined the wide street near the cemetery.

I handed Todd his official clipboard when he joined me. We were both wearing our regulation canary yellow Fourth Festival T-shirts. I'd voted for something in a red, white, and blue theme, but Adrienne had vetoed me. She wanted something that stood out. With his yellow shirt stretched over his belly, Todd looked like a stumpy version of Big Bird, except with a balding head and no feathers.

I knew he was divorced with a little boy he didn't see very often. I'd learned that from Mom, not from him. He never mentioned his son, which made me sad for the little kid. He had a good reputation handling real estate closings and other routine office work, but he'd told me himself that he preferred to avoid the courtroom. Having his clients end up in court was a personal failure, he said. I didn't agree, of course. Having as your attorney someone who didn't like—or was afraid of—the courtroom is the definition of doomed before you start, in my book. Neither of us brought up that topic again.

Todd studied his clipboard, flipping the pages. "You know," he said, "I've been doing some case research. I discovered why we weren't able to get the type and level of insurance coverage I thought advisable. I'd never considered the kinds of injuries that can occur at an event of this type. Children fall off floats and get run over, or they run in front of a car chasing after some candy. Those racing clown cars can run amok in the crowd. And that fair! Suppose one of the operators failed to properly bolt together one of the midway rides. It's sobering to think about the potential liability."

Standing in front of me was undoubtedly the source of the no-candy-throwing rule, all because somewhere, somebody had, at some time, been hurt and filed a lawsuit—a lawsuit that had probably been dismissed. I wanted to run to the grocery store and buy bags of wrapped candy by the armload.

"I doubt those injuries have happened often enough to worry about," I said.

"You should read the cases. Did you know that children are victims in half of all amusement park injuries?"

I didn't point out that a casual survey of the festival crowd would show that roughly half the attendees were short and probably children.

"Look at it logically," I said. "How many accidents resulted in severe injuries? How many of the lawsuits were settled or went to trial? Scant few, given all the people who have a good time at carnivals, fairs, and fun parks every year."

He raised his sheaf of papers as a shield, and I caught a glance at a headline listing accidents as far back as 1972. I didn't tell Todd he should investigate the number of traffic accidents and fatalities per people/miles driven. He'd never leave home again.

"It makes sense," I said, "to warn people to be

careful and speak to anyone who's doing something foolish. We don't need to stop all the fun or lose sleep at night."

He fixed me with a stern look, as if he were about to lecture an uncooperative client who refused to listen to reason. "As city attorney, I have a responsibility to keep Dacus out of trouble and out of court."

The lawyers who never spend time in court are the ones most petrified when someone threatens to sue. No use reasoning with him.

Why in heaven's name did Adrienne keep insisting Todd and I should "keep company," to use her phrase? I suppressed a shudder. I knew Todd was a good lawyer, but in a type of practice that would bore me. Had I reached "that age"? Did Todd represent a type, the only guy left for an early-thirties maiden lady? From where I stood, he was the one who acted like the old maid.

"I'm going to wander along the lineup," I said. "See if anybody has any questions."

I left him to his clipboard and his worries.

Someone had already put stakes in the ground with numbered cards attached, and all the entries had gotten their number when they registered. Todd and I were mostly just decoration and backup for the few who might have forgotten where they ought to be. By unilaterally declaring the no-candy rule a nol-pros, I figured I'd cut my workload to mostly nothing.

I was glad I'd worn shorts. Even in the morning shade, the air was already sticky.

Broad Street is just that—broad, with extra-wide tree-lined lanes on each side of a grassy median dotted with large oaks. It made a great parade staging area because people could drive down one side, spot their number, and come back up the other side to their place in line. The wide lanes gave the floats plenty of maneuvering room.

We only had two marching bands scheduled. Nice of the kids to show up, since school wasn't in session. The Dacus High band was piling out of its activity bus as I drew close to their slot. The kids were dressed in khaki pants, white golf shirts, and gleaming black leather shoes, like refugees from some tropical British outpost.

I waved at the director, who practically saluted in return. Mr. Paul, the band director, could tell me and everyone else how to run a parade. He was famous for demanding perfection, a wry martinet given to purple-faced passion whenever a parent thought something trivial, like a family funeral, was more important than band practice. That explained all the competition trophies they brought home every year—and why I waved and kept walking.

Because of the heat, the Fourth of July parade was always held at ten in the morning. I preferred the night-time Christmas parade, with the crisscrossed canopy of colored lights, bands from every high school in the county, Santa Claus at the rear (in front of the horses, of course), the elaborate and sometimes unintentionally funny church floats. My favorite last year had a littlest angel who rode almost the entire route with her finger up her nose. This parade made a good stop-gap until next Christmas, though.

I hadn't studied the list of entrants with the same attention to detail that Todd had given it, so the next arrival surprised me. I heard Dacus's resident motorcycle gang blocks before they turned onto Broad Street. At first, I had a shot of concern, but causing trouble is not really their style. Mad Max and the

Posse cultivated a "we're bad" attitude, but they were businessmen. Mostly the kind of business that wanted to avoid too much scrutiny.

Since regular jobs would violate their tough, free-spirit image and since selling Girl Scout cookies wouldn't keep up their gleaming Harleys, I suspected they engaged in the classic fund-raising schemes—drugs, prostitution, gambling, whatever presented itself. Whatever they were doing, they did it somewhere other than Camden County. Still, I was surprised to see the Posse Motorcycle Club on my parade lineup sheet. "Club," not "gang." Semantics make all the difference.

Every bike in the line sported a stuffed animal on back. Scooby-Doo, Pooh Bear, a giant floppy rag doll, what looked like a walrus—they all rode by in a slow sweep.

I'd met the boys when they'd come calling at my lake cabin in late November, to offer me some critical information and—without a single threatening word or gesture—to scare the daylights out of me. I'd helped them out by serving as a go-between with L.J., and we'd maintained a nodding acquaintance since then. I wasn't sure why, but I seemed to rank a "tolerable" rating in some book of unwritten rules.

They drove to the end of the block and turned back toward their lineup position. I arrived at Slot Number 16 just as Max pulled in at the head of the group. Talking over the roar of the mufflers was impossible, but I threw up an open-palmed wave. See, I come in peace—and a bright yellow Fourth Festival T-shirt.

Do-Rag—Clyde on his birth certificate—rode the shotgun slot behind Max. The two offered interesting contrasts. Max, with his bushy man-mountain beard, Christmas bow lips, and cold, flat, staring black eyes, offered me a barely perceptible nod. Do-Rag flung up his beefy arm, stretching the sleeveless denim shirt under his leather vest. His head rag today was predictable: a stylized American flag motif with swirling stripes.

The others stopped in formation. Most had to give the throttle one last punch so the engines roared, then *pop-pop-popped* before they quieted.

"Really like your passengers," I called to them.

Max stared at me with an intensity that looked as though it could sear flesh.

Do-Rag/Clyde yelled back. "We're early for the toy campaign, but thought the kids would love it."

At the same time, the kids' dads would love the bikes and the hint of the wild life they offered. Some of the moms might secretly wonder just how wild those biker boys could be. Everyone would smile at the incongruous scene with the stuffed animals.

The last biker boasted a gigantic American flag, mounted on a pole fixed to the rear of the bike. The biker craned around to make certain the flag wasn't touching the ground. If a cross-wind caught him while he was riding, I hoped he wouldn't have trouble controlling his bike. The flag was that big.

I kept walking, not worried he'd sue the city if he skinned up himself or his bike. We had enough people worrying about that kind of silliness already. Todd was probably worried the bikers would run wild in the crowd, raping and pillaging their way down Main Street.

I bit back a snicker just as I saw a real problem approaching.

From my vantage point near the Posse's lineup slot, I watched a familiar figure on a skinned-up scooter buzz softly down the opposite lane of the street, turn, and head straight for us.

I checked my clipboard. There it was. Slot Number 17: Donlee Griggs.

FIFTEEN

Tuesday Morning

Donlee Griggs is a goofball who'd nursed all through school a crush on me and any other girl unfortunate enough to be nice to him. Donlee's not quite right, as we say. He takes care of himself by working odd jobs, then gets himself in trouble by hanging out at Tap's Pool Room. Most of the time, that's okay, but when the guys there have been drinking, they forget about watching out for Donlee and they suggest stunts that can get him in trouble.

This looked like something Donlee had planned all on his own. He wore his glow-in-the-dark orange helmet with an Uncle Sam costume. At six-foot-seven, Donlee as Uncle Sam was an impressive sight, even though his pants legs barely topped his dingy white athletic socks, leaving his scuffed work boots fully exposed.

Donlee pulled up close behind the last two Harleys in the Posse line. His big face, squished at the sides by his helmet, beamed when he realized he'd scored a place of honor with his fellow bikers.

A biker at the rear of the pack rode with a potbellied plush bear wearing a flag motif head wrap; biker and bear looked like they were headed to a father-and-son fashion show. The biker traded a look with his closest comrade but never turned to look in Donlee's direction. The bikers could see all they needed to see in their round rearview mirrors.

Donlee didn't mind. He wasn't much for conversation. Whether that came from being teased as a kid because he stuttered or because most of Donlee's life was carried on inside his head, I didn't know. Donlee's thoughts always played on the revealing screen of his face, so he didn't have to talk. He was just happy to be there.

When he caught sight of me, he cocked his palm in a touchingly childlike wave and grinned as broadly as his tight helmet would permit, for a moment transforming his face into one of those dried-apple old men.

I waved back. "Nice costume, Donlee," I called and gave him a thumbs-up sign. With more squint-faced beaming, he returned the thumbs-up and settled proudly astride his scooter, his lanky red-and-white-striped pants akimbo on either side of his scooter and his blue coattails trailing in the dirt.

Before I could turn to leave, more trouble approached, this time from two different directions. The first to arrive was Donlee's runty friend PeeVee Probert, swaggering up the sidewalk to join us.

"Donlee, you nidgit. What the hell're you doin' dressed in that git-up?"

Donlee frowned and turned to face forward, pointedly ignoring PeeVee and waiting for the parade to start.

"What're you supposed to be, any how? You look like a frozen Tasty Rocket, all red, white, and blue and too big for your wrapper."

"You just jealous," Donlee said, still refusing to look in PeeVee's direction.

"Holy shit. Why didn't somebody warn me? I need my sunglasses." Pudd Pardee, head of the county Rescue Squad, had approached from the direction of Main Street riding half in, half out of a golf cart that leaned with his weight.

He made a soundless stop beside Donlee's bike. The Posse bikers continued to ignore Donlee and his crowd of hecklers.

"If it idn't the Jolly Green Giant in patriotic camouflage," said Pudd.

Donlee frowned as if confused by the reference.

Pudd leaned over closer, as if whispering to Donlee. "You gonna invite A-ver-ee here to ride with you? I hear she's hot for that kind of thing."

Donlee's eyes danced from one side to another, from Pudd to me and back again. He wriggled on his scooter seat, trying to process what Pudd had said.

I could've smacked Pudd. Donlee had recently had a girlfriend with a matching pumpkin helmet, who'd appeared in his life about the same time the scooter did. Some of us had assumed the girl and the scooter had come as a package, but then Donlee started appearing around town without his passenger. I didn't know the story, but I did know from long experience how difficult Donlee was to distract once his affections attached. I didn't need Pudd's help— and neither did Donlee.

Donlee knew to be wary of Pudd and his practical jokes, but Donlee also had an endless spring of hope bubbling in his barrel chest.

"No helmet," I said. "Pudd, you know better than that. It just wouldn't be safe for me to ride without one. What kind of message would that send to all the kids watching the parade?"

"This is South Carolina," Pudd said. "Who the hell cares whether you wear a helmet?"

"Nice advice from the county's safety expert," I said. "At least Donlee's got the good sense to send the right message."

Donlee's mouth twisted in a lopsided grin, though he never once looked directly at me.

I waved good-bye and headed to the command card table, in the opposite direction from where Pudd's cart was headed. He and his crude jokes have a limited shelf life with me.

About ten parade slots ahead of me, I saw Sheriff L. J. Peters herself walking in my direction. I expected to see her hassling the participants, making illegal searches and seizures of contraband bags of candy at Adrienne's instigation. Instead, L.J. was shaking hands. I thought I also spotted a smile, though it passed so quickly, I couldn't be sure.

As I drew closer, I saw her offer something to one of the convertible drivers. The beauty queen or politician passenger hadn't shown up yet. Was L.J. handing out tickets? For what?

"How do, L.J.?"

As she turned, her hand went with a deliberate reflex to her gun belt, which bristled with threatening implements.

"A-vry." L.J. returned my greeting with a curt nod.

She held brochures, printed on a cheap color laser printer, announcing *Reelect L. J. Peters—Sheriff. A Proven Record.*

"Getting an early start on November?" I nodded toward the brochure. She didn't offer me one.

"Might be a primary," she said.

L.J. tends to do little but growl around me. Today, though, I saw something in her eyes that I hadn't seen before. Maybe it was because she wasn't wearing her Oakleys, but she looked—vulnerable.

With a twinge, I remembered the negative comments about her around the festival committee table. A primary? Who was considering a run against L.J.? Now wouldn't be a good time to ask her, so I just said, "You've got my vote, L.J."

The look of surprise, followed by fleeting gratitude, made me glance away. I wasn't used to seeing L.J. so exposed.

If she'd been anyone else, I'd have patted her arm. Though I didn't always agree with Lucinda Jane Peters, I'd grown to grudgingly admire her. She hired good people, let them do their jobs, and she was honest. That's a good sheriff, in my book. We'd had lots worse.

"See you around." I waved and strolled on with a knot in my stomach. What the heck would L.J. do if she weren't sheriff?

I wasn't even sure what she'd done before she joined the Sheriff's Office. Had she been in the military? She'd come through the deputy ranks, but I doubted she could return to a patrol car if someone else became sheriff. That just wasn't done. What do defeated sheriffs do, anyway?

South Carolina appoints judges and hires police chiefs, but elects sheriffs and county solicitors. When a solicitor is defeated in an election, she can just go back to practicing law—and usually makes more money than she did as a solicitor. Not so easy for defeated sheriffs. I guess they have to move somewhere else to find a job.

I didn't think that would suit L.J. Her family, like

mine, were long-time Camden County residents. Of course, I was proof you could leave home—and even come back again. I had a knot of anxiety in my stomach for L.J., though. Odd how relationships change over time, even though the people involved don't really change. They just get more so, as Aunt Letha says.

I drew even with the first entries in line: the high school drill corps and the band. The kids moved and shuffled and danced without cease, a perpetual motion machine, their marching lines fluid with the pent-up energy of youth. The increasingly sticky air was filled with the constant chatter and occasional bleats and blasts and clicks from horns, woodwinds, and drums.

At command central, Lissie Caper, a woman I knew casually from church, stood in front of the folding table talking to Todd.

Todd faced her across the table. Something in his stance or the tightness around his mouth telegraphed that theirs was not a how-do conversation.

I slowed my approach, not wanting to interrupt what might be a confidential lawyer-client confab, being held in a decidedly unconfidential place.

Lissie caught sight of me out of the corner of her eye.

"Avery! How are you?"

"Fine, Lissie," I said and drew closer. "Is your daughter marching? How old is she now? Five?"

She gave the beleaguered Mom eye roll. "She's been so excited. She's a twirler this year. I just dropped her off with the dance troupe. Got to go find a spot on the shady side of the street."

"Nice." I'd been a dance-class twirler, too, when I was her daughter's age. It's hard to live that down, as Aunt Letha periodically reminds me.

Whatever I'd interrupted, both she and Todd seemed willing to let it drop. Lissie, though, shuffled in place with an awkwardness that she just couldn't leave alone.

"Todd and I were just talking business. Did you know Todd's been elected as secretary for the board of Manna Advisers?" She said it as though she was announcing he'd become secretary of state.

"Congratulations, Todd," I said. He acknowledged my words with a nod.

"And we just found out we have a mutual friend: Spencer Munn. Have you met Spence yet?"

"We met recently," I said, not admitting to much.

"If you need any help managing your money affairs, you really ought to talk to Spence. I was telling Todd what a great job he's done for me. You know, with the money from my divorce. A lump sum. That's got to last me."

I nodded again. What do you say to that? *Sorry it didn't work out?*

"So," she said, scrambling for another topic. "How's your mom and dad? And Lydia? I never see her anymore."

We both retreated into the comfortable, unrevealing exchange of life lived closely in a small town.

"They're all just fine. Thanks for asking. Where's your daughter in the parade today?"

"The Apple School of Dance. I'd better go find a spot. She'll be asking if I saw her." She waved goodbye.

Adrienne materialized at our card table, as if conjured from eye of newt.

"Everything under control here?" She sounded like a drill sergeant addressing first-week recruits.

"Yes, ma'am." My voice snapped like a salute. I

swear I didn't mean to mock her. It just came out that way.

As a peace offering, I searched for a question she'd love to answer.

"Adrienne, how—do the numbers look? For the festival, I mean. For everything."

She looked up from her clipboard, the harried executive with too many demands on her attention, gracing the little people who make it happen.

"Just fine," she said.

"As good as you'd hoped? In line with the Hellhole Swamp Festival? Or the Chitlin' Strut?"

Her eyes narrowed, as if she'd suddenly remembered I was the irreverent one who'd tried to sabotage both the dignity and the success of her event by reopening that scandalous fright house and pushing to allow Shriners to pelt small children with rockhard candy.

"We really can't tell this early, now can we? Besides, those are our aspirant festivals. We want to aim higher than we might hit, don't we?"

She made it so easy. It is, after all, hard to surpass festivals touting respectively the joys of being a tobacco-spitting redneck and the sublime nature of smelly fried pig intestines. I just smiled. "We've got the parade under control." I didn't salute.

Somewhere back in the parade line, a baritone horn gave a blubbery bleep and a Harley without a muffler restrictor fired to life. Adrienne's eyes narrowed, but the miscreants were saved by the singing of her cell phone.

"Yes? Who?"

She stepped away from our card table, her hand to her left ear to block some of the background noise. "What?"

The disbelief in her tone held my attention. Whatever was afoot had riveted Adrienne to the sidewalk. Apparently at the direction of whoever was talking to her, her gaze snapped toward Main Street just as a large white truck topped by a dish antennae came over the slight rise beside the Lutheran church.

Adrienne's mouth fell open as she clapped her phone shut. That's when I noticed Adrienne wasn't wearing a regulation yellow T-shirt. Guess her tumbled stone necklace and designer sunglasses would've clashed.

The truck's logo announced the arrival of one of the regional television stations from Greenville. Why Adrienne looked so distressed at the promise of parade publicity, I couldn't fathom.

SIXTEEN

Tuesday Morning

The television truck stopped in front of our folding table, heading the wrong way down the street toward the high school drum corps and the rest of the parade lineup.

"Hello," said Adrienne as she approached the truck's passenger window. Her greeting sounded brittle and forced, in danger of cracking. "So good of you to come cover our parade. It'll make a great special inter—"

"Are you Avery Andrews?"

Adrienne didn't look surprised by the question, though I certainly was. Adrienne stepped closer to the truck, rested her hand on the window ledge, and stood on tiptoe as if to shield the blond reporter and her inch-long eyelashes from me.

"You'll find better shots at the viewing stand on Main Street. I'll be glad—"

The reporter opened her door, forcing Adrienne back on her heels and away from the truck. She wasn't pushy, just persistent, her gaze for no one but me. I was leaning back against the giant tree trunk, hoping for shelter from the heat.

Over her shoulder, the reporter said, "Can you leave the truck here? Will the boom clear?"

He must have agreed that it would work because he began operating controls that activated all manner of equipment on the truck.

"Gray, you got the camera?"

Gray finished with the controls, stepped down from the truck, wrestled out a bulky camera, and slung it over his shoulder as if it didn't weigh more than I could have lifted.

Adrienne stepped up to the reporter. The woman with lacquered blond hair gave Adrienne a glance and no more than a quarter of a smile, offered with the air of someone who had deadlines and no time to waste. Even though the girl looked no more than twenty, she'd obviously earned her spot and planned to earn others.

Adrienne had met her match but seemed unwilling to concede.

"Ms. Andrews?" Microphone in hand, camera in tow, the reporter advanced on me. The cameraman switched on a blinding light the size of a car headlamp. Prisoners who appear on television doing the jail perp walk throw their arms over their heads—not to hide their identity but to protect their eyesight.

I'd been through this before, during trials that had captured media attention. It didn't happen as often with civil trials as it did with criminal cases, but it happened. This, though, was no courthouse, and I certainly wasn't handling any newsworthy cases.

"I understand you discovered the mummy in the amusement ride." No question. She made a statement and she waited for a response.

Had she already worked out her promo trailer? The *Amusement Ride Mummy.* Or maybe the *Mys-*

tery of the Mummy Man. That sounded like a Nancy Drew title.

I stood staring at the camera, a vacant smile on my face, but I didn't move or say a word.

"Could you just talk about what it was like?" She spoke louder, emphasizing each word as if she was talking to an imbecile. "What-did-you-see? How-did-it-feel?"

She knew she could cut her questions and just play my responses, with a voice-over lead-in that she'd record in the studio. She could make sure she sounded smart. She didn't really care that I'd look wan and shiny with sweat from the heat, the lights, and the lack of stage makeup. Her job was to look good and get film. She probably would've preferred that I have no front teeth, like the stereotypical folks who appear on TV after a tornado has targeted their Southern trailer park.

I just kept staring.

"Ms. Andrews? It's okay. No need to be afraid. Just-tell-us-what-you-saw." She leaned closer with the microphone, as if willing words to come out of my mouth. Any words at all.

I struggled not to squint or blink too much, even though the light bore into my eyeballs.

She stuck the microphone even closer. The camera recorded my pleasant though vacant smile, but not a single sound bite. Not even a slow-drawled "Well" or an "It'uz awful."

With an exasperated wave of her hand, she signaled the cameraman to shut off the camera.

I waited until I saw the red light on his camera blink off, several seconds after she'd let her microphone drop and he'd cut the light.

"Maybe you could have called ahead," I said. "Or

maybe you'd like to ask if I'm willing to be interviewed." My voice was measured and hard. My role
in this story didn't deserve an ambush interview. I
knew dead air and a pleasant smile wouldn't make
the evening news, but if I'd asked that she shut off
her camera or get the heck out of my face, that might
have made the lead promo. It had been safer to just
wait her out.

Her lips tightened, but she had the grace to look
chastised. "I'm on a tight deadline. The national out-
lets have been running this story since Saturday. My
boss is chewing my ass to get some new angle and
some visual. You're hard to track down."

Her tight size 2 skirt showed that she had no ass to
chew.

"I'm in the phone book," I said.

Her lips tightened a notch more.

"Miz . . . ?" I waited for her to offer her name.
Hers wasn't one of the pictures on the side of the
truck sitting a few yards away, its boom holding a
satellite dish at least two stories in the air.

"Phillips," she said, struggling to be civil. The in-
sult of my uncooperativeness was compounded by
my failure to recognize who she was.

"Miz Phillips. I appreciate that you have a job to
do, but so do I. You see, I'm an officer of the court,
and this is an ongoing investigation. I'm sure the sheriff's public information officer will be glad to talk to
you. I'm just not in a position to do so." I wasn't really
playing straight with her, but she'd picked the fight by
ambushing me.

"Everybody in the country's talked to the sheriff's
department. I don't need the same thing all over
again."

I kept my eye on the tiny, now-dark red camera

light. I didn't want them capturing some useful audio along with a visual of my sneaker-clad feet standing next to her three-inch gold heels.

"Parade video," I said. "That would be something nobody else has." I tried not to sound snotty.

She looked as though she wanted to bean me with her microphone. The cameraman—a burly fellow straight from central casting, with a bushy beard, baggy cargo pants, and sneakers full of holes—looked like he hoped we'd erupt into a catfight. Even if it couldn't go on air, maybe he could sell it to a tabloid news show or upload a million-hit YouTube video.

Adrienne had had the good sense to stay quiet until now.

"Nancie," she said, using Ms. Phillips' first name, a move which flattered Nancie, as Adrienne had hoped. "We're so glad you're here. The reviewing stand is full of dignitaries. I'm sure they'd be happy to talk with you."

I couldn't see whether Adrienne had her fingers crossed behind her back, hoping the dignitaries wouldn't come across looking like goobers. She should have known better than to hope for that.

Nancie Phillips sighed, exasperated with us all. "We'll see," she said, offering Adrienne only a crumb of hope. "Pack it up, Gray. Let's head to the festival."

Adrienne was too controlled to splutter—much. Nancie Phillips moved quickly to the waiting van and closed herself behind the tinted windows. She probably locked her door, since lowering the boom took some time and she didn't want to give Adrienne an opportunity to gather herself for an assault on her bastion.

Adrienne stood on the sidewalk, shifting from one foot to another, her cell phone in one hand, her clipboard clutched to her chest, planning her next move. She offered no "thanks for not talking about the town's embarrassing national news story" or anything. Without a word, she spun on her high heel and climbed into the golf cart that had carried her with stealthy quiet into our domain. Her driver, an earnest teenager sporting a bright yellow shirt that matched mine and Todd's, wheeled the cart around and raced toward Main Street.

Adrienne probably planned to lie in wait and follow the broadcast truck when it pulled away from the stop sign.

I was happy to leave them to their little game. We had a parade to start.

Fortunately no kids fell off or were run over by floats, no one set off cherry bombs and spooked a horse stampede, and Santa didn't show up drunk—okay, Santa didn't show up at all for the Fourth of July. But none of the scenarios Todd and Adrienne feared had materialized. A good time was had by all, and the parade broke up before eleven.

The heat settled in a damp, sticky blanket even before the sun rose high enough to leave too little shade. After our official duties ended, Todd asked if I wanted to join him at his neighborhood cookout for lunch. His offer was halfhearted, so I didn't mind letting us both off the hook by declining.

I mused on my lunch options. Maylene's was closed for the holiday, and my parents had gone to Asheville to see some handmade rocking chairs. I decided to try the fairgrounds.

The mile or so walk from Main Street was more attractive than sitting in my hot car and waiting through what passed for a traffic jam in Dacus.

I hadn't expected to run into Rudy at the foot-long hot-dog stand.

He didn't even bother turning around to acknowledge my arrival. He just snorted when I said, "Hey." I should've known he'd be there. On a day when everyone else was grilling out or fishing or playing somewhere, a guy with a long shift had to find a place to eat lunch.

Somebody had the foresight to set up picnic tables near the food trailers—whether that was the midway operator or one of Adrienne's army of volunteers, I couldn't guess. They hadn't seen their way clear to supply any shade, though. Guess the setup worked better at night, when it was cooler. Not cool, just cooler.

Rudy and I carried our hot dogs and drinks to the only unoccupied table, at the edge of the cluster. Rudy straddled the seat, turning sideways to keep the dribbling chili over the table and off his khaki pants.

"Any more information on where Rinda Reimann got those finger bruises?" It was too hot for me to engage in niceties, and that was a question Rudy should have known would come to mind as soon as I saw him.

He shook his head. "We haven't sat down with Rog yet," he said around a huge wad of hot dog. "He's been indisposed."

He said the last word with dainty derision.

"What about considering Rinda's boyfriend Ken as the source? Or that the bruises don't mean anything? That she just fell off the waterfall and those bruises happened some other time in some benign way?"

He shrugged and took a deep draw on his plastic straw.

"What if it really was just a horrible accident? What if Rog had nothing to do with it? What if he's just unlucky to have a wife who was running around on him right before she died? He's left with a double loss. He'd lost his marriage, and then he lost his wife, which is compounded by all the public rumor about her affair. Now he may even lose his freedom, just because he can't prove a negative. He can't prove he didn't do anything to her."

Rudy took another bite of his hot dog. I caught him eyeing mine, either to encourage me to shut up and eat or assessing whether I might decide not to eat and would instead offer it to him. I picked up my hot dog in its paper tray as a self-defensive move.

"Statistically speaking, it's more likely she slipped and fell," I said. "If she hadn't been having an affair, you wouldn't even be looking for a way to put Rog on that path last Friday."

Rudy balled up a wad of tissue-thin napkins and wiped the red chili stains from around his mouth before he spoke.

"She was fooling around on him, which is something most men don't take kindly to. Then there's the fact that he's the only one who stands to benefit from her death."

"Infidelity isn't an admirable activity, but it doesn't have to lead to murder. For Pete's sake, he fooled around on his first wife and nobody got murdered."

"True, but Rog did get a chunk of change when his first wife died. Maybe that just gave him a taste for the good life." Rudy's expression was a mild smirk. He was baiting me.

"Seriously, Rudy. You're looking at all the options, aren't you?" Not just leaping to a suspicious-cop conclusion, though I didn't say that out loud.

His eyes narrowed. "It's never easy—or fun—to accuse somebody of murder. Or even suspect them."

I'd ticked him off. I backpedaled.

"I know how careful you are. It's just—" I struggled for the words. "He looked so lost the other day when I talked to him, so completely out of it. I imagined what it would be like . . ." I didn't finish the sentence.

Rudy glowered. "So how do you think he'd be acting if he'd wanted his wife dead? Happy and relieved because he'd succeeded? Shell-shocked? Pretending to be dazed so he could avoid questioning? Maybe that's his problem. He's trying to figure out how he's supposed to act."

We locked stubborn gazes, both unwilling to concede aloud the merits of the other's arguments.

"Most falls are accidents," I said. I couldn't let the last word pass.

Neither could Rudy. "Most. Not all."

He stood and swung his leg over the picnic bench like he was dismounting a really short plastic pony. He gathered his trash and stalked to the waste can without looking back.

I sat in the boiling sun, steaming from more than the heat, and finished my hot dog.

"A-vry." Shamanique strode over, her tight denim skirt so high on her thin thighs that she looked like she'd borrowed some stilts. "Can't believe I found you. Why don't you ever have your cell phone on you?"

Lord, she sounded like her bossy aunt Edna.

"I left you a message to call me."

I'd turned the thing off after the parade, not wanting to be summoned to an after-the-parade debrief by Adrienne. The woman so loved stirring up tornados—in which, of course, she was the center— that the comparative calm after the parade was sure

to incite her to furious activity, especially since the
television station hadn't wanted to interview her and
since no children had been concussed by flying pep-
permint candies.

"What did the message say?" I prompted.

"To call me." She propped her forearms on the
table as she leaned toward me to make her point.

"And?"

"And I found out part of the story on your prune-
faced mummy man, but only part."

"Great! Any chance we can find somewhere in the
shade to talk?"

"Yeah, I don't wanna get a suntan."

I didn't know Shamanique well enough to know
whether that was a joke, but we both abandoned our
stained-plastic picnic table to a group of teenagers
with greasy plates of gyros and vinegar fries.

SEVENTEEN

Tuesday Afternoon

Shamanique and I left the midway and strolled toward the tree-shaded path that ran alongside the ball fields. The hot-air balloon hung in the hazy blue sky. As we walked, she typed a text message into her cell phone. I'd often observed kids strolling in pairs, ignoring their immediate companion to communicate with someone at a distance, but I'd never found myself the silent, ignored partner before.

By the time we reached a wooden bench in the shade, she'd finished and turned to notice my raised eyebrow.

"Telling Harmon where I was. He's not too happy with me working while we're supposed to be on a date but, with Harmon, somebody better be working."

I nodded, feeling a bit guilty that she was working, but not so guilty that I'd postpone hearing her news until her vacation time was over.

"So? What'd you find?"

"That mummy man has done some traveling, let me tell you." She crossed her hands on her lap. Her fingernails were extra-long fake party nails painted in tiny patriotic stripes in honor of the occasion. How did she text message with those dagger nails?

"Who is he?"

"I have no idea. We'll get there, though."

I knew she would, which is why I'm certain no disappointment showed on my face. She was a blood-hound, only sassier.

"I went over and talked to the Plinys," she said, "to see if they had any more details about that stuff they bought thirty years ago. They had just started reworking their show when Mr. Pliny had to start using a wheelchair."

She leaned toward me and lowered her voice, though no one was near enough to hear. "Some kind of circulatory problem. From smoking, his wife said. She said it also stunted his growth. It'n that a hoot?" She smacked her knee and smiled.

"Anyway, this guy, which they of course thought was a mannequin, was in with a bunch of other man-nequins and some electronics. Stuff I didn't really understand, switches and motors and such, though Mr. Pliny loved talking about it, every detail. They decided to put together a fright show—a really good one. Before he got sick, Mr. Pliny had always worked the tricks. Did you know he's sword swallower?"

Her hand flew to her throat. I couldn't have agreed more with her reaction.

"So he likes things to be really, you know, wow. He didn't want one'a those crappy fright houses most carnivals have. You ever been in one'a those? Dumb-est thing ever. Don't last but two seconds. You ride through in a little car with your knees jammed against the front and six shrunken heads pop up just after you've gone past. Just a dumb way to waste money."

I'd wasted my ride tickets on one years ago. That

hadn't broken me; I was still a sucker for something that promised a good scare, even if it didn't deliver.

"Anyway, when Con Plotnick, the guy who owned all these electronics and mannequins, died, his daughter had a big estate sale. That's when Mr. Pliny got the idea for a fright house, seeing all that stuff. You remember how the sack hanging from the ceiling swung out at you when you went through the door?"

I shook my head. Emma and I hadn't made it that far into the fright house.

"Anyway, it's run with a windshield-wiper motor. Can you b'lieve that? They rigged all kinds of stuff themselves. Miz Pliny made the costumes and decided what story should happen in each room."

I shuddered at the thought of wrestling Prune Man into his chain-saw massacre overalls. "Couldn't they tell he wasn't like the other mannequins?"

"That's what I wanted to know. I mean, after all, if he's a real man, he's gotta have real man parts, don't he? You don't reckon that fell off, like his leg, do you?"

Her face betrayed not a trace of guile. I was impressed with her initiative. She must have spent a lot of time with the Plinys, which was further evidence that she possessed more than a little of her aunt Edna's doggedness.

"Anyway, Miz Pliny said they didn't get him nekkid. His clothes were kind of lacquered on him. Some kind of brown suit, she said. So that's why he was wearing those baggy overalls. He was so wrinkly and dusty, they put him up high, so folks couldn't see him real close."

That made sense. She paused and I wondered if she was picturing dressing him.

"She said he was so stiff, he could've stood on his own, better than the plastic mannequins. They just

thought he was some kind of papier-mâché or something. Some of the others were stuffed cotton, real
stiff and tight. Two were straw, like scarecrows. She
said they throwed those away, they were so limp and
musty and full of bugs."

Shamanique shuddered at the thought of the bugs
and filth. She's an earthy, practical girl, but don't let
a spider crawl anywhere in view. Last week, one
had swung down over her desk on its thin filament,
just dropping in to say hi. The way she shrieked and
jumped, I thought she would climb the drapes to get
away.

"So Con Plotnick's daughter had no idea the
mummy was real when she sold it?"

"Nope. Least ways, that's what she said."

"You talked to her?"

"Found her in Alabama. She sells real estate.
Wanted nothing to do with 'the life,' she called it. I
took it that her daddy had sweet-talked her mama into
running off with him when the carnival stopped in
her little town one summer. He proved to be a better
sweet-talker than a long-hauler. I could'a warned her
about that."

Shamanique, in her very few years, had acquired
quite a database from which to study the male of the
species. Despite her experiences, she still collects
trifling boyfriends.

"Anyway, she said her daddy had bought a ten-in-
one, she called it, from someone back in the late sixties. You wouldn't believe the stuff she said it had.
She called them gaffs. A frog with a chicken's head,
a human head in a jar where the eyes would open and
close. She said that was a trick, that it was really just
a table with a hole in it and a big glass jar. When she
stayed the summer with her dad, she'd sit under the

table with her head in the jar and blink and stare at people. Said it was sweaty hot and cramped, and staring at stupid farmers who'd pay money to see something like that made them the real freaks."

What would that have been like? Staring at doughy faced kids and farmers or miners and their wives, all gawking at a little girl's head in a jar?

"Some of them wanted to be amazed," Shamanique said. "Some tried to figure out if they'd been taken. If a kid got obnoxious, she'd bug her eyes and stick out her tongue to scare him."

"I can see why she didn't want to stay with the carnival," I said. Selling real estate was a different sort of act, I was sure, but at least she didn't have to sit with her head in a jar in an un–air-conditioned tent.

"Her dad traveled into the early seventies, until he got sick. Came to live with her at the end. Even then, he kept thinking he'd get well, be back on the road. He was even harder to live with, cooped up in her house, than he'd been to put up with in a trailer on the road all the time. He got bad depressed. When he died, his stuff was in storage in Gibtown, which is a ways from her home in Alabama, so it was a couple more years before she sold it off, sight unseen. That's when the Plinys bought a lot of it."

"So when did Mr. Plotnick first get the mummy?"

"His daughter wasn't exactly sure. She remembers her dad traveling with his new ten-in-one when she was in the fifth or sixth grade, somewhere in the late sixties."

"And he owned it until he got sick?"

"Yep. Her dad lived with her two years before he passed, then she didn't get around to selling it off for another two years. That was in 1979."

"But she doesn't know how he first got the mummy?"

"No, but she gave me a name of a lady who might know something. I tracked down a phone number in Florida and left a message, but haven't heard back."

I studied her gamine face, the Cleopatra slant of her eyes extended with eyeliner. When Edna had hauled her into my office two months earlier, almost by the scruff of the neck, I'd been irritated at having her foisted off on me. I'd quickly learned she could talk information out of a sealed tomb, and I was learning to respect her instincts. I just couldn't reconcile her talent with her bad taste in boyfriends.

"Good stuff, Shamanique. Thanks for taking all this time when you're supposed to be off. Now get on and have a good time."

She waved a dismissive, talon-tipped hand. "Can't bear to think about that guy with the shellacked-on clothes and his family not knowing where he's been all these years. Besides, Harmon's always easier to handle when he's the one wanting you instead of the other way around."

She might choose bad ones, but she did seem to know how to handle them.

We would wait until we had the whole story before we shared it with the Plinys—or with Rudy. Maybe I'd earn some points with him, if we saved him some legwork at a busy time.

I stretched, stiff after spending all morning on my feet. We ambled toward the midway, moving slowly in the heat. Shamanique turned off toward the miniature Ferris wheel, where she'd told Harmon, her latest conquest, to meet her.

I decided I'd try to hitch a ride back to Main Street. Surely somebody would be ready to leave the fair and the sweltering heat. Which someone was—a lady from Mom's book club was herding her brood into a minivan as I reached the parking lot. The kids looked shiny and sticky from a combination of sweat and cotton candy—and irritable from the same combination. She offered me a seat up front—apparently anxious for a taste of adult companionship even if it lasted only a few blocks. Any attempt at conversation was drowned out by a wailing three-year-old.

I hopped out at the stoplight on Main Street, two blocks from my mauve Victorian, glad I wasn't the one responsible for hosing off the grime and tamping down the arguments.

I'd have my cool, dark, high-ceilinged cave all to myself. I smiled and pushed the damp tendrils from my forehead as I climbed the front steps.

The sight of lamplight in Melvin's inner office surprised me.

"That you?" I called, in part to alert him I was back, in part to alert myself if we had an intruder.

"Hey," he called. "You got a minute?"

"Sure." The French doors to his outer office were open, the lights off to maintain at least an illusion it was cool. "Why aren't you off enjoying holiday festivities?"

"I've enjoyed about all the heat, hot dogs, and beer I can stand," he said. "Why're you here?"

"Too much heat, hot dogs, and excitement for me, too. I gotta rest up for the fireworks."

"That's right." He sounded as though he planned to skip what I considered the best part of the holiday.

I plopped into the wooden chair in front of his desk. I didn't want to sweat on any of his elegant upholstery.

"Have you ever met Joe Pratchett? The president of Ramble College?"

"Nope, pretty sure I haven't."

"Would you be willing to talk to him? I'm meeting with him tomorrow morning. He's got questions about some dealings with their endowment. In case he's got legal questions to go along with his financial ones, it'd be useful to have you along, if you've got time."

"Sure." This was the first time Melvin had consulted me professionally—except, of course, when he'd been questioned last November about the death of his wife years earlier. We'd gotten that all straightened out—and I didn't count it in the same league as asking me to meet with one of his clients. I was flattered.

"The meeting's set for nine at Dr. Pratchett's office."

We agreed to allow half an hour to get there, and I bid him adieu.

I decided on a nap so I wouldn't sleep through the fireworks finale tonight. First, though, I rooted through my boxes and found a patriotic CD. With the top down and the speakers cranked up, we could sit on the grass and sync Sousa and *William Tell* with the fireworks. Emma would love that.

Emma rode with me to the ball field for the fireworks. We went early to claim a good parking spot.

Rather than hang around the carnival midway, Emma opted to play in a pickup soccer game with some kids who looked a little older than she did. I watched her dodge and weave, her thick plaited ponytail swinging behind her.

When her parents joined us, we headed off to the church tent for some barbecue and to kill some time as the sun set.

"Lydia! How are you?" A bosomy brunette with a big smile appeared at our table in the crowded tent.

"You must be Lydia's sister! How nice to meet you. I'm Lovey Pope. I've heard so much about you."

"Join us, Lovey?" Lydia scooted over to make room at the end of the bench.

"Just for a second. Where's Frank and Emma?"

"At the dessert table, I suspect."

Lovey laughed. "Same with mine. Good to have them old enough to entertain themselves, isn't it? And I mostly mean the husbands." She laughed again, a deep chime.

"Avery, I hear you've met Spence Munn."

"We-ell . . ." I didn't glance at Lydia. I doubted she was the source of the gossip, but if she was, now wasn't the time for a sister fight.

"I'm sure you know, he's quite the catch. And he can't do anything but talk about you. Is he here?"

She looked around as if suddenly aware that the catch himself might be in the vicinity, overhearing her not-faint praise.

I just shook my head.

"He and my husband knew each other at App State, you know. Bet he hasn't bothered telling you that his father's some admiral or something like that. Very successful. You know how those career military guys are, expecting great things from their sons. Spence has certainly continued the success, in his own way."

I nodded, figuring I really didn't need to speak.

"Spence has been handling some investments for us. Not that we have much, but let me tell you, he's incredible. We just think the world of him. Our daughter— you know Moira." She turned to Lydia. "She announced last year that she was going to marry Spence. Mind you, she's only four." More pealing laughter.

Lovey bounced up from the edge of the picnic bench.

"There's my crew. I'd better go see what they've been into. See you later!"

Lydia reclaimed her side of the picnic bench, putting a more respectful distance between her and the hulking man in the stained Cat hat sitting next to her.

"Avery's got a boyfriend. Avery's got a boyfriend," she sing-songed.

My only reaction to her childish falsetto was to roll my eyes. Anything more would've just encouraged her.

Emma, with no idea how grateful I was to see her, appeared at her mother's elbow.

"Dad says we can take our dessert with us. We don't want to miss the fireworks."

She carried a spidery mound of blue-green cotton candy twice as big as her head. I knew Frank hadn't been suggesting she go to his car with that sticky mess. He was pointing her toward my car. I owed him.

I'd need to find a place to rinse her off after she finished eating—and I was still glad to see her.

EIGHTEEN

Wednesday Morning

After the fireworks, I had trouble sleeping, either because I'd slept the afternoon away or because I'd eaten too much junk food. Whatever the reason, when I finally dozed off, snatches of conversations with Spence, with Todd, visions of the parade, the Prune Man, all played in an endless kaleidoscope in my head. I woke up exhausted.

Hot tea and yogurt with granola did little to revive me. I put on a suit, complete with skirt and heels, for our visit to the college. Somehow visiting the president's office sounded more impressive than I was sure it would turn out to be.

I was wrong. It turned out to be quite impressive, in a shabby-elegant way. I'd never been on the campus, set back off a country road as it was, but I'd seen the highway signs, had been faintly aware it existed. I knew Ramble College as a small church-affiliated liberal arts college with an indifferent academic reputation in a neighboring county; that was all I knew. Of course, I'd also recently learned that Spence Munn taught here, but I didn't expect we'd run into him.

Melvin turned his Jeep onto the oak-lined circular drive that led to the graceful Georgian brick administration building.

FOUNDED IN 1906 read the stone sign nestled on the carpet of green grass that stretched out from the highway to the front door of the main building.

A visitor's parking slot with a RESERVED FOR MR. BERTRAM sign sat a few yards from the grand stone entry steps. The reception area inside was part Victorian bordello, part rummage cast-offs.

A young woman in an office just to the right of the main entrance showed no particular interest in us and apparently felt no duty to serve as the college's official greeter. Her higher calling was to sit at a battered laminate desk in an office with wrinkled beige carpet, where she was sticking labels on stacks of envelopes.

Melvin was able to draw from her that President Pratchett's office was upstairs. With a shared glance, we agreed that asking her where the stairs were would take longer than finding them for ourselves.

The president's office was, predictably, the largest, taking up the end of a second-floor hall lined with administrative offices identified by plastic nameplates and titles such as DEVELOPMENT, BURSAR, and FACILITIES. The less-important functions, such as the library and classrooms, must be located in less-grand buildings elsewhere on campus, far removed from the president's view.

The president's office had a small plastic sign, similar to all the others along the hall, that read PRESIDENT but offered no more information. Inside the door was a suite of three spacious, high-ceilinged rooms, with fabric cubicle walls turning two of the rooms into subdivided tenements.

The original architecture included monstrous windows, the old-fashioned double-hung kind that probably rattled in a slight breeze, stuck when someone wanted them open, and leaked heat and cold like sieves. I recognized the problems they presented because I'd had to spend time and money to get similar windows in Melvin's Victorian house weatherized and functioning.

The benefit of such outsized windows was the sunlight, though the cubicles and oppressive beige walls swallowed most of the light, creating a strangled, closed-in mustiness.

A short woman packed tightly into a tweed skirt and ruffled blouse stepped smartly forward when Melvin took it upon himself to knock on what looked like the president's inner sanctum.

"May I help you?" she asked, sounding doubtful that she wanted to.

"Dr. Pratchett is expecting us." Melvin introduced the two of us. Her gray eyes underneath the iron-gray bangs of a pageboy haircut were unimpressed.

Just then, the door swung open and a man in pinstriped slacks, starched white shirt, and pink seersucker tie greeted us.

"Melvin. Good to see you. Come in, come in."

Dr. Pratchett was several inches shorter than Melvin, but he made up for that with a booming voice that could address a football stadium full of potential donors. His movements were quick and jerky. He reminded me of crack addicts I'd seen in the detention cells, although his clothes were much more expensive.

"Melvin, thanks so much for coming. And this is the smart lawyer you told me about?"

He inclined his silvery head over my hand as he

shook it, a facsimile of a courtly kiss on the hand melded into a more businesslike handshake. Was Ramble College stuck in a time warp—or just Pratchett himself?

"Nice to meet you, Dr. Pratchett."

He motioned for us to take seats on the brown, studded leather sofa, crinkled and worn smooth by countless gatherings around the scarred coffee table.

"Melvin, I know I don't have to ask, but I need to keep this in the utmost confidence." His voice lost its street-preacher bluster. Whatever had prompted him to invite us here—and Melvin hadn't given me any details beforehand—was serious, if the palpable worry in his voice was any indication.

"Certainly, Dr. Pratchett."

Dr. Pratchett didn't say, "Oh, call me Joe." Not that I would've expected him to. He seemed to like being Dr. Pratchett.

"I may be overreacting to a situation. I pray I'm overreacting, but I'd rather overreact than have to explain to the Board of Trustees why I overlooked the warning signs. That kind of thing gets college presidents fired." His nervous chuckle tried to turn that into a joke.

He leaned forward in his chair, his elbows on his knees, his hands clasping and unclasping in a nervous knot.

"What kinds of warning signs?" Melvin prompted.

"I'm sure you know how college endowments operate. Without our endowment, this little gem of a college would've been shut and shuttered years ago. The tuition the students pay doesn't come close to keeping the lights on. Thanks to the generosity of donors and the wisdom of generations of my predecessors, Ramble College survived when scores of other unique little colleges didn't. Thanks to the interest earned every year on the endowed funds, we can hire faculty, buy library books, mow the lawn, and educate our students."

Outside, I could hear the drone of a large tractor mower, probably manicuring the massive front lawn while we sat in air-conditioned comfort.

"There's a problem with your endowment?" Melvin asked.

Embezzlement was the first thing that popped into my head, but then I've spent much of my life working with large corporations, after which no bad element can surprise.

"Well." Dr. Pratchett didn't want to say it out loud, whatever it was. Because that would make it real?

He sighed, gathering his words. "We've always used a couple of different fund managers, to keep us diversified. The market goes bad, one fund may do better even if the other miscalculates, and one will sometimes hit an upswing in the market that the other doesn't hit quite as big. Guess that's obvious to you business types."

He waved his hand to include both Melvin and me. "I'm a history professor," he said. "Don't like to admit it, especially where those smart-ass economics professors can hear me. If you repeat this, I'll deny I said it, but I don't really understand all the details. Frankly, I'm not sure I want to. Too much akin to watching sausage being made. Or placing your faith in alchemy."

He took a deep breath. "Two years ago, we decided—by that, I mean the board's investment committee decided—to move some endowment funds to a local investment firm. We'd been using investment managers at two big banks, but frankly, their fees got steeper and steeper. We'd heard about the returns other investors were earning with this little outfit, which is based right here in South Carolina. And they didn't gouge their clients with high management fees. So we figured, why not?"

His nonchalant shrug echoed what had likely been the investment committee's carefree attitude at the time, but his tone presaged a bad outcome.

"Things went so well," he said, "we ended up transferring a third of our endowment holdings. The returns were meeting—and usually beating—the big guys. I knew the fellow, years ago, who started this little company. A straighter stretched string you'll never meet. Didn't realize until I called him last week that he'd sold his interest in the company, when he decided to retire, to the fellow running it now.

"As it turned out, the guy I knew isn't involved with the firm. I had always heard good things about him, associated him with this firm. Even so, like I said, it had been nothing but good news about this firm. Our earnings grew even during that little market blip not quite a year ago."

"But things changed," Melvin said. Pratchett was wandering around the edges of his story, avoiding the embarrassing central issue.

"Yes." Pratchett stared, without seeing, at a photo on the wall behind Melvin's head. It showed Pratchett in a tuxedo shaking hands with someone who looked like a bored but politely smiling Pat Conroy.

"Everything changed. The account even stopped paying dividends. I'm afraid it's turning into a train wreck."

"Do you have copies of the last few months' statements?" Melvin asked.

Pratchett's eyes reddened as he turned to Melvin,

his hands clasped as if in desperate prayer or appeal. "We haven't gotten a statement for the last two months. Our financial officer even went to the offices on Monday, trying to talk to someone in person when she couldn't get anybody on the phone. A sign on the door said they were closed all week for the holiday."

"What's the name of the firm?" I asked, hesitating to interrupt.

"Oh, I'm sorry." He slipped into his well-practiced role as host. "Manna Advisers."

I tried to maintain my cross-examination face and not reveal that this was the second time in two days I'd heard the name Manna Advisers, the first being the mention of Todd David's position as secretary of the board.

"What were they investing in?" asked Melvin. "Where did they put your money?"

Pratchett shook his head as he answered. "I'm afraid I don't have all the details. Greta, our financial officer, she can tell you more. She's off today, but I can call her to come in, if you'd like. I wanted to make sure this was something you could help us with, before I brought anyone else in." He didn't sound as though he wanted her—or anyone else—in on the sworn-secret meeting. He just wanted everything to be okay.

"We can talk to her later."

"She's been warning me for some weeks now." He knotted his fingers tight. That explained why he hadn't wanted to include her. "I have to confess, I just brushed it off. You know how those finance types can be, always full of doom and gloom and disaster. I just thought it was another of her Chicken Little moments and it would pass when the sky didn't fall."

He didn't acknowledge that Melvin was also one

of those conservative, cautious "finance types." And Chicken Little was looking downright prescient.

"From what I was told," he said, "Manna Advisers mostly puts money into home loans. That was one of their attractions for us, home folks helping home folks live the American dream. Because they don't have a lot of overhead, it being a local operation, they could afford to pay better returns."

I noticed a crinkle in Melvin's brow, almost imperceptible but telling.

"You want us to look into it, find out what's happening?" Melvin asked.

"I want you to get our money back." Some of Pratchett's animation and volume returned.

"How much are we talking about? Ball park."

"Greta can tell you. To the penny, I'm sure. But it's millions."

Melvin did a better job of hiding his surprise than I did, but not much better.

"Where would you like it transferred?"

Dr. Pratchett looked at Melvin like a drowning man offered a life preserver. "Um—back to the banks, one or both. Greta can tell you. You think . . ." He didn't dare finish his thought, no matter how hope-filled.

"Just wanted to know your preference so we can move quickly."

"I'll have my secretary call Greta, tell her to contact you."

"Thank you." Melvin stood to leave.

"Nice to meet you, Dr. Pratchett." I offered him my hand but didn't accompany it with any of my usual reassurances that I'd take care of things. As it turned out, I didn't have much I could offer, but the worry wrinkle between Melvin's eyes told me he and I had read the same reality in Dr. Pratchett's fears.

As the two of us descended the broad staircase to the first-floor hallway, Melvin said, "Sorry I roped you in on this. I thought he suspected some kind of embezzlement. What he said on the phone was that he was afraid somebody was stealing their money. I thought the college might need some legal advice."

"What do you think? Has he just got cold feet because of a bad patch in the market? Or is somebody stealing their money?"

"Lots to worry about here. The mortgage business in particular is struggling. I smell a general fishiness to all this. Smart money people return phone calls and answer questions. Otherwise, clients panic. In this case, there just might be something to panic about."

"Such as?"

"Sounds like Manna Advisers is offering interest-only or variable rate mortgages to people stretching to get into a house."

Even I knew that could be a risky business.

"So Manna would charge higher interest to borrowers and pay higher returns to investors to offset the risk. Problem is, there's been a bit of squeeze lately. Even a slight downturn in the economy, which we've seen locally with that plant closing in Anderson County, can push shaky borrowers over the edge."

"That would put a company that operates only in a limited region even more at risk."

"Exactly. If I had to guess, in order to offer such high returns, Manna has also been investing in low-rated debentures—unsecured loans which carry high risk."

The forecast for Ramble College's endowment was gloomy.

We exited into the bright sun and the heat. The lawn mower had done its work, smoothing the emerald carpet of grass stretched out along the broad alley of oak trees.

I wondered how far Spencer Munn's office was from the hallowed halls of administration. I couldn't see Dr. Pratchett consulting a professor about the college's woes. Spence was probably one of those smart-assed economists who doubted the history-professor president's business acumen. With good reason.

Melvin opened the passenger door for me. "Have you had occasion to meet Eliot Easton?"

His voice was casual, but the question hit me from an unexpected direction. "Why do you ask?"

He couldn't miss the surprise in my voice. "He's the one who bought controlling interest in Manna Advisers from Dr. Pratchett's friend. I just thought you might have heard of him."

NINETEEN

Wednesday Morning

I stood frozen, trying to reorder what I knew and whether it was important.

"What is it?" Melvin looked worried as he stared down at me, his hand on the car door. He looked as though he feared I was about to throw up on his upholstery.

"If something has happened to the college's money, this Eliot Easton's the one who stole it?"

"I doubt it was stolen. Mismanaged would be more likely. That's how these things usually develop."

"Then he'd be the one who mismanaged it?"

"He's the top dog. The buck-stops-here boss. That doesn't mean he's hands-on or he's the one directly responsible. Remember the young banker stationed in Singapore who brought down the British financial giant Barings Bank? The guys in charge didn't call the shots, and they certainly weren't responsible for the Kobe earthquake that sent Asian markets into a spiral, but they were the ones who let a kid run up a couple hundred million in losses with no internal controls to monitor it. So who really bankrupted Barings? The kid or his bosses?"

I remembered a little about the case. "It shouldn't amaze me that one person can have that much power over that much money, but it does. The guy at Barings wasn't even stealing for his own benefit, was he? Imagine what's possible with bad intentions."

Melvin, still holding the car door for me, said, "The intentions are seldom pure. Leeson, the kid banker, got huge bonuses for his performance at Barings. He would've gotten even more if the cards had fallen the way he'd projected instead of tumbling back on top of him. Some do it for the power. A few are simply incompetent. But there's always some risk they shouldn't be taking."

"Greed is good, as long as the cards stay stacked or fall the right way?"

Melvin gave a wry smile. "I don't think of my motivation, for myself or my clients, as greed. I have to admit, though, that I can't really think of another word to describe it. It's a question of degree, isn't it?"

"Most of life is, isn't it?" I climbed into the passenger seat.

He nodded, thoughtful, as he closed the door.

During the drive back to our offices, I mulled over how Spence Munn would answer the question about whether greed is good or a balance along a continuum. I also wondered how well he knew Eliot Easton. Did he just eat at Easton's restaurant and enjoy his wine selection? Or did he know anything about Easton's investment company? Could he help Melvin get some answers?

I didn't offer up Spence's name to Melvin. I didn't know Spence well enough or enough about his business to volunteer his assistance in unraveling Ramble College's problems.

The phone message light was blinking insistently on Shamanique's desk when I entered the office. Shamanique wasn't at her desk, and I hoped she was off somewhere having fun, though not enough fun to get her on the wrong side of her aunt.

The only message on the machine was from Eden Rand, in a voice so shrill it was difficult to catch every word.

"Avery! Are you there? Pick up! They've arrested Rog! That dumb-ass sheriff came to his house this morning and hauled him away in a patrol car. He was probably handcuffed. Who knows what's happening to him! They won't let me in to see him. You've got to do something!"

She hadn't taken a breath from the time she yelled my name to the time her message clicked off.

Her visceral anxiety gave me a chill. I pictured her storming the Bastille of the Law Enforcement Center. I thought I'd made myself clear when I last talked to her. Her presence—at the jail or in his life—would not advance Rog's cause. Having another woman could create in some minds a motive for Rog to want his wife out of the way.

I looked in the file for Eden's phone number because she hadn't bothered to leave one with her message. She didn't answer, so I gave my orders to her answering machine.

"Eden. Back off. Leave Rog alone. Do you understand? You aren't helping. I'll be back in touch." I hope she didn't ignore the anger in my voice. Not that I believed it would do any good.

Lord, help Rogert Reimann. I'd rather be interrogated by L. J. Peters and face life in prison than spend life in the commanding, desperate, lovelorn clutches of Eden Rand.

Rudy answered when I dialed his cell number. "You the one talking to Rog Reimann?" I asked.

"News travels fast." Rudy said. "What's it to you?"

"Has he asked for counsel?"

"No. But he hasn't said much of anything else, either, which is really pissing L.J. off. Talking to this guy is like trying to nail goop to the wall."

"Are you holding Rog?"

"Naw. He's already back home."

"Is L.J. going to charge him? For something that's probably not even a murder?"

"I know, I know. Statistically speaking, it was an accident."

"You ever waded out in that stream?"

"Hell, no. Got better sense than that."

"Every year in the Appalachian Mountains, some hikers don't have your kind of sense," I said.

"Speaking of not having any sense, how did Reimann get hooked up with that crazy Rand woman?"

So Eden had made her presence known. Rudy didn't seem to be jumping to any conclusions, though.

"I think she's the one that's got the hooks out," I said. "I don't think he's got a clue."

Rudy snorted again.

"See you later," I said.

My phone rang as soon as I hung up. I answered, expecting Rudy's voice. Instead, I got an earful of Eden Rand.

"Avery! Have you heard anything else about that life insurance policy? Rog is going to need a criminal lawyer, and he needs one of the best. That costs money but, with the funeral and the moving expenses and the new mortgage, he simply hasn't got the cash for that."

"Where are you, Eden?"

"At Rog's. They brought him home a while ago, but the way they acted, they'll be back. He's a stranger in this hick county and that makes him vulnerable, an easy solution for a sheriff who's getting heat about closing a case."

She'd been watching too many made-for-TV movies, or she'd bookmarked too many conspiracy Web sites.

"Nobody's pressuring the sheriff. She's just doing her job."

"They refused to let him call a lawyer. I kept insisting that they let him, but they refused."

"Did Rog ask for a lawyer?" I emphasized Rog's name. She didn't answer that question. She wouldn't listen if I explained that he had to ask for a lawyer, that she couldn't do it for him.

"They'll be back and he needs to be ready. He needs money to defend himself—a lot of money, unless he wants to risk being railroaded."

"Eden, there's plenty of time before that becomes a risk." I took a deep breath to clear my ire. "Eden, you've got to back off. Having someone who isn't his wife at his house, involved in his personal business, is going to look suspicious. You're giving them a convenient motive, Eden. Do you understand that?"

If I'd been talking to her in person, I'd have grabbed her by the shoulders and shaken her. Not that it would've had any more effect than my words. "I left a message on your answering machine at home. I don't suppose you've gotten it."

"He needs somebody, Avery. Who's going to take care of him? He's in shock."

"Eden, for Rog's sake, you need to back off."

"Well, that's just more evidence that I made the right decision. I told Rog you really didn't have the experience to represent him. He needs someone with a killer instinct, someone who isn't part of the good ol' boy network around here. Rog will be looking elsewhere for representation."

"That's a good idea, Eden. I wish him all the best." I hung up the receiver. I wished him luck in more ways than she knew.

Rog had a house and a job with a good salary. He should have money. He'd been behind or late on his payments lately, but Shamanique hadn't found anywhere he was squandering cash. Maybe his life—and bank account—weren't the open book to Eden that she thought they were. Something just didn't make sense.

The jangle of the front door startled me. Shamanique pushed into the outer office, breathless and glowing with perspiration and excitement.

"Thank the Lord, you're here. I found him."

She actually hopped like a lanky chocolate bunny on her wooden stilt shoes, her hands up in a praise dance.

"Who?"

"Burt Furder. That's who." Her polished white teeth glistened in a gotcha grin.

"A new boyfriend?" I got her back.

She rolled her eyes. Her gleeful bouncing ended in a shudder. "That's just gross."

"Prune Man? You found out who he is?" I felt like joining her in hopping with glee.

"Yep. None other. I want you to talk to this lady yourself. She said it was okay if I called her back today. You won't believe this unless you hear it for yourself."

She marched around her desk, punched the speaker phone button, and dialed a number she pulled from a shoulder bag sparkling with all manner of spangles and chains.

"Hello?" The voice broadcast into the room sounded as though she was glad the phone had rung, a sentiment I'm sure my voice seldom reflects.

"Miz Strange? This is Shamanique Edwards."

"Hey, there! And I told you, call me Dana. Dana B. Strange. I married him for the last name, but the first one is mine." Her laugh spread through the office along with the morning sun, filling the cool crevices.

"I've got Avery Andrews here, the lawyer I was telling you about?"

"Hey, Avery."

"Miz—Dana. Thanks so much for taking time to talk to us."

"Twice," said Shamanique.

"I'm just so thrilled to hear that you found Burt. Not that he was exactly lost, I guess. You know what I mean."

"We have been a bit—puzzled—as to how he got—misplaced," I said. I wasn't sure of her relationship with the dearly mummified, and I didn't want to be insensitive.

"It's quite a tale, I can tell you. Shamanique and I spent some time last evening piecing together his journey. He's better traveled than I am, and that's saying something."

I settled into a chair and smiled over the desk at Shamanique. From the expectant grin on Shamanique's face, I knew I was going to enjoy this story. I also couldn't wait to hear how she had tracked down all the pieces.

"How did you know Burt?" I asked.

"Never did in life. He'd already passed by the time

I made his acquaintance—and more particularly, that of his wife, Eufala. I was fifteen at the time, so it was about 1960. I remember it well, because that's the summer I left home and took off with the carnival when it left town. That's another story, but that's how I first met Eufala, and we ended up working the same midways for years afterward.

"Probably just as well I didn't know Burt in life. He had something of a reputation—petty theft, bad to drink and cause a ruckus at times. But Eufala had a certain fondness for him. Or a strong sense of duty.

"He got hisself killed in a brawl or something, somewhere in Texas. That was sometime back in the thirties. It was the Depression and his poor wife—Eufala—didn't have two nickels to rub, much less what the undertaker wanted for fixing him up. Apparently Burt's family was in bad straits and couldn't pay for the embalming that the undertaker had done, so Burt just laid there, all dressed up and no place to go.

"My guess was, the undertaker had his own hard times. Nobody had any money then, but that didn't keep folks from dying. He left Burt laying there for some months, all the while Eufala never could come up with the burying money.

"Then, as these things happen, a guy comes rolling into town with a traveling show. Eufala said they used to come quite regular through those little Texas towns. Maybe they did everywhere, I don't know. It was a way to make a living, I reckon, even if it was only coins at a stop.

"Anyway, this fella heard tell about Burt and offered to buy him from the undertaker, pay his expenses and then some. At first, the undertaker didn't want to. He thought it disrespectful, and Eufala kept saying she'd find a way to bury him proper.

"For some reason, the traveling fella had gotten quite an itch to take Burt with him on the road. He looked up Eufala. She told me he turned his snake-oil charm on her and witched her, but she never for a minute looked like she minded.

"To hear her tell it, she resisted as best she could, but by the time the traveling show was set to move on, the undertaker was paid off, Eufala was sitting up in the front seat of a DeSoto, and Burt was riding in state in the trailer in back."

"You're kidding." I knew she wasn't, but my words just came out in sheer surprise.

Dana's laugh sang from the phone. "That was my reaction exactly when she told me. But Eufala said this was in the day when people paid to see the bullet holes and bloodstains in Bonnie and Clyde's car. Heck, they paid to see faked-up versions of the death car. Did you know the real car earned thousands of dollars? Probably at no more than a dime a view. I can't even guess what that would be in dollars today. It was an eye-popping amount of money when I first heard about it, even in 1960. Somebody said the real death car sold to a casino in the sixties for around two hundred grand."

"Wow." As a comparison, I knew my granddad's new Mustang had cost about $2,500 in 1964, and a new version cost more than ten times that now, so $200,000 in 1960's dollars would've been some real money.

"Of course," Dana continued, "some dead guy from West Texas wasn't going to pull the crowds in like a bloodstained Bonnie and Clyde murder car, so Eufala's new beau—his name was Pete—created a story for Burt.

"The barroom brawling ne'er-do-well became a

famous West Texas bank robber, who consorted with the worst gangsters of the day. They dressed him up like a desperado. He was stiff enough, thanks to the embalming job, to almost stand on his own, so they propped him up in a rough wooden coffin. He even had a big dusty bandanna tied around his throat, like he was ready to pull it up and yell, 'This is a stickup.' "

She laughed at the memory. "Eufala said Pete spent good money on a hog-leg pistol and getup while she had holes in her cardboard shoes, but he more than made that money back. And in their years together, Pete more than made it up to her.

"I remember Burt's eyes were sort of half-open, which was creepy. That didn't hurt ticket sales any, him looking like he was about to wake up from a nap and go for the pistol they strapped to his leg."

I couldn't take in her tale. "She actually traveled around with a man who displayed her first husband's body in a sideshow?" I had to ask.

"I'll admit, when you put it that way, it doesn't sound good. But those were different times. And you'd have to know Eufala. She had a country dignity about her. And oh, did she love Pete. He treated her like a princess."

What had that conversation been like, I wondered. *I'd like to buy your dead husband and take him on the road. Want to come along?*

As if answering my thoughts, Dana said, "Eufala didn't have many options. Like a lot of us. This way, she said, Burt got the attention he'd always craved and she took care of him. Lots better than he ever took care of her, I'm sure. Said she didn't really know how bad Burt was until Pete came along. She was thankful for Burt, though, because otherwise she wouldn't have met Pete and she wouldn't have known how to appreciate what she got."

Pretty sensible, given the wackiness of it all—and surprisingly sweet.

"What happened to Eufala?"

"She died. Gosh, back in the seventies. Pete had died years before. She kept traveling with the show, though old Burt wasn't as much of a draw. At the end, he was just on display in a show without any mention that he was real—and really dead. Over time, people had gotten squeamish about that kind of thing. Got too proper and didn't want their neighbors to know they went and paid good money to stare at a dead guy.

"She missed Pete awful. I never met him, but my, how she loved that man. Guess it helps if you have something bad to compare against what comes next. I never could muster that kind of love for the guy I ran off with. When he took off and left me behind, I counted it as a blessing. I sure never took on another man full-time."

"What happened to Burt after she died?"

"He kept traveling with the show she'd put him in. Some guy bought her stock—or took it, who knows. She never talked about any family. Gosh, what had Burt become by then? A clown in the fun house, I think, last I saw him. I always knew which one was him. Those half-opened eyes were the creepy give-away. I steered clear of him, let me tell you. I could take a dead desperado in a wooden coffin, but that clown with those opaque eyes, that did it for me."

"What happened then?"

Shamanique stepped in with the answer. "That's when the concession was sold to Con Plotnick."

"That would've been the time when a lot of shows were shutting down," said Dana. "Everybody got so politically correct. Why come to the carnival when you can turn on your TV and see freaks and gaffs and tricksters pouring out into your living room? Not the same life as when I started, I can tell you. Which is why I quit."

"What do you do now, Miz Strange?"

"Dana, please. I own a restaurant. Down here in Gibtown. You ever down this way, you come in and see me. I'll serve you the best Co'Cola Cake you've ever had."

My mouth literally warmed at the thought. I doubted her cake could beat Jestine's Kitchen in Charleston, but I wouldn't back down from a taste test.

"Do Burt or Eufala have any kin, that you know of?"

"That's a good question. Shamanique asked me that yesterday evening, and I've been musing on it. I can't think of a soul. Eufala had lots of friends, you know, but no kin—especially none that'd give Burt anything but a good swift kick in his dusty ass."

"Well." I paused, torn between the thrill of the hunt successfully completed and the futility of it, in the end. "It's good to know the story, but it leaves us figuring out what to do with Mr. Furder's remains."

"Yeah," Dana said with a faint sigh. "It's surely time for him to come in off the road. Quite a run he's had."

"He sure has. Thanks so much for your time."

"You ever down this way, you come on in and visit. And bring that Pinner Pliny with you. Small world. I had no idea she was hauling Burt Furder around with her. Time she got herself a folding lawn chair and a beach umbrella."

"I'll let you tell her that," I said. Pinner and E.Z. might rather become mummies on the travel circuit themselves, instead of settling down, as long as they weren't the ones fretting over making the nut.

Shamanique disconnected the call, and we stared at each other.

"You gonna tell the Plinys, or you want me to?"

"I'll tell them," I said. "I take it they know Dana Strange?"

She nodded. "They eat breakfast in her restaurant when they're home in the winter. Been friends for years, she said."

I'd never thought about carnival people as such a close-knit family. They seemed so far-flung and separated. I could see the folks traveling with a particular show getting to know each other, but according to the Plinys, those shows broke apart and re-formed continuously, with everybody always looking for a better site and more reasonable fees and bigger crowds with easier money at the next stop.

"I'll stop by after lunch. The midway opens at noon today, I think."

TWENTY

Wednesday Noon

I headed to Maylene's later than usual but didn't expect to find a line waiting. The folks who normally came for their workday lunch would be off shopping in Greenville or goofing off and avoiding their usual routine.

A handful of us, though, were grateful Maylene hadn't closed for the whole week. While the locals were on vacation, tourists from other parts of the country came to town for the festival or to take a nostalgic soak in the small-town atmosphere, even though the quaintness is largely a figment manufactured by outsiders who moved to town to open shops and create an image.

The vestiges of real small-town life remain—the Feed & Seed store with the rump-sprung cane chairs outside, the hardware store selling electric fencing and leather work gloves and nails by the pound but no cute kitchen accoutrements, and Maylene's, with its cracked and slightly greasy vinyl booths and scratched faux-wood tabletops.

I walked the block to Maylene's Restaurant and saw the welcome sight of an unmarked patrol car parked in front. Sure enough, he was ensconced in his usual booth. The crowd was thinner than usual, and the only waitress working the floor, a relatively new entry through Maylene's revolving door of waitresses, looked more surly than usual. She wasn't much of a morning person, but I wasn't sure she was happier during any other part of the day, from what I'd observed since she'd started waiting tables here.

Despite her mood, it didn't take long after I slid into the booth opposite Rudy for her to deliver my fried flounder.

"I thought you might be taking the day off," I said.

"Naw, I'm saving up time for later in the month, go fishing down near Murrell's Inlet when it's not so crowded."

I took a bite of my sandwich. A blob of tartar sauce oozed out the bottom. The bun was fresh, the fish was crispy and hot. Not bad. Not as good as salt-and-pepper catfish pan-fried in cornmeal batter, but still good.

"Did you see Ken Tharp leaving as you were coming in?"

I wiped the corner of my mouth and shook my head. "We must have missed each other." I felt a pang of sadness, remembering his struggle to find words for his illicit grief—and relief that we'd had no reason to talk.

"Wish I'd missed him. I never in my life saw somebody go so far around his elbow to come up with some reason why he ought to be harassing the police about a case. He hit me with some nonsense about how it was his civic duty as a member of the city council to make sure that murderers don't wander free in this city. Can you believe that crap?"

When the waitress brought Rudy's tea, he was

kind enough to point to my empty glass. She didn't roll her eyes. She seemed to like Rudy.

"Why doesn't he just come out and admit he was sleeping with her? I'd have a lot more respect for him. What's he think he's hiding? Everybody in town knows about him and Rinda." Rudy leaned close. "He had the nerve to lie to L.J. about it when she asked him point-blank. His hind-end would be on the hot seat for sure if we could find anybody who'd seen his car anywhere near Bow Falls last Friday."

"So you've been checking into that?"

He gave me that narrow-eyed stare I get when I've crossed the line with him. "His alibi held up. He was in Greenville that day. Shopping with his wife and her sister."

"Did you check his cell phone records, just to make sure?" I kept talking, knowing I was about to get another slant-eyed stare. "Rinda was on the phone constantly that morning. Some people assumed she was talking to Ken."

"We know that. And we did check. His alibi held, I said."

I did sound as though I were second-guessing him.

"I just wasn't sure anybody'd mentioned all the calls. Don't get in a snit."

"I thought you wanted it to be an accident," he said. "Don't tell me you're entertaining a few possibilities now."

"Keep an open mind. Isn't that what you're always preaching?" Okay, he didn't preach it, but he did do it. I wanted him to know I realized that.

"You think we're locked in on your buddy Rog, but I can assure you we're walking all the way around this. It just keeps coming back to those bruises on her arms and the money. Follow the money, right? Those insurance policies weren't tiny."

"Maybe Rog is just smart and plans ahead. Nothing wrong with having the foresight to buy insurance."

"If he's so good with his financial planning, why is he having trouble paying his bills on time?"

He and L.J. had been busy. I didn't have an answer for that, despite Shamanique's digging. Obviously Rudy and L.J. hadn't found an explanation, either.

I changed the subject. "They had life insurance on Rinda. How about Rog? Is his life insured?" I hadn't thought to ask Rog.

Rudy's food arrived, and he took a few seconds to douse it in salt and pepper, close his eyes over it, and shove in a forkful of shredded cabbage.

"Yes," he said after a few chews.

"How much?"

"More than she carried."

"Well, that helps make the case, doesn't it? They bought insurance as part of a good financial plan, to provide for the lost income the other would suffer if one of them died."

"Even if I give you the good financial planning," he said, "what's that got to do with him having his butt on fire to get his hands on that insurance money?"

"Rudy, you know good and well he's not the one who called the insurance company."

"No, he got you to do it. You and that airy-fairy professor flake that showed up when we were questioning him."

"He didn't get me to call. Eden Rand—that airy-fairy professor flake—is the one who asked me to call."

Rudy smirked. "Okay, Counselor, how about you

explain why it's not odd that he's got a girlfriend all over him before his wife's body is even found. The wife's having an affair. He's having an affair. Not exactly a Hallmark card home life, is it?"

"You don't know that he's having an affair. Eden's just taken him in, like a lost puppy. None of that means Rinda was murdered."

"Why're you so insistent she wasn't?"

That stopped me. I sat for a moment, processing my impressions. Why was I so certain?

"I was there," I said. "I saw them both. Rog wandering around in a fog, which seems a permanent state with him. It's deeper now, but he's never totally plugged in to the real world, if you know what I mean. He seems to invite people to take care of him."

"Women, you mean."

"Okay, women. Eden works with him. She's got her mother-hen instincts fired up and focused on him. I also saw Rinda that morning."

I pictured her in her trim white slacks, her head bent over her cell phone, her stylish ponytail flicking with energy. "She wasn't angry or upset. She was just talking on her phone. Away from everybody, where no one could hear."

She'd reminded me of high school girls making furtive calls from the hall pay phone to boyfriends who were too old to attend school or who were at home on suspension for some dire offense. The bad-boy boyfriends. The ones they weren't supposed to be caring about, much less calling during school hours. That's what she'd reminded me of—a girl with a salacious secret.

"Rog acted like he was oblivious. I didn't see any— passion. I just don't see how it could—erupt, with no warning, no sign, no aftermath. I was there."

"You haven't been called out on as many domestics as I have. Passion, as you call it, just erupts. Lots of people claim they had no warning. I'm not sure I believe that in most cases. A trash can overflowing with empty beer bottles ought to be some warning, but whatever."

"That's my point, Rudy. There's usually some hint, even if it's nothing more than a trash can full of empties."

"Avery, we're not locked into one theory. We have to investigate everything. It may have been an accident. I admit that. But I can't ignore the money. Follow the money. That works more times than you know. Until we're comfortable about all the variations, we'll keep asking questions. Okay?"

"Okay." Standing in his shoes, I had to agree that two dead wives and two large insurance policies looked like more than just good financial planning. Even though I was there and I couldn't believe Rog had anything to do with killing her, I had to admit that money in large clumps had its own gravitational pull.

TWENTY-ONE

Wednesday Afternoon

"Avery!" Melvin called out when my entrance jangled the bells hanging on the front door. I jumped, startled, because yelling wasn't his normal form of greeting. He sure had been hanging around the office a lot during the holiday week.

He came to his open office door. "You got a minute?"

"Sure."

The professional calm with which Melvin approached even the most bizarre events had melted into a quick urgency.

I followed him back to his office. He slid into his chair, his computer screen at his elbow.

"I just got some information on Manna Advisers. Apparently Dr. Pratchett at Ramble College isn't the only investor with questions. The state attorney general has just issued a statement that Manna is under investigation. I would expect the next step to be an announcement that Manna has temporarily ceased doing business."

Like a bad restaurant, would a CLOSED TEMPORAR-

ILY FOR REMODELING sign taped to the front door presage Manna Advisers' permanent demise?

"What's happened to the college's money?"

"I've been trying to get Dr. Pratchett on the phone. One of the trustees offered him the use of a condo at the coast, and he took some vacation time to play golf. His assistant is trying to track him down. Even if they'd pulled their money out before now, though, a bankruptcy judge would come looking for it."

A bankruptcy judge usually declares any payments or withdrawals made on the eve of a bankruptcy as improper or even fraudulent transfers. Even if Ramble College had withdrawn its money, a judge could demand that it be returned so it could be divided among all the irate creditors first, with the even more irate investors like Ramble at the end of the line.

"You think it will come to that? Bankruptcy?"

Melvin shrugged. "The drumbeats are sounding."

Ramble College needed a lawyer to protect its interests. Rog Reimann needed a lawyer to settle Rinda's estate while fending off whispers that he was responsible for her death. So many end-of-life issues, personal and corporate. I didn't feel particularly useful. Maybe I should have specialized in something other than the terrifying glamour of trial work.

Melvin turned from his computer screen to face me. "You said you don't have anything invested with them."

"No."

"How about that investor friend of yours? Spencer Munn? Does he know Eliot Easton?"

Melvin sure pays attention to details. "They know each other. I don't know anything beyond that."

"Do you know Munn well enough to call him, let him know what's going on? I believe he has money in Manna. It might be helpful to get a group of investors together early. Once the government gets involved, it can get a little muddled about what its mission is and who it should protect."

I'd never had reason to contemplate the intersection between creditors and investors outside the sterile confines of a textbook. Securities law tries to give investors the information they need to make investment decisions. Arguably somebody could offer to sell shares in the Cooper River Bridge, as long as he told potential investors he didn't really own the bridge. With such a material fact available when they made their decision, investors would be free to buy up as many worthless shares as they wished.

Bankruptcy law, on the other hand, spells out debtor and creditor relationships. The goal is to give those who've gotten in over their financial heads a way to climb out, dry off, and start fresh. The court apportions what assets are available and pays off the creditors, but only after paying off the lawyers, the accountants, and the IRS.

If any assets remain, they go to those who'd chosen to loan money to the bankrupt person or company, whether to buy a house, start a business, or run up vacations, restaurant bills, or get-rich-quick schemes on a series of credit cards. The lenders supposedly went away having learned to be more careful about those to whom they loaned money in the future. The investors who owned the bankrupt company stood at the end of the line. They usually got nothing.

I knew the law. I just never had reason to contemplate where the two federal legal schematics collided. In a corporation, creditors were the biggest focus since the investors—the owners—presumably knew what they'd gotten into. However, with Manna Advisers, did the investors really know what they were doing with their money?

"The creditors get in line first," I said. "Who is that likely to be?"

"After your brethren at the legal bar get paid?" Melvin said with mild sarcasm.

"Of course." I couldn't see that an investment firm would have a long list of creditors, not like a manufacturing firm, for instance, with suppliers, truckers, employees, and such.

"Manna Advisers had expanded its operations recently, so it has several new long-term office leases, new employees for each office, new furniture, and so forth. From what I've been able to pull up, their board members are also well compensated. I don't know whether the state or federal tax authorities have anything owed to them, though nothing has gone as far as a formal lien."

"Still, Manna ought to have enough assets to pay the creditors with something left over for the investors, right?"

"Ought to, but these things usually don't turn out well."

"What do you mean, these things?"

"Small hometown investment schemes gone bad."

"You make it sound doomed." I had a knot in the pit of my stomach as I thought about the carefully patched gentility of Ramble College. In a flash, I remembered Lissie Caper and her tight-faced conversation with Todd David at the parade—Todd, who was secretary of the board of directors at Manna Advisers.

"By the time the government publicly announces

an investigation, the investigators have already done plenty of quiet digging. No official wants to panic the public and cause a run on a firm that's hit a bad patch but still has a chance to pull out. That would be tragic."

"Like the Enron guys tried to claim: We had it all under control. If you hadn't scared people off, the market would've proven us right."

"Exactly," Melvin said. "Sometimes they can pull it out, given a little time. You can't always tell from the outside when something is simply volatile and when it's doomed."

"But if the watchdogs wait too long to start barking, innocent people can lose everything."

"As you said, Enron."

"So regulators tend to err on the side of caution and wait too late," I said. That would explain the tenseness in Melvin's voice.

"Yes, especially given this attorney general. He's the cautious type. I did some checking. His office had been getting heads-up calls and e-mails from one investor for several months, so this has percolated awhile."

"What upset the guy enough that he alerted the attorney general?"

"According to what I heard, an investor in Columbia got suspicious when Eliot Easton first bought Manna. He said Easton started spending more money than a small-town savings and loan ought to have to spend."

"But it's not a savings—"

"Exactly. To me, that's the most damaging part of this situation. Have you seen one of their offices?"

I shook my head. "No. Just driven by the one in Seneca, but I haven't paid much attention."

"They look like banks, complete with tellers' windows and a nice lobby. A lot of investors treat it like a bank or an S&L—and consider it to be as safe as one. Trouble is, Manna Advisers isn't covered by the same regulations or safeguards."

"It's still covered by state and federal securities regulations, though."

"True," he said. "And, like any regulation, those rules do a great job keeping in line those who are in-clined to follow the rules. But rules don't keep people honest if they're bent on being bad."

"You think Manna Advisers was bent on being bad?"

"No, not on the face of it. They were making in-trastate offerings to a limited number of investors, as allowed by law."

Securities sold within a state don't have to comply with federal securities reporting requirements as long as the amounts sold and the number of investors stay below certain limits.

"On the face of it," said Melvin, "investing with people close to home gives an investor a chance to know the company personally, to keep an eye on them. So these intrastate offerings make a lot of sense—in theory, at least."

"But aren't intrastate investments usually sold to institutional investors?" I said. "What if the investor isn't a large, savvy institution, but instead is a small group of not-very-canny good ol' boys?"

"Ah, therein lies my worry about Manna Advisers. Some of the investors weren't very savvy. I'm afraid too many of them thought they'd found a bank that paid really good interest rates—except it isn't insured like a bank, and those rates were bought with high risk."

"That's scary."

"Anybody can be fooled by a good story. Enron had some of the nation's most sophisticated investors on its shareholder roster. From the time Carlo Ponzi began talking his neighbors into the wonders of trading on international currency fluctuations—and, more important, getting them to convince their neighbors to join in—the more unbelievable the investment scheme, the more attractive it often is."

"But this isn't a con or a Ponzi scheme, is it?" I asked.

"Not in the technical sense. But face it, all investment is a sales job—a good one, if you make money; a con, if you don't. That's how people see it. It's supposed to be a sure thing."

I hadn't thought about the client expectations Melvin dealt with every day. Most of my clients knew why they were sitting in jail or why their wives were leaving them. Sometimes they wanted to blame me, but even they knew that wasn't going to stick. On the other hand, Melvin took other people's money and played with it. They would get touchy if something happened to it, no matter how careful Melvin was.

"What was Easton investing in that made the irate investor blow the whistle to the attorney general?"

"Former investor. He got his money out, after a little tug-of-war with Easton." Melvin shrugged. "Manna was listing a private jet, a yacht, expensive trinkets like ink pens and art as investments."

I frowned. "Those could be investments, right?"

"I personally wouldn't put my clients' money in art or collectibles and call it an investment. Investors expect a return on their money, in case they want to make a mortgage payment, pay their granddaughter's orthodontist bills, or buy their own private plane. As to a plane or a boat, I haven't seen any cases where those were anything but money pits. Not what I'd call investments."

"Lose a little money on a little boat, big money on a big boat." I quoted my grandfather with a smile.

"Unless you use it to catch fish and supplement the family food budget," Melvin said with mild irony, quoting his brother's rationale for his recent bass boat purchase. Melvin enjoyed fishing, but I noticed he didn't own a boat. He used his brother's.

"I can call Spence Munn. What do you want me to tell him?"

"Test the waters. See if he's read about the attorney general's announcement. Depending on his reaction, you can decide whether to ask if he'd like to attend a meeting to discuss next steps. If he's intensely loyal and has absolute faith in Manna and Easton, leave it alone. I don't want to stir up trouble for them and don't want to start a stampede. That's in no one's best interest. That's why I'm not calling him. It'll be better coming from a friend, somebody he knows, not somebody out of the blue."

"Sure." I agreed with his reasoning but didn't have a clue what I would say.

TWENTY-TWO

Wednesday Afternoon

As I walked into my office to call Spence, Rudy's voice replayed in my head: *Follow the money.* Quite a lot of money had been floating around Camden County lately. Where would it land? And when?

I'd planned my voice-mail message, but Spence surprised me by answering his cell phone.

"Are you in your office at the college?" I asked.

"Just leaving. As a matter of fact, I was about to call you, see if you wanted to meet for coffee."

"Sure," I said. I was glad not to have our conversation on the phone, where I couldn't judge from the body cues what he was thinking.

The coffee shop he suggested in downtown Seneca was closer to my office than to his, so when he arrived I was waiting at a circular metal table in the front window. The spindly metal wire chair wasn't as comfortable as the squishy stuffed chairs in the rear of the shop but, despite its deceptively public location, the little table was farther away from any accidental eavesdroppers.

"Oh, you already have something to drink," he

said when he spotted me. "Anything else? A slice of cake or a cookie?"

I waved away his offer and sipped my ice tea. I really don't like coffee, but coffee bars are nice creations. Neutral turf, with a contrived sense of homeliness.

"Thought you might be traveling, taking some vacation," I said when he carried his ceramic mug over and joined me.

"Why?" His face looked as if he was trying to decipher a strange message.

"No reason. Just that it's a holiday, lots of people leave town."

"Oh. More reason to stay, I figure." He balanced himself on the round chair seat and tested the heart-shaped wire back with a tentative lean.

I took a deep breath to focus myself. I tend to splutter when I have more to say than I have words for. "Have you heard about the attorney general's statement today?"

"No." His puzzled frown said that wasn't what he'd expected to chat about. "Why? Should I?"

"He sent out a release this morning, announcing an investigation into Manna Advisers."

Spence stiffened. The movement was almost imperceptible, as if he was drawing himself up so the chair wouldn't tip over, but he didn't say anything.

"Isn't that your friend Eliot Easton's firm? The guy from the restaurant?"

"Um—yes." He was paying more attention to something in his head than to me.

I waited out his silence.

"How did you—find out?"

"Like I said, an announcement. A friend of mine

told me about it." I didn't mention Melvin by name or remind him he was also an investment advisor.

"It's just an investigation," I said, "but I know that can panic investors."

He nodded. His hands were wrapped around his white mug, but he wasn't drinking any coffee.

"Would you be interested in joining a meeting of other investors?"

His head snapped up. "What meeting?"

"Just to explore options."

"Who's calling this meeting?"

"I don't know. Just some others who have clients or are invested themselves, to see what they can learn."

"Are they going to force a regulatory seizure? An involuntary bankruptcy?" His voice had a sharp edge.

"No, that's the last thing they want to see."

That seemed to calm him. His shoulders relaxed. "Sure. Tell them to include me."

I sensed a wary caution. Spence hadn't denied having money invested with Manna, so had I made the right assumption there? Or was he hoping to report back to Eliot Easton about what was going on? Melvin wasn't dumb. He would have considered that possibility. Besides, Melvin wouldn't know anything that Easton didn't already know.

"That's sobering news." Spence played with his coffee mug, turning the handle to first one side, then the other. "So much happening lately. I saw the funeral announcement in the paper this morning. How's Rog doing? Have you heard?"

"I think he's still in shock."

"Who wouldn't be, especially with the sheriff harassing him."

"I don't know that the sheriff is harassing him." I acknowledged my double-mindedness on that subject only to myself, feeling oddly protective of Rudy and even L.J.

"The idea that he had anything to do with her—with his wife's death is just absurd," he said. "To anybody that knows him, it's inconceivable. He'd just never do anything like that."

I didn't point out how often serial killers' neighbors say, "What a nice young man he was—a little quiet, but nice."

"I know," I said. "But look at it from their perspective. They've got to do their job. It's an unusual death. They're doing Rog a favor by answering the natural suspicions people have, especially since his first wife also died in an accident."

Spence gave a mild snort. "The sheriff's more worried about her reelection chances. These things are always political, Avery. I know these people are your friends, but a prolonged investigation has made the insurance company suspicious. Rog told me they're refusing to pay until the investigation is finished 'to their satisfaction.' And I quote. You know insurance companies love an excuse to delay paying a big claim."

I didn't point out that Eden Rand had done more to raise suspicions at the insurance company than the sheriff's investigation had.

"Do they plan to charge him with anything?" Spence asked. "If so, he'll be in a really tough position. Needing a lawyer without the resources to hire one. Do you guys work on spec, in cases like that?" His tone wasn't snide or sarcastic. He seemed genuinely curious.

"What happened to all his money? I understand

he got a nice settlement when his first wife died, so why's he in such a fix?"

Spence didn't act surprised at my question. "It's not in liquid investments. He just can't get his hands on it right now."

He didn't volunteer whether he served as Rog's investment adviser, and it would be unprofessional to ask.

We both sat silent, staring out the storefront window at the occasional car that passed along the side street.

I also didn't ask if he'd like to go up the mountain for a walk. For one thing, he had a lot on his mind and was probably as anxious as Melvin had been to dig into the Manna Advisers mess. Whether he had his own money invested or that of his clients, or whether he was just worried about Easton, the news I'd brought was not good.

As another impediment to even a casual stroll down a wooded path, he was dressed in sand-colored silk slacks and what was likely yet another expensive silk Hawaiian shirt, this one covered with red poppies. Slipping on a patch of damp red clay would ruin his braided leather thin-soled loafers.

"I'm sure you have things to do," I said. He seemed content to continue our coffee date, but I granted him a reprieve so he could get to his computer or phone.

"Yes." He breathed with relief and stood, almost tipping over the wire chair before it righted itself.

"I'll give you a call," he said. "Maybe this weekend?"

I nodded, and he bent down and gave me a kiss on the cheek, an unexpected offering. I understood better than he could know the draw of work, of an overwhelming responsibility for other people, for their money or their livelihood or their reputations. I respected that. No need to apologize for ditching a date to take care of business.

As I walked around the corner to my car, I mused on what to do with the rest of my afternoon. A summer blockbuster movie? Naw, not in the mood for all the testosterone in one of those. I really wanted to take the canoe out on the lake, but that would have to wait until October when the Jet Skis hibernated. A walk in the mountains? Home to read a book in the front porch rocker? To Clemson for some ice cream? Would the student-run store be open today? It would only take a ten-minute drive from Seneca to answer that question, during which I could decide what to do next.

This vacation thing was an unnatural act for me. Before I'd returned to Dacus, I'd had plenty of cases crying for billable hours. Relaxing was just too much work. What do you *do* when you relax? That had always been a troubling question for me.

At the Clemson Student Center, I ordered a chocolate walnut sundae in the bright, sparkling shop. I missed the institutional gloom of the old Agricultural Sales Center where I'd first eaten Clemson's home-grown ice cream as a little girl on outings with my granddad in his Mustang convertible. I drove the convertible now, and every time I came to this part of campus, I missed him. He'd taught me to roller skate on the broad sidewalks surrounded by the agricultural and forestry classroom buildings. Things changed and moved on, but those ice cream memories still tasted good, even if the ice cream shop had changed location—and the scoops were smaller.

I crammed the change into the pocket of my shorts and carried my sundae outside to one of the metal tables lining the center's massive portico. These tables felt less risky than those at the Seneca coffee shop. Scattered among the other tables sat students with laptops and backpacks bulging with knowledge bound in books larger than those I remembered carrying. Most looked like graduate students taking summer classes, older and a bit scruffier than the undergraduates scooping ice cream inside.

Even in the shade, the heat wrapped around me like a steamy, damp sweater.

Follow the money, Rudy had said. A lot of money to follow lately. Melvin—and likely Spence—were haring off after money that had been entrusted to Manna. I didn't envy them the political delicacy required in a situation like that. To panic or not to panic, that was the question.

Then there was Eden Rand. Maybe not in a panic, but certainly in a fret. Not so much following the money as herding it.

I agreed with Rudy, following the money often leads to the source of a problem. I'd seen it in high-stakes civil cases. Having large amounts of money at risk drives people to extremes. Money does make the world go around, faster for some than for others.

The one person who didn't seem motivated by money was Rog Reimann. Of course, he might be the consummate actor. As I often reminded myself, I'd been fooled before. But I just couldn't see him taking such a risk, shoving his wife off a cliff in broad daylight with a score of his friends and colleagues within shouting distance.

But Rog was the only one who would benefit from the insurance—unless Eden managed to run him to ground. Money didn't seem to be her motivation, either. Even though she'd helped create official suspicion about Rog's insurance greed, I sensed she was prompted more from a need to make herself useful by guarding and protecting him than from any interest in the money for herself.

She had a good job. Was she just desperate for companionship and Rog was a malleable prospect? Security, companionship, validation, even sex—I could see all those as driving forces for her. But what did I know?

If I followed the money, where would it go? To pay a lawyer, if Rog was arrested. Gosh, I thought wryly, could that make me a suspect if I represented him?

If things had a happier ending, Eden would see that the money was invested. Her lecture on the time value of money sounded like something Melvin would deliver. Something he and Spence had in common, the put-your-money-to-work mentality. Couldn't disagree with that, what with compound interest being one of the wonders of the world.

I smiled to myself. If you really followed the money, it would end up in an investment portfolio somewhere. It would cease to be liquid, like the rest of Rog's money. Would Eden mind?

By the time I'd scraped the bottom of my plastic ice cream bowl as clean as I could, I'd decided I needed a long walk. Probably guilt over ordering a chocolate walnut sundae with two scoops of butter pecan. I usually enjoy walking on the sprawling campus, but not today. The pavement, even when shaded by the heavy oaks, looked too hot in the shimmery heat.

I pointed the Mustang back to Dacus and up the mountain road. A few hundred feet in altitude would lower the temperature a degree or two, and the idea of a tree-shadowed path felt cool. I'd make sure I stayed away from the path to Bow Falls. No need to revisit that.

TWENTY-THREE

Late Wednesday Afternoon

I didn't want to drive far, didn't want a lot of people around, and didn't want a strenuous hike or anything near falling water. That narrowed my options. I decided to take the trail from the Oconee State Park toward Tamassee Knob. I didn't plan to hike to the top of the Knob; that would be too demanding in the heat. But the path along the old logging road would be quiet, shaded, and hot but not blistering.

As soon as the noisy shouts of swimmers at the park's lake dimmed in the distance, I wished I'd stopped by the house for my S&W .38. I'd never encountered trouble on any of my solitary hikes, other than the occasional snake that was less thrilled with our meeting than I was, but both my mom and my granddad had drilled it into to me to carry a gun in the woods. "You never know," Mom would say.

A sunny holiday afternoon on a popular trail was a safe bet, though, so I trudged along the path, tamping down the frisson of worry born of my family's constant caution.

The undergrowth closed in along the path, encouraged by recent rains and the warm summer to stretch for new territory on the sun-dappled path.

My mind flashed back to the weedy, overgrown creek banks above Bow Falls, where the woody stalks and vines had clambered over each other, stretching for the opening in the tree canopy that offered more sunlight and water and elbow room beside the creek.

I broke out in a light sweat. Not dripping wet, but perspiring enough that I could feel the air brush my face like an invisible, faint flannel.

"Ow!" I stumbled as I jerked my leg back. A blackberry briar had imbedded itself in my calf. I eased it out so it wouldn't dig in deeper or break off the tip under the skin. A dot of blood pooled up.

The berries were scant and not dull enough to be ripe. I wondered if Lydia had any of the really sweet blackberries left in her back pasture. Blackberries wanted more sun than they got here or at Bow Falls. I needed to go by Lydia's. I didn't want to miss blackberry season—the jelly was worth the briars, the heat, and the snakes.

I stepped around the spot where the brambles stretched onto the path and glanced down at my scratch. I'd live, but it reminded me that I'd need to check myself for ticks when I got home. The scratches on my arms from last Friday were fading. Had it only been five days?

Had Spence been able to fix the bramble tear in his pants? Probably not. That had been a much bigger tear than the little prick on my leg.

I stopped suddenly, frozen on the path. That tiny tear, no more than an inch, in the delicate silk fabric. Where had he gotten that?

I was headed back to the car for my camera. The

blackberries weren't growing on the path to the parking lot. That path was wide, with granite slabs almost as smooth as paving stones, in deep shade. Blackberries grew in the sun, along the creek at the top of the falls.

A wave of adrenaline shot through me. I'd have been less frightened if a copperhead crawled over my foot.

I stood frozen, my brain jumping from one snapshot memory to another, checking to see whether things made sense in a new, less dappled light.

I turned, dodged the grasping bramble branches, and ran back the way I'd come, anxious suddenly to hear the shrieks and laughter from the swimmers in the lake.

TWENTY-FOUR

Early Wednesday Evening

I drove farther up the mountain and took the shortcut over toward Bow Falls, my tires squealing on every curve. As much as I wanted to avoid it, I needed to go back to Bow Falls, to reassure myself that the heat had gotten to me, that I was imagining things.

The path to the photo-op overlook was crowded, but, once I passed the overlook, I had the path to the top of the falls all to myself.

I jogged as quickly as I could over the broken ground, scanning the sides of the path for the telltale red and purple berries and the tiny jagged leaves on spindly runners.

Retracing the path along which we'd carried our picnic supplies, I spotted not a single blackberry or any other kind of bramble or thornbush. Not until I turned along the creek did I find tangles of blackberry briars choking the weedy, narrow edge. At least ten feet downstream from where the path crossed the creek.

The roar of the water over the rocks grew in my head as I studied the clumps of blackberries, some of the leaves yellow-tinged in the sun.

I would let the sheriff's crime scene folks come and crawl around looking for any beige silk fibers caught on a bramble. The experts might find something, but more likely, a bird had carried any threads away to its nest by now.

I walked slowly back to my car, studying every plant alongside the rock-strewn path, hoping to find just one that would convince me I'd been overcome by the heat. Maybe he'd caught his pants on a sharp twig. Maybe—something else. But no blackberries, no brambles, no sharp thorns close enough to the broad path, the only path to the parking lot.

I was headed back to the car for my camera.

In the car, I dialed Rudy's direct office number and got his answering machine. I desperately wanted to talk to someone in authority. I wanted Rudy to tell me I was irrational and incorrect. I wanted him to discredit my amateur sleuthing and tell me about a dozen other explanations for the tear in Spence's dress slacks.

He could've caught it on a twig, right?

I took a deep breath and tried to dissect the reason for my panicked certainty that something was amiss.

That tiny tear could have other rational explanations. Why was I so certain? I realized the torn pants had not been the only prompt for my panic.

Follow the money. If Rog followed his past pattern, the money would be invested—with Spence. Eden lectured on the time value of money and fretted over the insurance company's delays because of what she'd learned from Spence.

Spence knew Rog couldn't get his hands on any cash because his investments weren't liquid. Rog and Spence were friends, so it was likely Rog had invested the insurance proceeds and his other assets with Spence.

I dialed Rudy's cell phone. It rang so long that I'd begun planning what message I could leave in the allotted time when he surprised me by answering.

"Rudy. This may be crazy, but have you talked to Spencer Munn about Rinda Reimann's death?"

Rudy took so long to reply that I feared the connection had been broken. "Now it's a *death* rather than an *accident*?" His tone had an undercurrent of derision.

"Have you talked to him?"

"He was interviewed just like everybody else who was there that day."

"You need to talk to him again."

By the time I finished outlining everything—how his investment advice pushed Eden to hound the insurance company, the bramble tear on his pants leg, the absence of brambles along the path, Spence's likely role as Rog's investment adviser, Spence's relationship with Eliot Easton, and the investigation of Easton's investment company, I was down the mountain and on north Main, blocks away from both the Law Enforcement Center and my office.

After a long silence, Rudy spoke, the derision gone from his voice. "Might be worth another chat," he said. "Where you going to be, in case I need to get hold of you?"

"Back at the office," I said. I needed to be inside my cocoon for a time.

Later that evening, after I'd made myself a peanut butter and blackberry jelly sandwich and curled up to watch part of the BBC miniseries of Dickens's *Bleak House* on my laptop, Rudy called.

"Can you come over here? I'd like you to see part of this, if you have time."

I clicked the pause button on my movie. Lady Dedlock had just shot the lawyer Tulkinghorn. "Sure."

When I got to the Law Enforcement Center, the deputy at the desk directed me to a back hall lined with small interview rooms. He took me to a room with a table, two chairs, and a mounted television monitor linked to a nearby room.

The deputy left me alone in the room and knocked once on a doorway in the hall. Over the television monitor, I heard the sound and saw the back of Rudy's head turn to acknowledge the single knock, but he didn't make a move to open the door. A signal I'd arrived?

"Mr. Munn," Rudy said, "I want to make sure I've got all this straight."

I wondered how long they'd been talking. Spence Munn sat at one end of a small table, his back to the wall, his face to the camera. His legs were crossed and he leaned back in the chair, his body language as relaxed as if he was having drinks on Lydia's deck. Even on the washed-out video, though, his eyes looked wary, his fingers tightly laced together in his lap.

Rudy faced Spence with his back to the camera, giving the camera a view of his dishwater blond hair sticking out in short spikes from the back of his head. His deliberate tone gave the impression he was a slow-witted cop, not quite able to understand everything the sharply dressed professor was telling him, so he had to ask for clarification.

"You said you were walking along the path to the parking lot, then you turned back."

Spence paused, as if searching for a trap, before he said, "Yes."

"You didn't walk toward the top of the falls."

"No."

Spence spoke as if short replies created a smaller target.

"You walked a ways along the creek at the top, though, didn't you?"

Spence sat without responding. Was I imagining the tension?

"You must have. You had a tear in your pants."

Did Spence realize I was the one who had reported that? Were the pants in his closet at home, or had he destroyed them?

"That ought to be easy to explain." Rudy offered him an escape hatch.

Spence said nothing.

"Did you see her when she fell?"

Rudy let the question sit there in a long silence.

Spence shifted in his seat. "I told you, I heard her."

"Did you call to her, tell her to get back from the edge?"

Spence's gaze lifted slightly upward, to the left, away from Rudy.

"Did you warn her it was slippery?"

Where had Spence grown up? Norfolk, on the coast, but he'd gone to college in the mountains. Surely he'd been hiking before. He couldn't claim he didn't know about slippery rocks.

Spence blinked and looked down.

Of course he'd known the rocks were slippery. He'd been standing near them, hadn't he?

"What did she say that made you angry?"

Still no response. In a cold wave, I realized what

was happening. He was using the Kennedy Smith defense, he was keeping his mouth shut, refusing to talk. If he'd been as smart as he thought he was, he'd never have agreed to sit down with Rudy, never let himself and his tight control, his involuntary reactions, be captured on videotape.

Rudy leaned forward, crowding him but not blocking the camera's view.

"You pushed her, didn't you?" His voice was loud, insistent.

"No!" Spence's words came through clenched teeth. "I told you—" He cut himself off like an angry dog who'd run full tilt to the end of its leash.

"So you just let nature take its course, didn't you? You didn't tell her to stay away from the edge."

Rudy was offering him a safety rope, a face-saving alternative: *I didn't do it. I just didn't stop it.* If Spence reached for the rope, he'd put himself closer to where Rudy knew he'd been.

Every step Rudy could draw Spence along the weed-choked path near the top of the falls, the closer he admitted to being with Rinda when she fell, the stronger the case against him. With every question, Rudy tried to put him closer and closer.

Most interrogations didn't play out like television cop shows. Spence wasn't going to collapse and confess. He'd been living with whatever guilt he felt. He wouldn't feel compelled to confess, to cleanse his soul. He'd had the time—and the intelligence—to make some peace for himself, to reach some equilibrium that he could maintain, no matter how ill-founded.

Like any good con man, Spence had managed to convince himself of the rightness of his views, at least in part. Fooling yourself always made it easier to fool others.

Maybe I was fooling myself, reading something into an upward left shift of his gaze, his tight knot of fingers, his careful posture, frozen and tense. Even though he thought he was playing it smart, he'd let Rudy place him on the path close enough to hear Rinda's one scream—which was very near the only place he could've torn his pants, close enough to the edge to either save her or push her.

Rudy let the silence lay, and Spence made no move to fill it.

"Tell me a little something about your business," Rudy said.

Spence shook his head. "I've said all I'm going to say."

Why wasn't he asking for a lawyer? Why wasn't he leaving? He wasn't under arrest, he didn't have to stay. For someone who thought he knew how to play the system, he'd missed a couple of key game pieces. He wasn't under arrest, he didn't have to stay.

"Can I get you some water?" Rudy said, pushing his chair back with a loud scrape on the tile floor.

"No, thanks."

Rudy left the room. Almost as soon as I watched the door on the television screen close, Rudy's bulk filled the doorway in my dim room. On the television, Spence sat frozen in the chair, staring at the floor.

"Any suggestions?"

"He hasn't asked for a lawyer." I didn't ask, simply stated the obvious. I knew Rudy would play by the rules. If he hadn't been, he'd never have called me.

"And he's not talking."

"You believe he was there?" I asked.

"I'd expect somebody who wasn't to be protesting his innocence a lot louder. Not sitting there like some drunk trying to keep from swaying on camera so the jury might believe the video instead of the breathalyzer."

Rudy was referring to a trial last week where an assistant solicitor ended with a hung jury in a drunk-driving case. Rudy was still steamed. The jury wasn't allowed to know it was the defendant's third offense, which would have taken him off the road and into jail for a while. The driver had, though, learned from his several arrests and two prior convictions. He'd stood frozen in front of the jail intake video and given monosyllabic answers to the questions so he appeared sullen, but in control. The jury had mistakenly believed their own eyes and the video.

"You could ask him about his relationship with Eliot Easton." Questions about Easton's financial difficulties and the state attorney's investigation might rattle Spence. "But it would be better to wait on that."

Rudy, his rump propped on the table edge, stared down at me. "Yeah," he said after a long pause, mentally running through the options. "I'll cut him loose for now."

He stood. "You heading on home?"

I appreciated the head start. No point in letting Spence see my distinctive burgundy Mustang in the parking lot.

As I traced my steps down the cement block–lined institutional hall, I wondered what I'd do if Spence should ask me to represent him. What attorney would I suggest he call? Could I maintain my poker face, not reveal too much, the way he'd done in his interrogation?

I'd need some time to get into character, ready to play the role of innocent. I doubted I'd ever be able to play it as well as what I'd just witnessed. Despite the outward control, though, I couldn't believe a word of his silence. Not a word.

TWENTY-FIVE

Thursday

On Wednesday afternoon, I left the Law Enforcement Center and drove up the mountain to the lake cabin. I didn't want to have to talk to anyone, but I didn't want to be alone with the scenes circling in my head.

The noise of Jet Skis and squeals of kids playing on the water gave me the backdrop I needed in the shaded cabin, curled up on the sofa with one of my grandfather's journals tucked in my arms. I didn't read any of it, just held it.

Only after the sun set did it get quiet outside. Only after dark came fully and I knew the sad hour had passed, those long moments as dark approaches that can leave me melancholy, did I stir from my cave.

Sitting on the porch, I listened to soft voices float across the water, watched lights blink on, the blue screens of televisions materialize. The tree frog concert echoed in deafening crescendos, eventually drowning out everything else.

I stayed in the porch rocker until the other human sounds disappeared and most of the lights in the houses around the lake flicked off, leaving only the protective circles from the outdoor security lights scattered among the cabins, the pulsing tree frog calls, and the moon path laid out on the glistening smooth water.

The next morning, I got up early, before the noise started on the lake. I'd had enough of the noise and the solitude. Nothing to eat in the cupboards or small refrigerator except black beans and Spam and freeze-dried ice cubes.

Force of habit took me straight to my office and apartment. The vase of flowers in the front hall greeted me with an overpowering funeral home smell. Without ceremony, I carried the whole thing out back to the giant rolling trash can, then thought better of it.

I dumped the flowers in the trash and poured the water under the boxwoods next to the garage. The vase, I carried inside. I'd rinse it and take it to the rummage. Someone would enjoy it.

I dialed my parents' number. Dad answered.

"You had breakfast yet?" I asked.

"I'll scramble you some eggs," he said, which meant he'd already eaten. No matter how early I get up, I can't beat him.

"I'm on my way."

"Your mom had some meeting at the church. Don't know what world-beating endeavor this is."

Something worthwhile, I was sure.

"You still got your office closed?"

"Mm-hm," I said. Even though he never said anything direct, Dad probably worried that his eldest child would starve to death or end in debtors' prison. The fact that debtors' prison went the way of Dickensian England didn't mean it wasn't a specter that could visit a concerned parent.

"Dad, you ever met someone you totally misread?

Somebody you thought you had figured out, but you were completely wrong?"

My question wasn't mere self-searching specula-tion. My dad has an uncanny ability to read people. When I was a child, I was convinced he had some sort of secret mind-reader power. Over the years, I'd watched him size up in a single meeting what, for me, was revealed only after someone's character flaws had time to work both their charm and their damage.

"We've all done that," he said. He bent over the eggs in the skillet, stirring them slowly in a swirl of butter and cream. The grain bread in the toaster smelled like toasted nuts. My stomach gave a soft growl.

"Sometimes it just takes time to know all we need to know," he said.

"You put it together pretty quick."

He snorted, but didn't offer any examples of his failures to make me feel better.

"When people want to hide themselves," he said, "it's hard to see past the mask. Let's face it, they spend a lot of time trying to be like the rest of us. They get good at it."

"Yeah." I rested my chin in my hands, propped on a stool at the breakfast bar like a drunk visiting his bartender therapist. "Granddad always said the best liars fool themselves first."

"Something to that." He chuckled. "Trust me, your granddad knew some con artists and horse trad-ers of the first order. He knew whereof he spoke."

Did heredity count for nothing? I had discernment genes on both sides of my family, so what had hap-pened?

"This about that guy at Lydia's picnic?"

I glanced at him, then away.

He focused on the eggs and didn't try to probe my

brain with his mind-reader gaze. "He's been arrested, I heard," he said.

News was really traveling fast—especially considering that Dad is usually the last person plugged into the gossip network. Odd for a newspaper owner, but that had been a later-life job calling for him.

"Arrested for what?" I asked, curious.

"I'm not sure exactly. Something about some investment scheme. I don't rightly know and don't like to say."

Dad didn't ask if I'd fallen for him or if I'd invested any money with him or anything else. Never one to pry. He just knew.

"Seems he fooled a lot of folks, from what I hear." He cut off the heat under the pan and gave the eggs a few more stirs.

"Ought to be able to see through somebody like that," I said.

"Can't say that. If you could think like him, that'd make you as shifty as he is. Best to know you're protected by something bigger than yourself and not fret over what you can't know. You get insight when you need it, not before."

Nice to hear, but I wasn't quite believing it. Maybe it only made sense if you were a mind reader.

He spooned the eggs on a plate for me as I buttered two pieces of toast.

Had I been falling for Spencer Munn? Was that why I felt all sodden inside? I certainly hadn't felt any of that giddy girlish rush I remember from crushes past. Had I simply lived past the giddy age? Were my emotions crusted over with cynicism, accreted over time from making foolish decisions and watching others become fools?

Had I thought something might develop there? Or

was I just flattered by the attention and now embarrassed by my lack of judgment?

I took a bite of the creamy eggs and gave an appreciative murmur. Regardless of where I'd been headed, I was now left even more doubtful of my own judgment, at least in affairs of the heart.

Dad carried the skillet to the sink to wash it. "We get older, but I'm not so sure we get wiser. Maybe we just make so many bad calls, we get cautious. The wise part is understanding that we can't see and know everything. I'd rather be someone who can be fooled. Wouldn't you?"

I laughed and blinked to squelch the tears that threatened to gather.

Over the next few days, the fraud case against Spencer Munn and Eliot Easton became front page news—and not just in the *Dacus Clarion*. As the details unfolded, it became clear that others would be caught in the net, including Todd David. As an attorney and the secretary of the board, he was named along with other board members in a civil suit brought by investors whose losses totaled millions. Todd should have spent less time worrying about candy-tossing injuries and more time studying up on the fiduciary duties of a corporate board. A snide part of me congratulated myself on having the good sense not to go out with him.

Spencer Munn hired a criminal defense attorney from Greenville, who often represented high-profile defendants. The attorney promptly applied to the court for funds, claiming Munn was indigent, his assets frozen or nonexistent.

Angry prosecutors and civil attorneys were coming at them from all sides. I knew how those stories would end. The civil settlements would pay out only pennies of what the investors had lost. Some of the jail time might be suspended, but the major players would serve enough time to scare guys who normally wear suits to work.

Spence's defense, according to his lawyer's statements to the Greenville paper, was that the government had started a panic by announcing an investigation and had caused the collapse. "My client's investors would have been protected had the government not started a stampede. Investments fluctuate. He just needed a little more time, and the government denied him that."

The interesting part of the story took a few weeks to unfold. When it did, it blew the financial fraud case off the headlines.

Spencer Munn was indicted for the second-degree murder of Rinda Reimann. The solicitor claimed she'd been killed in a complicated attempt to get her insurance proceeds. Rinda's husband had money invested with Spencer Munn, and Munn needed an influx of cash to pay off investors clamoring for their dividends. When investors whose funds he'd placed with Manna Advisers had gotten suspicious, he was desperate to stave off a panic. Getting control of Rinda's insurance money was his last frantic hope.

That day at the falls, had she been harassing him about why their dividend checks had stopped coming? Had he planned it? Or had he just not stopped it? No matter how many trials they held, I doubted those answers would ever be clear.

Rog Reimann had known nothing about the scheme. The news reports listed him as one of Manna Advisers' ten largest investors.

I watched it unfold from a distance, as if watching

a movie unfold, one in which I had no emotional stake. I felt detached, not viscerally involved, even though I'd known many of the players.

I marveled at my lack of emotion, my lack of anxiety for Spence or Todd. I felt a twinge when I thought about Lissie Caper and Dr. Pratchett and Rog and the others who'd been sucked into Eliot Easton's get-rich-quick scam. Should they have known it was too good to be true?

Another part of me—buried deep because I didn't want to study it too closely—knew it could have been me, but for grace.

Ironically, a funeral proved the fun part of the week. I found a cheap airfare from Greenville and flew into Tampa to join the Plinys, Dana Strange, and others in paying our respects to Burt Furder.

I shouldn't have been surprised that the carnival crowd would throw a heck of a party, though I admit it gave me a shock when I came face to face with Burt himself, dressed in a classy black suit with his top hat resting on a bar stool nearby.

They had propped his coffin up so that he could join the party. Judging from his half-open eyes and slight smile, I'd have to say he enjoyed his funeral more than any corpse I'd ever seen.

As the social column in the *Dacus Clarion* would have reported it, had the funeral been covered, a good time was had by all. Dana Strange wasn't lying a word when she boasted about her Co'Cola Cake, though I'm still partial to the cake at Jestine's Kitchen, which fortunately isn't as far as Gibtown is from my own strange hometown.

A FEW FINAL WORDS
ON FRAUD

REAL LOSSES.

The actual incidence of financial fraud is difficult to calculate. However, I spent most of a year researching "small town" financial fraud cases and found the amount of money stolen and the number of people harmed staggering.

Interestingly enough, the type of scams I've explored in this novel are not the most prevalent, though South Carolina alone has had four high-profile fraud cases like this in the last six years, with investors losing almost half a *billion* dollars! Note, that's just in South Carolina, and that's thousands of investors who've lost their life savings.

MOST COMMON FRAUDS.

According to one government agency, the most common frauds include:

- *Identity theft.*

- *Check fraud* (stolen or altered checks, often cashed with the aid of an accomplice at a store or with false identification matching the check).

- *Advance-fee scams* (the plea to "send me some money to cover fees and I'll share my fortune with you," seen in the now-common Nigerian scam offers).

- *Theft of credit, debit, or ATM numbers* (often stolen with high-tech aids like hidden cameras and card skimmers at ATMs or skimmed by waitstaff or retail clerks).

- Automatic bank transfer payments to a *false account.*

- *Internet fraud* (someone posing as a legitimate business e-mails [or phones] to "update our records" and asks for private information).

- *Predatory home loans* (loan consolidation or foreclosure "rescues" that either steal information or acquire mortgaged property through fraudulent promises).

For a detailed discussion on "Common Cons . . . and How to Avoid Them," see an excellent article at www.fdic.gov/consumers/consumer/news/cnspr03/cons.html.

The best scams work on our own innate greed. In

the right circumstances, anyone can be convinced that they can get something for nothing.

Another common ploy is to play on our desire to help someone in need. We want to be helpful, likable people. You don't want to be anything else. But you also want to be safe. Ask questions, check up on claims—legitimate businesses and charities won't mind. And report suspicious activity to the proper state, federal, or private agencies.

PROTECT YOURSELF.

What can you do to protect yourself?

1. Once a year, get copies of your credit reports (in the name of everyone in your household) from www.annualcreditreport.com or call toll-free 877-322-8228. These reports are free, once a year.

   Read this Web site carefully; don't click to buy anything (such as your FICO score or credit monitoring) unless you want that.

   Lots of "sound alike" Web sites exist that want to sell you credit-monitoring services, but you are entitled to one free report from each of the three credit bureaus each year at this Web site.

2. Check up on those with whom you do business. Links to just a few of the organizations and government agencies who can give advice or to whom you can complain include:

   • www.bbb.org/alerts/tips.asp Better Business Bureau links and tips.

- www.ftc.gov/idtheft FTC's Identity Theft site. Or call toll-free 877-FTC-HELP (877-382-4357) to report fraudulent, deceptive, or unfair business practices or to get information.

- www.aarp.org/money/wise_consumer/ AARP links and reports.

- www.pueblo.gsa.gov/scamsdesc Descriptions of scams and frauds. Browse the Web site or call toll free 888-878-3256 for free information from the government's Federal Citizen Information Center.

Con artists and scammers are very good at what they do. Plenty of smart people become victims. Don't be embarrassed or shy about refusing to send money or refusing to give information to people who call you or come by your house or approach you on the street.

3. Remember:

- If it seems too good to be true, it probably is.

- High returns are *always* linked to high risk, in legitimate investments as well as illegitimate ones.

- Do business with well-established firms—and keep your eye on them. Bricks-and-mortar buildings and fancy monthly reports are no guarantee of stability.

- Ignore the "hot tip" from a friend, even people at church or civic clubs. Several

successful scams have targeted trusting
church members or clubs. Check everything
with independent ratings sources.

- Some "con artists" start out legitimate but
  panic during a downturn and take crooked
  shortcuts. Get out while the getting is good.

- Diversify. Learn what that really means.
  Don't invest all your money in a single stock
  (ask the former employees of Enron about
  that). Be aware that investing in several of
  the same types of mutual funds (such as all
  small companies or all foreign funds) also
  means you've got your eggs in too few
  baskets. One starting point is to buy a
  mutual fund that "buys the market" and
  has low management fees.

However, don't let this scare you away from saving
and investing.

- First, *save*. Even a few dollars a month in a
  savings account will add up. Shop around at
  your area banks, savings-and-loans, and credit
  unions for the best interest rate. Choose an
  account insured by the FDIC (Federal Deposit
  Insurance Corporation) for banks and savings
  and loans. For credit unions, choose an
  account insured by the NCUA (National
  Credit Union Administration).

- When you've saved a nest egg large enough
  to cover three to six months of your living
  expenses, then you can start to *invest*. When

you're starting, no need to get fancy. For more information, try *Personal Finance for Dummies* or *Get a Financial Life: Personal Finance in Your Twenties and Thirties* (don't worry if you're no longer in your thirties; it's full of good advice).